Ovation for Zachary Lazar's

Sway

"A compelling novel . . . deft and persuasive. . . . Plunging his readers into 60s counterculture, Lazar merges episodes from the lives of the Rolling Stones, the Manson family, and experimental filmmaker Kenneth Anger. But the novel's central character is that era's strange energy. Lazar's real-life figures are emblematic of a fascinating cultural shift: Something was being born, yet no one could say quite what it was or where it was headed. The energy Lazar evokes was far more powerful than any individual. Impersonal, indefinable, thrilling, and dangerous, it seized people and brought them just to the brink—if they were lucky—of chaos."
— Gregory Leon Miller, San Francisco Chronicle

"Zachary Lazar begins where Joan Didion left off in his fiercely imagined, kaleidoscopic novel."
— Jonathan Ringen, *Rolling Stone*

"Mesmerizing. . . . A nightmarish journey through the era, a guided tour through the excess, violence, and occultism. . . . It takes Lazar's deft touch to evoke the cult of death in the early Stones."   — Amy Woods Butler, *St. Louis Post-Dispatch*

"Rendering fictional characters from public figures is a dodgy business at the best of times—especially figures who have lived as publicly as the Stones and Charlie Manson. But Lazar makes the ploy work by keeping a cool, myth-sustaining distance from his players, focusing instead on the thread of black magic he's weaving. . . . As a kind of novelistic tone poem, *Sway* has a dark and propulsive power."

— Geoff Pevere, *Toronto Star*

"It's not easy to say exactly why I was so blown away by *Sway*. Was it the scintillating intelligence of Lazar's prose? His cunning characterization of an era? The sense of every sentence taking me to a new place? His brilliant portrayal of life as a legend? Surely some combination of all of these, and more besides. But I hope many, many readers will soon find themselves in this position of inexpressible admiration."

— Margot Livesey, author of *Eva Moves the Furniture* and *Banishing Verona*

"*Sway* makes a convincing case that dark forces can be summoned with the right incantation. . . . This is the story of a bizarre convergence of real lives overlapping. . . . It's about the compulsion to find the edge by plunging over it."

— Patrick Beach, *Austin American-Statesman*

"*Sway* is really brilliant. I savored every sentence with as much exquisitely protracted languor as humanly possible. To inhabit and animate and choreograph the psyches of these mythic icons with such delicately registered emotion is simply extraordinary."

— Mark Leyner

"This brilliant novel is about what's to be found in the shadows, the most terrifying crannies of twisted souls, the darkest gleaming gems. . . . What Lazar evokes is unlikely to please either those who condemn the decade as a body blow to decency and authority, or those who celebrate it as a trippy carnival of raised consciousness and experimentation. Lazar's is a book that has no time for preconceived ideas, that tells the reader exactly the things likely to disturb any cozy notions. He's a bad-news bear and thus the most valuable kind of cultural commentator. . . . With its motifs of homosexuality, Satan worship, drug addiction, promiscuity, nihilism, and general decadence, *Sway* reads like your parents' nightmare idea of what would happen to you if you fell under the spell of rock 'n' roll."
—Charles Taylor, *New York Times Book Review*

"Hypnotic. . . . It is not the now-historic acts of violence that make *Sway* so riveting, but its vivid character portraits and decadent, muzzy atmosphere, all rendered with the heightened sensory awareness associated with drugs and paranoia. The near miniaturist precision with which Lazar describes Keith Richards's attempts to master his guitar, Brian Jones's acid trips, and Anger's obsessive desire for Beausoleil bring this large-scale tableau into stunning relief."
—Liz Brown, *Time Out New York*

"Joseph Conrad said that fiction is primarily a visual art; he would have loved Zachary Lazar's *Sway* for the thousand indelible visual details of a startling originality—and for Lazar's ability to shine a light into the contemporary heart of darkness."
—Edmund White, author of *A Boy's Own Story*

"Lazar's hugely impressive achievement is to evoke the energy of an over-documented time in a new way. . . . His feel for the dialogue of Jagger and Richards, for their louche humor, is so instinctive that you forget that what you're reading is an extrapolation. As dark and enigmatic as its central subjects, *Sway* often feels like a whole new genre of folklore fiction. . . . It's irresistible." —Tom Cox, *Daily Mail*

"A rare find, both violent and beautiful." —*GQ*

"A coruscating, kaleidoscopic vision of the 60s, *Sway* is at once an intimate re-imagining of iconic figures and an expansive meditation on an epoch that reverberates to this day. An enthralling read, shot through with flashes of edgy beauty and dark wisdom." —Peter Ho Davies, author of *The Welsh Girl*

"Visual imagination pervades the novel, whether meticulously redescribing the shots in Anger's films, or tracing the acid-fuelled hypersensitivity of Jones to the sights of Marrakech. . . . A disorienting, densely imagined view of allure and danger." —Bharat Tandon, *Times Literary Supplement*

"As a painter might do with a brush and canvas, Lazar uses words in *Sway* to fashion a restrained but seductive portrait of lives intersecting in the tumultuous 1960s." —Stephen Williams, *Newsday*

"Almost every page contains an arresting observation. . . . *Sway* is a study of layers of manipulation and control. . . . But in the end, the most haunting spell is the one that Lazar casts over the reader." —Mick Brown, *Telegraph*

SWAY

A NOVEL

ZACHARY LAZAR

BACK BAY BOOKS
LITTLE, BROWN AND COMPANY
New York Boston London

ALSO BY ZACHARY LAZAR *Aaron, Approximately*

Back Bay Books / Little, Brown and Company
Hachette Book Group
237 Park Avenue, New York, NY 10017
Visit our Web site at www.HachetteBookGroup.com

Originally published in hardcover by Little, Brown and Company, January 2008
First Back Bay paperback edition, February 2009

Back Bay Books is an imprint of Little, Brown and Company. The Back Bay Books name and logo are trademarks of Hachette Book Group, Inc.

Illustrations from the Rider-Waite Tarot Deck® reproduced by permission of U.S. Games Systems, Inc., Stamford, CT 06902 USA. Copyright © 1971 by U.S. Games Systems, Inc. Further reproduction prohibited. The Rider-Waite Tarot Deck® is a registered trademark of U.S. Games Systems, Inc.

The conversation with Zachary Lazar reprinted in the reading group guide at the back of this book originally appeared in Bomb (Spring 2008, number 103). Copyright © 2008 Bomb Magazine. Reprinted with permission.

Library of Congress Cataloging-in-Publication Data
Lazar, Zachary.
Sway : a novel / Zachary Lazar.—1st ed.
p. cm.
ISBN 978-0-316-11309-0 (hc) / 978-0-316-11311-3 (pb)
1. Nineteen sixties—Fiction. 2. Rolling Stones—
Fiction. 3. Anger, Kenneth—Fiction.
4. Manson, Charles, 1934-—Fiction. I. Title.
PS3562.A969S93 2007
813'.54—dc22 2007009920

10 9 8 7 6 5 4 3 2 1

RRD-IN

Designed by Iris Weinstein

Printed in the United States of America

For Sarah Lazar,
Peter Gallagher, and
Christina Carrad

AUTHOR'S NOTE

Sway is a work of fiction. Among other things, it is an examination of the way several public lives were detached from the realm of fact and became a kind of contemporary folklore. As such, the book should not be read as a factual account of events or as biography. While many of the characters in the novel bear the names of actual people, they and their actions have been imagined by the author and should be considered products of the imagination.

PART ONE

"Energy is eternal delight."

—WILLIAM BLAKE, from *The Marriage of Heaven and Hell*

THE HOUSES, 1969

FROM A DISTANCE, they had the demeanor of prisoner and guard. Bobby looked down at the frayed cuffs of his shirt, pushing them back over his wrists as he followed Charlie away from the house. His truck stood in the sun, its fender dented, the bed enclosed by weathered wooden boards. Beside him, Charlie looked silently ahead, his hair covering his face and beard, his hands crossed behind his back. He was an ex-convict, maybe fifteen years older than Bobby, but it was hard to think of him as being any particular age. He had taken just one look at the beat-up piano in the back of Bobby's truck and his face had gone expressionless, as if it disgusted him.

"We'll take the Ford," he said, holding out the keys to Bobby in the flat of his palm. Then he smiled a little facetiously, a smile at nothing, as if they both knew there were intricate layers of pretense between them and Charlie was inviting Bobby to admit it. "Do you mind driving?" he said. "I don't really feel like driving right now."

There were two men coming up the road on motorcycles, some girls walking back from the corral, carrying empty buckets. Dogs slept in the shade beneath the broken planking of a shed. It was an abandoned ranch. The first time Bobby had seen the place he'd felt oddly protective of it because it had seemed so doomed. The buildings were falling apart—shingles missing, holes in the walls, windows covered by black garbage bags

3

or sometimes just left as empty frames. There were drawings everywhere of peace signs, animals, birds. His first day there, with his girlfriend Kitty, they had all fallen in love with his teen-idol face, his jeans with the colored velvet patches. It was like a lot of other places he'd been in the past two years— everywhere along the coast now there were groups of young people with nowhere to go and no money to spend. It was as if they were living in a fort or a tree house. They scraped meals together out of plants they grew or things they scavenged from the trash outside of supermarkets.

He looked back at his truck as they got into the car. The piano was strung up with lengths of rope, a battered upright with a few deep scratches on its side. He was a musician—that had been his plan, to be a rock musician—but it struck him now, with Charlie there, that the plan had become unreal somehow, that it had been diminishing so slowly that he hadn't noticed. Two years ago, he'd starred in an avant-garde film about the rise of Lucifer, a kind of rock-and-roll god who seduced the world not into peace and love but into something more brutal, something more like ecstasy. He'd thought of it at the time as just a stepping-stone to other ambitions, but the role had also appealed to him, had spoken to his particular gift—"charm," "charisma," none of the words captured its unpredictability, the way it was sometimes in his grasp, sometimes not.

Yesterday, in one of the barns, he'd been looking for some twine or rope to secure the piano to the back of his truck when he'd come across a gun sitting in a tool chest, wrapped in a towel. Kitty had been with him—she was hardly even a friend anymore, just another one of the girls he would see when he was at the ranch. She watched his expression as she pulled up the halter strap on her shirt, her face a mocking reflection of his surprise. The gun was a revolver, the wooden grip splintered on one side, the wood as dry and smooth as bone. When he looked back at Kitty, his head tilted a little to the side, her eyes seemed to say, *Who do you think you are? You're really just some good-looking fool, the kind of boy I would have had a crush on in high school.*

"Be quiet for a minute," he said.

She looked at him, her arms crossed in front of her chest. "Cut it out, Bobby."

"You can stop staring at me like that. I know what you were thinking just now."

He brought his hand to the back of her neck and tried to kiss her. She turned her head away at first, but he turned it back, his fingers on her jaw. His chest was heavy, his face unsmiling. He moved away from her a step, letting his hand slide from her neck down her back, the gun still in his other hand, pressing against her arm. Her hair was sheared off at different lengths, standing up in clumps. She was so small, so delicate, that he was almost afraid, his hand on her back, feeling the flat muscles beneath her shirt. She kept her eyes open, watching him, as he backed her toward the table behind her, propping her up a little in his arms. He just stood there for a while, close enough to brush his body against hers, to feel the rise of her breasts against his rib cage. Then he unbuttoned the front of her jeans, using just one hand, the other one still on the gun.

"You know, you've been here so long you can't even remember your own name anymore," he said. "I thought you were a little smarter than that."

"I don't really care what you think."

"All this 'Charlie is Christ' bullshit. Or is it 'Charlie's the Devil'? I forget."

"My parents were strange people," she said, leaning back, her hand on the table. "They never really talked. They just sort of policed each other. I never understood what they were so afraid of. What are you so afraid of?"

The words and ideas were not exactly hers. She had become smarter than before, but also dreamier, smarter but also absent. He thought of the first time he'd seen her walk off with Charlie, maybe a month or two ago, her hand in the back of his jeans, sloppy and blatant and stoned. "Turning them out," Charlie called it, "breaking them in." If you seduced them like a father with his daughter, if you scared them a little, got inside their heads, then any kindness you did them afterward would seem like an act of God.

He pushed his fingers down through the opening of Kitty's fly, feeling the rise of muscle beneath the tangled wedge of hair. She looked right into his eyes and seemed to barely see him.

This morning, he'd found her in the kitchen, washing dishes in the ragged slip she sometimes wore as a dress, her nose and the skin around her mouth burned red by the sun. She was all forearms and shins, barefoot on the dirty kitchen floor, even smaller than he'd remembered.

"You just need to leave me alone for a little while," she'd said.

He thought of her hips rising toward him in the barn, the freckles on her rib cage reminding him somehow that she was sixteen, a girl from a house with a swimming pool in Brentwood.

He told her that he was going to take the used piano over to his friend Gary's place, pick up the twenty dollars profit, use the money to buy some motorcycle parts. He asked her if she wanted to come along. He spoke in a purposeful voice, as if nothing had happened between them, but she just smiled at him in a disbelieving way, as if she knew that Charlie was about to walk in and say that he and Bobby needed to go have a talk.

He got in the Ford with Charlie and they headed south toward Los Angeles, listening to a faint scratch of music on the radio, not speaking. The rocks outside were gray, the plants a grayish green, the dirt tan. Everything was the color of dust, except the sky, which was a washed-out blue behind a thin yellow haze. At the little store outside of Chatsworth, they pulled over and Charlie bought a six-pack of beer and some things for the girls: a booklet of find-the-word puzzles, some candy bars.

Bobby started the car and backed up, looking over his shoulder. When they got on the highway, Charlie lit a joint, examining its smoke as it leached out the cracked window. He passed it over, his hand low, down by Bobby's knee.

"You're kind of quiet," he said.

"I'm not quiet, I'm just wondering where we're going."

"We're going to a friend of mine's house. It's nice there, peaceful. You'll like it."

They were on Highway 118, heading toward Topanga Canyon. They drove for a while, looking at the sparse houses surrounded by trees—oaks, sycamores, a few tall eucalyptuses. After the hills, they came eventually into the suburbs: gas stations, coffee shops, a movie theater.

"I always thought you were a nice kid," Charlie said. "But

I guess maybe there's more to you than that. Like maybe you weren't just bullshitting me about the time you spent in that reform school, for example."

Bobby looked ahead at the road. "This is about Kitty, isn't it?" he said. "Whatever Kitty told you."

"What does that mean?"

"This little talk we're having. Whatever this is. She knew about this."

Charlie looked down at his lap, rubbing his knees with his hands. "You need to stop thinking so much," he said. He brushed something off the dashboard with the side of his hand. "Turn up here," he said. "Take a left."

"Left?"

"Up here at the light. Put your signal on."

Bobby turned from the wide boulevard onto a two-lane street, steering with one hand, the other on the vinyl armrest between them. They passed a Safeway supermarket on the corner, then a post office and a school, then they were in an ordinary neighborhood of small houses behind sidewalks and fences.

"That piano you had in your truck back there," Charlie said. "I was just wondering, where were you taking that thing?"

Bobby looked at him blankly, not even understanding for a moment. "What?"

"That piano you had in your truck. I was wondering where were you taking it."

"I was taking it to Gary Hinman's. He's buying it from me. I got it cheap at one of the auctions."

"Yeah, well, I figured something like that. I was just wondering where you got that piece of shit in the first place. I wanted to make sure you didn't find that on the ranch somewhere."

"I bought it at an auction."

"That's what you said."

"Yeah. That's what I said. What is this?"

Charlie stared at him with an expectant frown, as if waiting for more. Then he turned away, and Bobby wished he had never seen the piano, or that he had found it on the ranch, that he had stolen it.

"I just wonder what goes on in that head of yours sometimes," Charlie said. "Selling a used piano like that. Wasting your time."

Bobby turned the knob on the radio. "I'm trying to make some money."

"Yeah, well, money. There's lots of ways to make money." He passed the joint, not looking at Bobby. "What day is it today?" he said. "Friday?"

"I think it's Thursday."

"Not bad. Just driving around on a Thursday, getting high. Why don't you just cool off and relax?" Charlie nodded then, his mouth half-open, drifting into some sort of sarcastic daydream. He had a way of miming his emotions, acting them out so that they came across as artificial and sincere at the same time. It was the way he played his guitar, dipping and bucking his head, giving himself up to the song, but also making fun of the idea of giving himself up to the song, making fun of you for believing it.

They drove on in silence. It was like this sometimes when you were Bobby. The way he looked—the fact that he was good-looking—made it hard for people like Charlie to believe that he really was who he was. They were always giving him nicknames — B.B., Cupid, Bummer — as if "Bobby" was too intimate, as if saying it was like kissing him on the lips. He remembered being out in the desert one time, just he and Charlie riding around in one of the jeeps, when Charlie had spiraled off into one of his moods, suddenly angry, hectoring and strange. The world was always at war, he'd said. It wasn't just Vietnam, it was the nature of people, the way they made sense of things. Look at a newspaper and all you'd see were soldiers, riots, assassinations. You'd see things being pulled apart, sides forming, rifts widening: black and white, rich and poor, young and old. It was like everyone had looked down and finally seen that they were standing on a tightrope. They didn't know which way to walk (that was the problem), they didn't know how to choose. Some of them were so scared that they just wanted to fall off. They might seem harmless, but you had to be vigilant, because they wanted you to fall with them — that was the peculiar thing about their fear.

Bobby was usually embarrassed when Charlie talked this way. It seemed involuntary, a way of showing too much of his hand.

They turned at the next stop sign. The house on the corner was invisible behind its high brown fence, garbage pails in front, thick tufts of palm trees pushing out over the wooden slats.

"That's it up there," said Charlie. "Park up there a little ways."

He raised his chin at one of the houses across the street. It was a Mexican-style bungalow with a carport off to one side, a front yard covered in smoothly raked gravel. There were cactuses and yuccas planted in little islands behind white bricks. It was so neat that it looked almost like an old toy that had been pressed into service as something real.

"I don't think anyone's home yet," Charlie said. "Why don't you let me have the keys."

Bobby looked at him skeptically. Then he handed him the keys and Charlie nodded, clasping them in his hand.

"Just wait here for a minute," Charlie said. "I'll go and see if anyone's there."

He got out of the car and crossed the street, heading up the sidewalk that bordered the gravel yard. He had the sack of beer cradled in one arm, his free arm dangling at his side like a little boy's. Bobby watched him walk around to the side of the house, following a winding path of concrete disks. Then he disappeared around the back, his head down.

Bobby wiped his eyes. He looked through the windows at the houses: ranch houses, Spanish houses, a miniature Tudor house with a lawn and a chain-link fence. The neighborhood seemed empty, abandoned for the day of work and school. It was like the neighborhood he'd grown up in: middle-class, somehow accidental. There were sidewalks, but nobody outside to walk on them.

He thought of Kitty, the way she had leaned her head on her shoulder last night, looking down at Charlie's hand on her wrist, then back up at Bobby, her eyes sleepy, dismissive. Maybe she was just acting a part—you would see it happen around Charlie sometimes, a certain carelessness in people's faces, a faint edge of sarcasm. Bobby had just kept talking—he'd been acting a little like Charlie himself, he realized now—staring at Charlie to show how little it mattered: he could have Kitty back, she was Charlie's girl now, there were others. But the more he thought about it now, the more distorted the memory became, his face not calm but twitching a little at the cheeks, like a rabbit's.

He looked at his face in the rearview mirror: his dark hair coming down over his forehead, his blue eyes beneath the hatch marks of his eyebrows. His head felt empty, full of air. The longer Charlie was gone, the less he trusted him. Charlie said that fear was the end of thought, the end of lies, an opening up to what was real and true about someone, his soul. But that had always sounded to Bobby like just more of Charlie's bullshit, words for the others, not for him.

He got out of the car and crossed the street, flicking the hair out of his eyes. He walked across the gravel yard—the cement circles, the cactuses in their little islands—but everything he saw was slightly blurred, as if he were looking at it through a smeared pane of glass. At the back of the house, he found a wooden door, a flimsy thing with a windowpane and a rusted brass knob. It was still open a crack, as Charlie must have left it. He stood there for a moment, hesitating. He had felt like a child in the car—*just wait here for a minute*—but now he felt even more like a child, standing outside the door.

Inside, there was a small laundry room, a kitchen beyond it, all of it dark. There was something hanging from the ceiling—three baskets connected by woven strands of yarn that held fruit and boxes of tea. The kitchen counter had all kinds of domestic things on it: a ceramic cat; several canisters for flour, sugar, and the like; a notepad by a telephone. He could see through a rectangular opening into the empty living room with its dim walls. Above the sectional sofa hung a clock shaped like an exploding star.

Charlie emerged from a hallway off to the side. He turned to Bobby with a kind of disgusted shrug, his hands crossed before his waist. Under his arm, pressed to his side, he had what looked like a rolled-up extension cord.

"Not what you thought," he said.

He turned and walked into the living room, his hair covering his face. In the faint light coming in through the picture window, the furniture looked strangely abandoned.

"What is this?" Bobby said.

"I told you that already. It's a friend's house."

"What friend?"

"Right now it's just a house. It's just here. What difference does it make whose house it is?"

He sat down in a padded armchair, putting the extension cord down on the coffee table before him. The sack was on the floor at his feet, hidden from Bobby's view, and he reached down into it, rattling the paper. He brought out a can of beer and offered it to Bobby with an upturned, cupped hand.

"You knew something like this was going to happen, didn't you?" he said.

"I don't know. I don't know what this is."

"This is kind of like the experiment where you break into someone's house in broad daylight and decide whether or not you can handle it."

Bobby looked back to the kitchen door. It was still partly open, sunlight brightening the little curtain in front of the windowpane, a bleached pattern of inkblots on pink fabric. In the living room, Charlie looked almost like a doll, dwarfed slightly by the overstuffed chair. He was small, only five and half feet tall, and yet the dark room seemed to gather itself around him, as if habituated to his occasional presence.

"You came all this way, you might as well have a seat for a minute," he said. "Nothing's going to happen to you here. Just trust me for a minute."

Bobby was still in the kitchen. He looked down at the floor—linoleum with a pattern like Mexican tiles, the shapes fixed and identical, like bored eyes. Charlie pushed the beer to the far edge of the coffee table, toward him. Then he sat back, one of his elbows on the armrest, his fist beneath his chin, and Bobby stepped into the living room, sitting down on the floor, bringing his knees to his chest, looking down at the carpet as if being careful.

————

They were friends, Bobby had always thought. They played music together and rode motorcycles and drank beer, slipping off with the girls, and usually after a few days Bobby would leave. Other people came to Charlie as if he were a visionary, some sort of guru, but to Bobby he was another musician, someone with connections. He knew the Beach Boys, Neil Young, a man named Terry Melcher who produced the Byrds. The music they played together was coiling and improvisatory, a current that Bobby helped guide, leaning in toward Charlie to hear his voice, a controlled presence next to Charlie's endless wandering. They were going to make a record together, that was the plan, but it never seemed to happen. There was another Charlie who didn't care about plans, cynical and distant, and it was this Charlie, oddly, whom you could most easily imagine becoming a star, swaying the crowd like a revivalist preacher, fully believing in his act until the moment it was over. This was the Charlie who always kept a special eye on Bobby, aroused and suspicious. He seemed to anticipate Bobby's thoughts, to always find them a little disappointing, evidence of squandered potential, close but never quite there. There was something compelling about dodging Charlie's moods. It was one of the reasons Bobby kept coming back, one of the main reasons. Sometimes a frightened daze would overcome him in Charlie's presence, but even the daze had an adrenaline sheen that felt almost like self-confidence.

———————

They sat there for several minutes, neither of them talking. Bobby looked at the room, the pictures of family members on the walls, or what he assumed were family members. There was a middle-aged woman, her hair pinned back above her head, smiling behind cat-eye glasses with black frames. Her husband was off to the side, almost cut off at the edge, a man with thick creases in his face and a striped tie loosened around his neck. There were pictures of their two grown daughters: in their graduation gowns, separately, and gathered with their mother around a platter of food on the back patio. On the wall opposite the window was a crucifix and a print of an angel. There was an oil painting of a girl in the woods being serenaded by a man with a lute.

"We shouldn't leave that car sitting out there much longer,"

Charlie said. "We need to get it out of here. You're going to need to make a choice about that."

He sat back in the chair with his hands on the arms, his elbows a little cocked, like someone posing in an old photograph. The brown carpet stretched across the living room toward the opening into the hallway. Its nap had been brushed back in swatches by a vacuum cleaner.

"I don't know who lives here," Charlie said. "It doesn't matter—we're not here to hurt them. I don't know anything about them other than the fact that they live in this house and they wouldn't want us to be here. That's why we have to be here."

He smiled, a fatherly smile, almost helpless. It was full of a skeptical candor, as if he knew that no matter how hard he tried to communicate what he was about to say he wouldn't be understood.

"Those people at the ranch, they all come from places like this," he said. "I think you know what I'm talking about. It does something to them, I don't know what. They never stop struggling with it, even after they leave. It's like they have to hurt somebody or hurt themselves, it doesn't matter which sometimes."

Bobby turned his head and looked at him. "I don't want anything to do with your little private army back there," he said. "And if this is about Kitty, then all I can tell you is she's yours, fine, she's your fucking zombie."

Charlie looked down at the coffee table. "This has nothing to do with Kitty. I already told you that. This has to do with you now. How you're any different from those people back there, all those boys, those girls, the zombies, if that's what you want to call them."

There was some shift in the room's shadows that a moment later didn't seem to be a shift at all, just a deeper stillness. Time and space — these were favorite subjects of Charlie's, the prison of time and space, the way the mind was always desperate to escape from that prison. He leaned forward in his chair, sizing up Bobby's face, his thumb moving across his beard, his breath filling the air between them, staring at Bobby like an opponent.

What did Bobby suppose made him any different from those people out at the ranch, he asked again. How was Bobby any different from those people out there who were just waiting for some sign or some change that never came? Did he want to put himself above them? Did he want to be a star like Elvis maybe, or like Sonny and Cher — or maybe he wanted to be something more serious than that, a rebel, a criminal, Jack the Ripper maybe, or Jesse James. But what did Bobby want really, and did he even know, and why did he just keep drifting around, never asking himself these questions?

Charlie leaned back into his chair, his face in shadow. "Those people at the ranch are my people," he said. "You need to remember that from now on. They're not yours, they're mine. You can't just keep treating them the way you treat yourself, like it's all just a game or a waste of time."

He raised one of his hands, as if to pluck something small from the air, then did the same with the other hand. "Moving a piano, making a few bucks like that," he said. "One moment, the next moment — that's who you are after a while, all those little moments. They're not something you can just go back and change. They're like rooms. They stay there after you leave."

Bobby tilted his head back toward the ceiling, his eyes closed. "If you wanted me to leave, all you had to do was say 'leave.'"

"I don't want you to leave. I wouldn't have brought you all the way over here if I wanted you to leave. I want you stay there, if you want to stay there."

He steepled his hands beneath his chin. His hair was falling into one of his eyes, but his impatient, put-upon gaze was absolutely still.

"I'll do this for you this time, if that's what you want. I've done this plenty of times and it's very simple. One of us has to go move the car. The other one of us is going to stay here and meet these people, take some money off them, whatever. I don't have much else in mind, do you? You tell me what you want."

Bobby shook his head. "I don't know what you're talking about."

"Yeah, well, maybe you're just like I used to be. All wrapped up in yourself, not seeing anyone else very clearly."

"I don't know what you're fucking talking about."

Charlie reached into his pants pocket and held the car keys out in his hand. He dangled them in front of his face, staring at Bobby, then held them out in his extended palm, just above his knee, the pose somehow biblical, deliberately so.

"I don't want to keep you here," he said. "If you want to leave, then maybe you should leave. You do whatever makes you feel comfortable. This is an easy one. This is almost like practice."

"Practice for what?"

———

He wanted to be taken seriously. He wanted to be different from those people at the ranch, but he couldn't even sit there in an empty house without being cowed by his own thoughts. Maybe he was the kind of person who spent his whole life sleepwalking, daydreaming, barely scraping by, never going too far or pushing very hard. Or maybe there was more to him than that. Maybe he could think of just one thing he'd ever done that would show there was more to him than that.

They were Charlie's words, not Bobby's. They were Charlie's words in Bobby's ears, Bobby's mind, shared words. It didn't matter after a while whose words they were.

———

Charlie left the keys on the table. Then he sat back in the chair, slouched a little, one foot up on the table's edge. The light through the window was a wedge of moving dust, a field of rays that rotated and shone. Outside was the car, parked in front of a neat yard with a low chain-link fence. Everything on the other side of the window was still, brightly colored, like a slide lit up by a projector.

"None of this is too complicated," Charlie said. "I'm just telling you some basic things you knew all along."

He worked one of his hands into the pocket at the side of his denim jacket and pulled out a balled-up wad of fabric. He shook it out in his hand—it was a black nylon stocking—and laid it out on the table next to the extension cord.

"Maybe you should go outside for a little while and think about it," he said. "Take a little walk, get a breath of fresh air. I'll stay here for a minute."

Bobby shook his head. "You're serious."

"Of course I'm serious. These people who live here, I don't know what they mean to you, why they matter so much. They don't think, they don't know anything they haven't been taught by someone else. You'd just be showing them another side of things for a few minutes. Just like what Kitty did for you yesterday. You and your little gun."

It turned out that all along Charlie had had it in a shoulder holster beneath his jacket. It was the same gun from yesterday, the .38 with the wooden grip splintered on one side. He worked it slowly out from beneath his jacket, tugging with his right hand, then set it down on the table beside the extension cord and the stocking.

Bobby looked down at his hand, his fingers on the carpet, not quite seeing them, lulled for a moment like a child. He looked at the things on the table. When he finally stood up and walked toward the kitchen door, the walking had as little to do with his body as if he were dreaming it. There was the kitchen — the telephone, the notepad, the ceramic cat. There was the door with its inkblot curtain. Outside, in the backyard, was the afternoon sunlight, flashbulb white and then a widening yellow haze.

There was nowhere left to go. Malibu, Topanga, Mendocino, Big Sur — in the last year, Bobby had crossed these places off one by one as overcrowded, menaced by cops. It was the war in Vietnam — the war had somehow permeated everything, even things that had no relation to the war itself. It made everyone feel like fugitives, wary of the same people they would have looked to as friends just a year before. It was why Bobby had kept moving, sleeping in the bed of his truck or on someone's floor, fixing up old cars and trying to sell them, bartering, helping out on drug deals. He had been trying to stay out of the war, but the war kept following him in its different forms. It was what made places like the ranch so confusing—dreamy but combative, childlike but also desolate.

They wanted you to grow up into some helpless combination of old person and infant. They wanted you to have a house and a family and a refrigerator and a TV, and not know how any of it worked. They wanted you to spend your life working on something that was never concrete, never anything you could see or hold in your hands, and if you didn't do that they wanted to put you in jail. Cutting down forests, poisoning the earth—it was a country driven by stupid, blind impulse. It was a country where nobody knew where their food came from or where their garbage went, they just flushed the bowl, kept eating it and throwing it away, building bombs and computers, cars and TVs, sending people off to Vietnam so they could set it on fire. It was a country that had turned against everyone he knew, cast them out like garbage, and all they could do was smile to themselves at all they'd learned and wait patiently for the fires to start here at home.

He stopped walking and looked again at the houses. Sidewalks, fences, lawns. It was a dead world. There was no point in pretending it wasn't, or that he could go back to it and find anything there but emptiness. What was he afraid of? What was Charlie asking him to do that he didn't already believe in, even if he'd never had the courage to really imagine it?

He thought of the pictures on the living room wall—the woman in her cat-eye glasses, the man's loosened tie. He saw them coming home, turning to find the stranger sitting in their living room. It would all become a paradise then—the living room, the kitchen, the star-shaped clock above the sofa. It would all become something precious he was about to take away, had already taken away, just by being there.

But what did they mean to him? And what would they think if they'd seen him on the street some afternoon, driving a beat-up pickup truck with a broken piano in the back?

To live inside Charlie's skin. To be empowered by fear, to use it like a tool. To go back to the ranch as someone transformed, not the pretty boy you had a crush on in high school, not a musician or another lost soul, but a harder, truer soul he had always known was waiting there inside him.

He turned and walked up the sidewalk toward the gravel yard. The house was a living thing now, the watchful center of the empty neighborhood. He thought of the man and woman who lived there, and he had a sense that they were all bound by something he had never been aware of and had no name for. It made him sick to feel them inside him now, pulsing like the blood in the veins of his throat.

ROCK AND ROLL, 1962

IN THE SMALL ROOM, two guitars surge in and out in chaotic alternation, an amplified noise that seems to revolve. It's on a dilapidated street in London, called Edith Grove, in the southernmost part of Chelsea. It is the coldest winter there in a hundred years.

The flat has mold on the walls. Its gray paint is blistered and chipped, the carpet flaked with bread crusts. For now, the singer, Mick, can only sit and watch. The other two, Brian and Keith, are learning their parts from a record player, blankets over their legs. Their hands are cold and they play intermittently, nodding in silence when it starts to work.

The room feels as cold as it is outside. The radiator is silent, dented, its paint scabbed. To set it pinging they have to feed the gas meter with coins they don't have and even then the result is only disappointment.

Brian has shiny blond hair and accusatory eyes. He is the only one who can be called handsome, though his neck is thick and he is short, almost stocky. He is the leader—it is his band, he came up with the name. He stares at Mick and plays seven notes on his guitar with a bent note in the middle. The message is something like *You are tolerated for now, but only tolerated.* Brian is two years older than the others, twenty-one, and he is already the father of two illegitimate children.

Mick blows smoke, and his hand travels up to the collar of

his bathrobe, affecting disdain. His ugliness is eye-catching; in his movements there is a patient strategy. He is a student at the London School of Economics, still hedging his bets. He can leave here at any time and end up slightly better off than his father, who is a physical education teacher in Dartford. But he is also the only one of the three who has ever performed in public, singing every Tuesday night in Ealing with another band.

Keith raises his chin, and he and Brian start in on an American song called "Carol." They trade leads and the two-string vamp of the rhythm part. Keith is gangly, ridiculous. He is still a little in awe of Brian. He makes cutting remarks under his breath, and he sometimes snaps to with a belligerent grin and grabs someone's nipple and twists. He knows every lick from every Chuck Berry record ever made, an indication of how much time he's spent alone.

They have a groove going now. It's impossible to say who is leading whom. Brian plays with his eyes closed, head bowed, his blond bangs falling almost over his eyebrows. Keith's style is more aggressive, more rhythmic, his crossed legs moving with the beat. Mick is tapping his knees and bobbing his head with his eyes closed too. His chief talent for now is a lack of embarrassment. He starts singing in a voice that is not his own, a lucky stroke of mimicry. It is part Cockney, part black American, and though neither half is authentic, the mix is somehow a joining of strengths.

They come from quiet towns and near suburbs, terraced houses thrown up in the aftermath of German bombs. Places you don't see until you leave them, and why would you want to leave them, the same roses on the same trellises?

Mick is watching Brian now, whose head is still bowed, intent only on the sound he is making. The sound from his guitar has no meaning, it is only a set of tones, but it seems to imply a range of ominous meanings. Maybe part of Mick already suspects that in that grim flat he is in the right place at the right time.

The flat smells like vegetables and cigarettes. The ceiling is ringed with the black stains from the candles they sometimes burn in place of lightbulbs. They put their socks on top of the radiator until they smell the wool start to burn and then they put them back on and have a minute or two of relief before their toes are numb again. It is so cold they sleep with all their clothes on. They sometimes have to sleep together in the same bed.

Mick is the only one who ever talks about money. For the other two, money is an abstraction, something you get in exchange not for labor but for demeaning yourself in front of other people. Brian works in the electronics department of a large store in Bayswater, but he will soon be fired for stealing. Keith subsists on whatever his mother sends him from home. The two of them have only the vaguest sense of living in a physical world: a place where windows keep out rain, chairs make it more comfortable to sit, electric lights allow one to see. When they get drunk, they break the furniture and imitate Mick's queenly gestures, and one night they burn his bathrobe in the sink.

They play for hours at a time, their two guitars the warp and weft of the same fabric. They weave minute variations on a single pattern, forgetting themselves in the trance of detail. They spend days and nights in this way, almost wordless, signaling to each other until their fingers bleed. When the pipes freeze, the toilet down the hall won't flush and so they piss in jars. When the water comes back on, they leave the jars in the basin. Over time the basin fills up with cigarette butts and the newspaper wrappings from food. Mick thinks about quitting, concentrating on his economics course, but the more he has to sit and watch, the more he needs to stay.

Italian suits and Cuban-heeled shoes. White dress shirts with tab collars. Narrow black ties that look even better when he lets the slack end dangle free of the clasp. These are some of the clothes that Brian has managed to wangle out of his various girlfriends, or to steal from his job at the department store in Bayswater.

A week before Christmas a girl arrives just before dark, standing behind the iron fence. Her wild hair makes her ordinary topcoat look misplaced, somehow severe. She looks more lost than she really is, which is her odd way of deflecting the hostility of this strange city. She has a pram with her and inside it is Brian's infant son.

When she won't stop ringing the bell, he goes outside to greet her. Upstairs, he and Keith have been practicing, and he knows that Keith is mocking him now in his mind, thinking of dishrags and nappies, and so the thing to do is to act responsible and concerned, to surprise him in this way.

"Tricia," he says.

She looks shaken for just a moment, but then turns on him with a familiar, disappointed smile.

"I'm here for just a day or two," she says. "I'm staying with Claire. You know, my cousin Claire, the one you used to fancy."

He looks at the baby, touching its cheek with two fingertips. "It's cold," he says. "Is he all right?"

She touches his hair as he's still bent over the pram. She

brushes it back behind his ear. "The bohemian look," she says. "So unruly. But it suits you, though. Really."

He stands straight and looks off down the row of identical stone buildings, his hands in his pockets. "We've been practicing," he says. "Getting some numbers down."

She nods her head. "I just thought you'd like to see Christopher." She bends over the pram and nuzzles the baby, her nose and lips on his face. "London," she says. "We're in London."

After a few drinks with Keith and some friends, he takes the train to Clapham to visit Tricia at her cousin Claire's. It turns out that Claire has a husband, Neil, a tall and chinless man with a shock of black hair who works as a pharmacist. The four of them have a home-cooked dinner and Brian drinks some wine and finds himself relaxing into a magnanimous mood, riding a wave of sincerity that he begins to believe in. He holds his son high in the air and makes airplane sounds. He and Claire's husband talk about Algeria, where there has been a revolution. As he speaks, Brian looks almost like a child. It's clear that his enthusiasm has less to do with politics than with enthusiasm as an end in itself.

"One more loss for Europe," he says. "But it's all down to America and Russia now, isn't it? Just a matter of which side they join up with."

"Do you believe that?" says Neil.

"Believe what?"

"That it's just a matter of which side they join up with. That the world is split in two like that. That there's no chance for real socialism in Algeria."

Brian smiles at Tricia, then back at Neil. "I don't know," he says. "What do you think?"

"Well, there's no point in *not* thinking so, is there?" says Neil. "There's no point in being fatalistic."

Brian pours out another glass of wine for Neil, then tilts the bottle slightly toward him as if making a toast. He pours for Claire, and then for Tricia and himself. The conversation turns to safer things — London, the cold weather, the cost of heating a flat. When they've finished eating, Brian and Tricia do the washing up, and they splash soapsuds on each other and sing songs the way they used to, childish songs about the people back in their hometown of Cheltenham. He is not quite insincere; in this particular moment he sees himself as fundamentally playful, a spreader of good cheer. But when he feigns sleepiness, it's obviously a ruse, and Tricia does what he knows she'll do. She lets him spend the night, leading him back into the extra bedroom with the baby.

She feeds their son with a bottle, patiently and gravely, then bounces him on her shoulder for a while, singing to him, until he burps. When he's finished, she wipes his mouth with the large white napkin on her shoulder, then carefully lays him in his crib. For a long time, she makes faces over him, mewing and speaking baby talk, as if they are the only two in the room. Brian notices how bare it is: the half-empty bookcase with a lamp on one corner, Neil's pharmacology diploma on the wall, the slanted cot with its creases visible through the sheets and the thin pink quilt. The neatness of the room — its air of a newly married couple just starting out — inspires in him a surprising resentment, then a desperate, half-convinced pride in the mindless shambles of the flat in Edith Grove.

"Do you think there's a chance for real socialism in Algeria?" he says, moving toward her.

She is still doting on the baby as he runs his fingers through her tangled brown curls. "I don't know what he was on about," she says. "They wouldn't let him in at Oxford. He's never gotten over it."

"I bet he has a stash of pinups in here somewhere. A leather mask."

"What?"

"You know, he serves Claire a dinner in the nude, wearing just a mask. Eats his own meal from a dog dish."

She pushes his hand away with a distant, skeptical smile. "I thought you were sleepy."

"I'm going to thrash you, Neil. You've made me very upset," he mocks.

She doesn't seem to be hearing him. She lies down on the cot in her bathrobe, crossing her bare feet and closing her eyes. Her arms are folded beneath her head and she smiles faintly, a girl again. He switches off the lamp and takes off his shoes. Something about her competence with the baby has made it feel as if it were nothing more than a game they had both been playing. He can't see her exactly, can see only her blurred image in the near darkness. In the sepia light, he sees the curve of her hip, the length of her body beneath her robe.

There is that moment when they finally take off their clothes and he feels her skin against his and his vision fades out almost completely. There is only a vertiginous blur, a torrent of inexpressible messages. What binds him too closely to girls like Tricia is this deluge of feeling. He is not very careful or skillful, but almost always he is strangely sincere, moving over their bodies with an obsessive slowness that verges on the embarrassing.

In just a few hours he sees what's really there. The baby is screaming. In the bald lamplight, Tricia stands over the crib and tries to soothe him in her arms, tired and puffy-faced, sore but also somehow alert. He can see how natural this is for her, how bound she is to their son, and he feels suddenly displaced, confused by the idea that Tricia might think that this has anything to do with him.

Onstage, they are all awkward, all except Brian. His face is almost feminine, pale and wide-lipped, but his hands are large, blocklike, and they handle the guitar like a shovel. He attacks the strings with wide up-and-down sweeps of the wrist, forms the chords with wide-stretched fingers, making his playing look more difficult than it is. He does this while standing still, not looking at the crowd, his face unaccountably stern.

They have a bass player now, and a drummer. They are basic and direct, steeped not only in blues but in jazz.

There is no stage — it is not a club, just the basement room of a pub called the Wetherby Arms, where there are thirty people or so drinking pints and smoking cigarettes, not necessarily interested in music. What they hear now comes across as deliberately abrasive. They've never encountered anything so unpolished, as if the whole point of the music is to be aggressively unmusical, knowingly a fraud.

Mick moves with little head-bobbing steps around his microphone stand, pigeon-toed. What he doesn't realize is that the collar of his shirt has ridden up above his suit jacket, bringing with it the knot of his tie, which makes his neck look comically long. The noises he makes have nothing to do with singing. But his sheer persistence is a provocation because it's clear that he isn't joking.

They're playing Muddy Waters. Their version is faster, less free. The two guitars veer in and out at different angles, never touching. Brian moves his shoulders in a strange, fluent way, as if the music were somehow circular and he hears its center in the space between the beats. There's something misplaced, something feyly undergraduate, about the length of his blond hair in combination with his somber three-button dress suit. Across the stage, Keith pounds out his chords, crouched down by the drum riser, his thin frame hunched around his instrument. He had never bothered to put on his tie and now he has taken off his suit jacket as well. He has no showmanship, but he is the one who is secretly guiding them forward, the drums following the lead of his guitar.

Some of the boys in the crowd are starting to taunt them now. They can see what is starting to happen, see that these boys with their instruments have started to believe in their own act, especially the singer, Mick.

He sneers in his weird drawl, *Well I could never be-e-e-e satisfied and I jus-s-s-t can't ke-e-e-p on crying.* He looks sideways at Keith, pursing his lips. There is a jostle of guitars. He twitches his head, chin raised, marching in a slight crouch or stoop.

Their hair is long and they look both ugly and vain. They look like women, that's what people will say, but in fact they don't look like women at all, it's just that they're sexual, aware of their bodies. If anything, their hair makes them look like very careless transvestites, with something devious and brittle beneath their outer resolve. The music is making them move in ways that might be embarrassing, but they're trying to master that embarrassment by seeming not to care. This sense of fakery has something vaguely to do with being English and playing the music of black Americans. They're trying to be serious and

31

sarcastic at the same time, emotional but also cool. All the helpful commonsense distinctions are being made pointless by their grating, persistent music.

The crowd breaks the tables and one of the bass player's amplifiers. They smash a few pint glasses on the floor. Brian is set upon by six boys who claw at his long blond hair and tumble after him in a scrum up the broken stairs.

After that, the gigs start to draw crowds. It's the violence that draws them, the violence in the music, and the violence that ensues. They play every Wednesday at a new pub in Ealing, weekends at a hotel bar in Richmond. Almost all the shows end in some sort of confrontation: a skirmish in the crowd, a verbal brawl between the band and some heckler, a fistfight broken up by bouncers and then continued on the pavement outside. There is always a tension in the rooms, the darkness and heat accentuated by the tight jostle of too many people in too small a space. The anticipation of what might go wrong becomes central to the music, which gets louder and more jagged in response.

One night when they're onstage Mick notices the way that Brian rattles his tambourine. He smirks at the crowd and gives it a single hard shake, as if he's cracking a small whip. The next night Mick taunts the audience along these same lines, turning his face in profile between phrases, laughing at some private joke, then sneering and pointing his finger. All the lights seem to be on him. He pushes it further and further but not too far.

In February, Brian meets a girl at a pub in Soho. He's trying to get another booking for the band, and he's brought some money—he's borrowed it from the band's common fund without telling them—so that he can make an impression on the bartender. But he forgets this mission as soon as the girl comes in out of the rain with her group of friends. From the bar he can see her hair falling in wet strands over her narrow face. She's tall and thin and she wears a shiny black raincoat, a coat that seems to be made of some rare, expensive kind of plastic.

Within a minute or two, he has become the center of attention at their table. He's wearing a tweed jacket and a narrow black tie whose ends dangle free of the clasp. He buys a bottle of champagne and has it brought over to the girl and her friends. The girl in the black raincoat regards him at first with a comic skepticism, a feigned hostility, but he pours her a glass of the champagne nonetheless. Before long she is speaking in a way that almost mirrors the way he speaks, sarcastic and deliberately peculiar, as if they are in together on some secret.

He asks about her raincoat. He says he had a dream once about a girl in a raincoat just like hers. He asks her if by any chance she speaks German, or if she's ever been to Germany. Her raincoat looks German to him.

She looks down at the lapel of her coat as if she's never noticed it before. When she looks back up at him with the same suspicious smile, he notices the little gap between her front teeth, the faint groove on the underside of her nose, between the nostrils. When she asks him for a cigarette, he tells her that she will have to fight him for it, and after a confused pause she raises her two fists to the level of her cheeks and pretends to stare him down.

That same evening, Tricia arrives at Edith Grove, this time having left the baby with her cousin Claire in Clapham. Her hair has been cut shorter, curled at the ends like Jackie Kennedy's. She's in high spirits, planning to meet Brian on his own terms, but it turns out that he isn't even home; he's somewhere in the West End at a jazz club, looking for gigs.

It's Mick who tells her this, after he's invited her inside. He's loafing around the flat in a new bathrobe and a worn pair of pajamas that look as if they've been twisted in tight knots and left for a year in a damp trunk. A textbook is spread out on the sofa beside a parcel of fried potatoes wrapped in newspaper. As he sits down on the sofa, he indicates a chair for her to sit in with a wave of his hand.

He puts his feet up on the table and lifts a martini glass filled with something tepid and brown. He has a long strand of dried toothpaste on the lapel of his robe.

"Didn't he know you were coming?" he says.

The chair he's offered her is piled with dirty clothes, which she picks up in a clump and places on top of one of the amplifiers. In recent weeks, her disappointment over Brian has reached an apex and turned into something resembling exuberance, a desperate, unashamed yearning.

"Do you think I would have come all this way if I hadn't told him?" she says.

She sits down and lights herself a cigarette, breathing out with closed eyes. She's wearing mascara and a new green dress beneath her topcoat.

"That's our little till," Mick says. He points to a cigar box on the floor, lying sideways with its lid agape. "We keep our savings in there, to make the payments on the instruments? As you can see, there's not much in it now. Nothing at all, in fact. Keith just ran off a little while ago to try to find him."

She leans forward with her elbows on her knees, her feet splayed out dejectedly in front of her. Mick raises his glass awkwardly and sips some of the strange liquid.

"Beef tea," he says. "Would you like some?"

She stands up and starts to appraise the clutter in the room. On the wall near the kitchen is a long Bakelite-covered table stacked with dirty plates, ashtrays, newspapers stained different shades of bright yellow and beige.

"Are you sure?" she says.

"Sure of what?"

"Are you sure that it was Brian who took the money?"

Mick stands up. He yawns, stretching his arms by clasping his hands in a bridge behind his waist.

"It's his band," he says. "You know that. He needs that money to keep himself in shampoo, I suppose. Shampoo for that lovely hair of his."

He is standing right behind her now. She can feel him pausing there, watching her with a kind of scorn. She closes her eyes and feels a warm swelling inside her, not anger or guilt but some fusion of these that brings with it a tinge of her earlier anticipation, her excitement over seeing Brian.

She imagines him making one of his funny faces, jabbing two fingers up his nostrils and sticking out his tongue. She sees him doing this in a circle of girls whose faces she can't see, wearing the dark suit she gave him as a present when they lived back in Cheltenham.

"I'm sure he'll be back soon," says Mick. "Why don't you come sit down?"

When she feels his hands on her shoulders, she stands very still for a moment. Then she turns and stares at him. Their kissing is a way to avoid having to look at each other any longer.

If anything, she tries too hard. Her breath is stale and she keeps thrusting her chest out at him. He moves her clumsily back toward the couch. When he sees her eyes roll back blankly in the vagueness of succumbing, he realizes how determined she is, how little this has to do with him.

The music is simple on the surface. On the surface, it's a matter of three chords that even a boy like Keith, sequestered in his bedroom in his parents' house, can learn to play along with on his guitar, until he begins to listen more carefully and hear what's actually there. After that it becomes a matter of how many layers he's able to discern, how much he's willing to commit to in terms of patience and repetition. For a boy like Keith, the willingness is all but infinite. He's a shy dreamer, prone to isolated fantasies, preyed upon at school by older boys who call him a faggot and a girl. They throw rocks at him from the building sites of unfinished council terraces. They inspire in him confusing, shaming acts of cruelty, tormenting animals mostly. The music he listens to when he's alone is like the angry essence of the boys who taunt him, the aggressive force in them that he can't help but covet. Its sound is otherworldly, impossible to connect to his drab suburb of identical brick flats, muddy roads, dustbins.

The three chords are usually only alluded to, he finds, approached from various, jarring angles in massings of two or three odd notes that are sometimes not even in the same key. He struggles with half tones and quarter tones, dozens of tiny, hard-to-discern variations in rhythm and pitch that he has to match somehow on his thick-stringed, high-fretted guitar. To hear any of this requires an ear acute enough to pick out several tones at once and isolate each of them, even as they change, and this in turn requires a nearly autistic willingness to move the phonograph needle back, groove by groove, in order to assess again the same two-second snatch of song. It is a tedium exceeded only by the painful, fumbling labor of trying to finger these notes on a fretted board, going only by ear, by trial and error, one awkward voicing to the next. The music raises blisters on his fingers, causes him to pound the guitar in frustrated fits or to stare at it from his bed. It defies him to internalize even a portion of its alien power, to play it just once with his body and not his mind.

A hundred and fifty people in Ealing. Almost two hundred in Richmond. They've begun to draw followers who come every week in leather and black sweaters to dance on the tables with such violence that a reporter from the *Record Mirror* feels threatened and denounces the band as "thugs." A kind of culture has started to evolve. Everyone under thirty has decided that they're an exception—a musician, a runaway, an artist, a star. There are no more wars to fight, no more ration coupons, nothing to do but study graphic design or live in Paris for a month busking in the Métro. They have no experience of fear, or violence, or patriotism, or duty. What they have instead is an obsession with style, a collage of half-understood influences from other times and places. It is a language of pure connotation, of suggestion and innuendo, and once it gets started it has to move faster and faster, it can never stop working.

It's something Keith has begun to feel a little suspicious of, when he's not belittling it in his mind, the way the unspoken se- cret between Mick and Brian—their mutual awareness that Mick has slept with Tricia—has had the odd effect of bringing them closer. Keith sits with his guitar now, idly playing little bits of music, while Brian tries once again to teach Mick a riff on the harmonica. They are weirdly eager and solicitous with each other, rising to careful heights of consideration. For Keith, who's never even kissed a girl, whose only contacts with girls are sarcastic and self-defeating, it brings a confusing kind of envy.

It's a Little Walter riff they're trying to learn, impossible to duplicate without a microphone, but when Brian plays it he manages to catch some of its menace and depth. He takes Mick's hands and cups them around the harmonica, places his fingers on Mick's and holds them in place. Then he brings his own hands to his mouth and mimics the waving motion that pro- duces vibrato, raising his eyebrows at Mick, who takes the cue by just barely shaking his head. He stares seriously into Brian's eyes and tries once more to reproduce the sound. He sits up straight and raises his shoulders, the instrument cradled in one hand and completely covered by the other, which flutters be- neath his thumbs in the deliberate way of someone making birdcalls. He closes his eyes and blows harder, and Brian nods his head at the ground, unimpressed but patient, almost re- signed in the way he's passing on his skills.

·   ·   ·

Even in March it is still cold in the flat. Through the window, the crusted snow glows a faint blue between the rails of the iron fence. At three in the morning, Keith has passed out at the far edge of the bed where the three of them are curled up for warmth. Brian and Mick are snuggled against each other, both drunk, both moving back and forth between deep, stuporous sleep and lulled, half-waking dreams.

It is so dark that when Brian opens his eyes, Mick's face is a blue vagueness that seems asleep but also not like a human face at all. It seems large and made of highly pumiced stone, a monument that emanates a kind of numinous comfort that has nothing to do with Mick's actual self. He seems to be faintly smiling. Then his face seems blank and tranquil, the remembered smile a faint nimbus that fades in and out.

Brian twists a little and Mick groans. For a moment, the look on his face is pained, but then he moves his head down against Brian's shoulder, and they enter a space that is almost indistinguishable from sleep. They are pressed up against each other, front to front, and each of them has a hand buried deep in the warmth between the other's legs.

Then Mick's hand slackens and stills. His mouth is open and his eyes stare at Brian without recognition.

They're still holding each other in their hands. There is a moment before the shame has time to register, and Brian closes his eyes, opting to continue, but Mick takes his hand away and turns on his side, rolling over toward Keith on the other side of the bed. It occurs to Brian then that he has been deceived, that Mick has been awake this whole time, and now he is awake himself, unable to move.

· · ·

They get their next big break a few nights later, a Saturday night gig at the Marquee Club, the most important club in London. The sound is bad and they play a sloppy, fast-paced set, but there is a young publicity man in the audience who wants to speak to them anyway, a twenty-year-old former design student named Andrew Loog Oldham. He sees that this band with its aloof antistyle, drawing the crowd closer to the stage to fight for a space in which to dance, is in some way a rough successor to Elvis Presley. He's encouraged to think this way because a band from Liverpool of all places has just sold a million copies of its own song.

Backstage, he speaks to Brian, who is obviously the leader. He offers to get them into a recording studio. He says he has an older partner with connections at Decca Records. He says that they need a different singer, though, because Mick has no voice.

Brian raises an eyebrow. He's never thought of this before — it's a guitar band, and Mick can't even play an instrument. He has no voice, that's obvious, but it's never occurred to him that Mick would ever be more than a secondary figure anyway. What he feels now, at this first glimpse of success, is a kind of generosity born of his own power, made keener by a perverse reluctance to make any concessions at all to this person who wants to be their manager.

He tells him that he'll make the demo, but that Mick has to stay. Then he tells Mick what has just happened. He tells him that this is it, that they are on to something, that he had better call it quits with the London School of Economics.

That summer — 1963 — they make a first tour of the hinter-lands. They follow the old vaudeville circuit through Epping and Slough, Bradford and Spalding, dim ballrooms with spot-lit curtains where the last of the big bands still go through their paces. It's a failure, one failure after another. They come onstage and half the seats are empty and there is too much space to move around in, all that old-fashioned stage to some-how inhabit and use. In London, the crowds had gotten so dense that people fainted from lack of air. The band some-times had to strip down to their bare chests it was so hot. Now they come on in their street clothes, the way they did in London, and nobody responds. They play seven songs to quiet indifference, then they do the same thing an hour later for a different audience, then they drive somewhere where the tea shop is closed and the petrol station won't sell them fuel.

It's hard to remember what they thought they were doing, playing blues to tiny crowds in the Midlands. The ballrooms are damp and cold and they can't make out the faces in the room, the strange austerity of the spectators. On the wide, empty stages, they move around in some effort even to make them-selves seen. They play to forty people in Watford. In Morecambe there are twenty-two. They arrive in provincial high streets, where a few girls wait outside in kerchiefs and plastic pumps, and always there are the stares of the local constables, skeptical faces in a changeless gray drizzle.

The only thing that seems to work is aggression. The sound gets angrier and angrier. In the van afterward, they sometimes turn this aggression on one another.

Keith writes a letter home to his mother:

I thought I'd see the countryside but all I see is the inside of this van. Two weeks now and not a minute to myself. The other night Bill, who's playing bass, gets into it with the police. They spot him pissing on a wall. There's a restaurant won't let us in to use the toilets, so we have to piss outside. Then the cops take each one of us individually behind the building and make us walk a straight line, count backwards from a hundred, pat us down with their hands. Three of them and one of you and it's dark, some town you never heard of, they're shining a light on you, none of it makes any sense. Last night Bill pissed himself because we wouldn't stop the van, just kept jabbing him in the kidneys, telling him it's a long way back to London and would he like a warm cup of tea?

On the road, Brian sometimes gets his own car. He sometimes even gets his own room at some shabby country hotel while the others sleep in the van. He's supposed to get to the shows early, settle accounts with the management. That's the arrangement he's come to with Andrew Loog Oldham, who has sent them on this futile round of engagements. But something about his privileges, his isolation, along with the shaming drudgery of the tour, has given him a sense of experiencing things from a distance, as if he's not quite present for what's really happening. He places his phone calls back to London and counts out the nightly receipts and writes in his book what they've spent each day on petrol and food, but there's often a feeling that somehow it's coming to an end, that the band is on the verge of failing, no matter what he does.

He's started to think about the Beatles, to envy their growing fame. There's the temptation to clean things up, to wear matching suits, and then the realization that it wouldn't work for them anyway.

One night in Sheffield he arrives almost an hour late for the first show, so drunk he can hardly get inside the backstage door with his briefcase and guitar. He greets the others with a tone of fuzzy dismissal, a complicit blear-eyed shrug, as if the whole thing is just some minor hassle that they should be hip enough to not even notice, much less mention. But then he sees the way Mick is sitting on his dressing room stool, smoking, not looking at him, and it causes him to drop his things to the ground, newly animated, suddenly raising his arms and opening his eyes wide in some strange parody of spookiness.

"What's wrong?" he says. He walks over and puts his face right in Mick's, leering at him in a way that Mick has never seen before. It causes him to stare back for a moment in challenge but then to recoil inside himself, realizing that Brian isn't seeing him.

"What are you so afraid of?" Brian says. "What is it? Are you afraid that I might lose control? That I might bite you, or touch you somewhere dirty? Is that what the long face is about?"

Mick closes his eyes, struggling to compose himself in the small space between himself and Brian. He nods his head then, his eyes heavy-lidded, and lets out a disdainful sniff.

"You're right," he says. "We're all afraid of you, Brian."

Keith is strapping on his guitar, impatient. "What the fuck are you on about?" he says. "Get your gear on."

"He looked so displeased just now," Brian says. "Like this was the whole point, this little gig in fuck knows where. Sheffield. You think you can handle it, Mick?"

He turns back toward Keith, smiling at him in a weirdly complicit way. "Everything he's ever done, I thought of it a thousand times before. Now he has the nerve to just sit there like that. Like anyone can even see him."

"Right," says Keith. "Get yourself together, yeah? You ought to have a look at yourself in the mirror."

He looks not drunk but fluish. His eyes are gluey and his face is blanched, pink only at the edges of his cheeks. He paces around the dressing room for a few more moments, incredulous and lost. Then he takes his briefcase and his guitar and walks back out the door.

It's a small crowd, only a few dozen people, but by the third song they've all moved close to the stage, standing in the first rows and waiting as if the spectacle before them might collapse. It's the first time the band has played without Brian, the first time Keith has had to fill up all that space with only one guitar. He moves back and forth toward his microphone stand, raising himself into place for his vocals. For some of his chords, he crouches down by the drum riser, his head lowered almost to his knees. Others he attacks with a sudden upswing of the wrist, a windmilling motion that makes the chords seem like small, controlled detonations. He knows without looking at the crowd that they're watching him as much as they're watching Mick. What he's playing is not quite the blues, and it comes out as if the band is playing it through him, a kind of revenge for Brian's desertion.

That night Brian has a dream. He's walking through a court-yard full of rubble — it's in London, during the war. The courtyard ends in a patch of stubby weed trees, then opens up on a whole city block in ruins: burnt-out cars, sidewalks folded in on themselves, trunks and boxes lying on the ground cov-ered in white dust. What keeps him moving is the sense that he's being pursued. His pursuer is not quite a person, but like the distorted essence of someone he knows: a middle-aged man with a wrinkled suit who can't stop smiling. Above them, the sky tilts and veers, invaded at its edges by the branches of trees. The man is stepping through a hallway now, swinging a closed umbrella at his side, grinning. There is a sense of panic before an immense, unending futility. Now they're in a gray room and the lights surge to an intense white, the walls and ceiling emit a high hum. It sends Brian to the floor, on his back, grasping his knees, paralyzed by the bright exuberance of the man's gaze. He wakes up with a feeling of intense shame, a sense that whatever happens now will be tainted by the violation of this dream.

———

Life pivots all at once and suddenly they are stars. One night they come onstage to a hall so full, so crammed with bodies, that they seem on the verge of falling onto the stage. They're al-most all girls — girls with bouffant hairdos and scarves, girls in black jumpers who elbow their way to the front. For a moment, they struggle to find the dials on their guitars; it's as if they've outgrown their bodies and become some quality of the air. The sound the girls make is the strangest they've ever heard, not the high screech of adulation but an eerily sexual keen, a thickening moan.

Their arms and legs and chests and heads suddenly feel ridiculously stiff and crude. They feel magnanimous for just standing there in the torrent of noise and not walking off the stage.

What has happened is that their record has found its way onto the radio. It is a basic pop song, not much of a song at all, distinguished by a simple guitar riff, a hitch in the rhythm, that gives it angles and contours. They had recorded it a little more than a week ago, but already it seems like something from the distant past.

Every gesture they make now is magnified, triggering panic and exaltation. Everywhere, they're met by the same horde of plucked and powdered faces, pallid and swollen and lost. It's impossible to hear what they're playing, but they're not there to be heard. They're there for this swishing around in front of a thousand girls with sprayed hair and defiant, tearful glares. They don't realize they're even making a gesture until the screams get louder, and then they have to just accept it: they're performing, they're putting on a show.

They're suddenly matched up with American stars—Bo Diddley, Little Richard, the Everly Brothers—people they have idolized. It happens so quickly that the band doesn't have time to parse all the different implications of this mistake. The girls are screaming, but it's for the English boys with their one hit song, their ill-fitting jackets, their scruffy, unwashed hair. If they stop to think, they are lost, but if they keep moving there's a chance it will cohere into a kind of sense. Bo Diddley plays with them onstage. The moment Bo Diddley leaves, the screams get much louder. They finish their next song and girls start to throw themselves from the balconies: they get their friends to give them a handhold, then dangle for a few bewildered seconds, twisting and dazed, then fall shrieking onto the crowd below.

Already, Mick can see what's happening. He can see that no matter what he does he's about to become the focal point of the band. He's in the middle of the stage, taller than the others, and he is the only one not obscured by a large, hollow-bodied guitar. Each night, he watches Little Richard leap and collapse and raise himself up, brandishing his microphone stand, everything deliberate, calculated for maximum impact. Little Richard can be draining to be around backstage, queenly and round-faced now that he's cut his hair, but he's always performing, and Mick himself has started to dance in a way that no one else in the band would dare to try.

A sudden rise onto his toes, seizing the microphone. A quick spasm that jerks his head upright and carries out into his back-stretched arms. A lazy slouch, hips slung to the side, one hand up, one down, drunken and sliding. A pause before he rights himself, turning his head and clapping, a sideways glance at no one, guarding his space.

It turns out that the point of touring is speed. Time moves faster and faster, the moments bunching up on top of one another, so that it's difficult to experience any of them as real. To stay awake, they take pep pills, the same pep pills that performers have been taking for years, but it affects each of them in different ways. Onstage, Brian has started to smile between postures of menace. He's started to act a little bit like a pop star, standing with his feet apart, raising his eyebrows wistfully when he plays harmonica. It's mostly a joke, except when he gets frantic and starts vying with Mick. He winks at the girls as they're carted off on stretchers, grins at them as they pull out their hair. The speed gives him an intense feeling of focus for a while, a sense of presence and wit, until the details get exaggerated to such enormous proportion and significance that time becomes impossibly dense. His face stares out into the crowd and either acknowledges them or shrugs them off, it's never quite clear. It's a face he's had all his life, one that has molded his personality, and now it's a face that carries him as the personality begins to fade.

Backstage, the girls hover around him — the assertive, the shy, the fat and devoutly hopeful. He speaks to them in a faint, spacey lisp, mixing good manners with a sudden spice of profanity. They let him do whatever he wants, but they're not seeing him, they're seeing what they'd imagined they'd see, some projection of their awe. They can seem like predators, especially the shy ones, and he begins to take pleasure in the ways he makes them leave: feigning a helpless, melancholy fugue that requires immediate solitude. Retreating into the toilet to emerge a few minutes later as an older, businesslike stranger. Pouring himself a drink, then tossing their clothes out the door in a pile and telling them to get out before he calls the front desk.

When he misses another show in Newcastle, their manager, Andrew, has a talk with Mick and Keith. They don't realize that Andrew has taken a sharp, animal dislike to Brian, almost from the moment of their first meeting. It's the fact that he's vulnerable and arrogant at the same time, the fact that he gets so many girls. In the dressing room, Andrew tells Mick and Keith that according to his records Brian has been paying himself an extra five pounds for every show.

Keith punches a hole through the dressing room wall. He can't speak; he has to leave and stand in the alleyway, staring at the dampness that steams and drips off the black stone building. His anger and disgust are compounded by the apprehension that this stupid rivalry among them is somehow at the heart of their sound. It's a sound that even Bo Diddley has told him would make them famous if they persevered. But he knows that the sound starts with him, that the drums follow the lead of his guitar so that the backbeat always comes just a millisecond late, lazy and blunt and stamped with his imprint.

"Forget it," he says to Mick a few minutes later. "Now's not the time to fuck around."

"Not now," says Andrew. "But when we get back to London, we're going to sit him down, have a little palaver."

"I think we should do it now," says Mick. "How much longer are we going to carry him?"

"He has style," says Andrew. "Do you know how to speak like he does? I don't think so. Brian speaks like Hollywood."

"It's two guitars," says Keith. "That's what I'm talking about."

"We need his bloody face," says Andrew. "His image."

"Image?" says Mick.

They arrive in America and are treated like a comedy act, a scrofulous, second-rate version of the Beatles. A deejay drives them around Detroit in a convertible Ford while a loudspeaker plays their songs to empty streets. Their songs are too much like American songs, too raw and unmelodic, and they seem on the verge of failing once again, faking their way through an America they'd always imagined as their rightful home. They pose like teen idols with a circus elephant in California.

But it turns out they've only gotten started. The tour will go on for much longer than they'd expected—in fits and starts, it will go on for another three years—and they will have no time to assess what has happened or how they've changed. They play a week of sold-out dates in London, and everything reverts to violence. The fans charge the stage, smash the instruments, pull off the band's clothes. Every show erupts in a riot. When they make their way into Europe, the tour becomes like a military exercise: attack dogs, tear gas, truncheons, armored vans. They see through their limousine windows a row of cars with flames rising from the hoods, coalescing into startling blossoms of thick, dark smoke. In Paris, the fans are joined by student mobs who smash windows and throw cobblestones at the mounted police.

In West Berlin, Brian gets sick and spends two days in bed. He misses the entire city, doesn't see the Reichstag or the rubble of Potsdamer Platz or the newly erected Wall. He dreams of stray dogs running through the rubble of a blacked-out London, taking cover beneath the piles of beams and crumbled stones. He wakes with a smothered sense of distance that makes it difficult for him to move. It comes as an ironic surprise, how ill-equipped he is for this life he's always wanted. He has an odd relapse of his childhood asthma, a sudden fluttering in his heart that leaves him light-headed. He misses all four shows, and Keith has to fill up all that space with only one guitar.

But it doesn't really matter what Keith plays anymore, it doesn't matter if he plays at all. The crowd is screaming. The stage is overrun before the first song is over, and the band races for the limousines through the fire door. The next single goes to number three.

All Brian can think to do is push himself harder. He splashes water on his face, steels himself with liquor and barbiturates, liquor and speed.

When the tour makes its next brief stop in England, Andrew locks Mick and Keith in his back bedroom and tells them they can't come out until they've composed an original song. He doesn't mention any of this to Brian. He explains that this is the next step, the way they will be like the Beatles. It's where the real money is anyway, not in some five extra pounds on a package tour of England.

The short film *Invocation of My Demon Brother* had its premiere at the end of 1969. The images rush by like a strobe light, rapidly intercut, sometimes super-imposed: Mick Jagger's face, Keith Richards's face, the face of Bobby Beausoleil, a rock musician whom nobody would have heard of at the time. In the film, there is a violent merging, a trance, all of their im-ages blurred into one. The filmmaker, an older man named Kenneth Anger, is shown conducting an oc-cult ceremony while helicopters land in Vietnam; Hells Angels menace fans at a Rolling Stones con-cert; a nightmare begins to unfold. Within months of the film's release, Bobby Beausoleil would appear for the first time in newspapers in the company of Charles Manson—he had committed the first of the Manson murders. That same week, a fan would be killed by Hells Angels at a Stones concert at Altamont Speedway. The sixties would come to an end.

An invocation draws forces in. It can lead to an evocation, which spits the forces back out.

— from *Dream Plays: A History of Underground Film*

The dream starts with Bobby Beausoleil, the would-be star. He's walking by himself at night, his clothes soaked through to the skin, cuts on his hands. People hurry by with bowed heads beneath umbrellas, water pools on the sidewalks, lights burn dimly in the liquor stores and bars. Bobby thinks about how he used to know people like that, but now they don't see him, the hunch-shouldered kid with his hands in his pockets, the runaway fingering his change.

The entrance to the theater is a tiny vestibule of darkness that seeps into his lungs, a musk of cigarettes and mold. He finds the gap in the heavy blackout curtains and pushes them open with both hands. Before him, the screen is enormous, maybe six stories high, far enough away that a fog of blue light seems to waft in the air before it. He goes up to the balcony, where a few people whose faces he recognizes are passing around a skull-shaped pipe. Ron, Carol, Sharon. They stare at him but don't say hello.

He sits down by himself, his face hidden in the darkness, his hands cold and stinging where they're cut. Hanging from the ceiling is a silver eagle gripping a swastika in its talons. The theater is more like a warehouse or a hangar, he sees now, with catwalks on the ceiling, lights hung from girders, condensation trickling from the gridwork. He recognizes it without knowing from where, a forgotten part of some recurring dream.

The lights go out. There is total darkness. Then a pale half-moon of light slowly rises over a man on a stage before the screen, accompanied by a sound like the purr of distant helicopters. At the man's feet, there is a blue nimbus of fog. He raises his arms, extends them fully so that his heavy sleeves form the shape of a cross. In his left hand he holds a wand. Above him, on the screen, a shirtless boy sits and stares. He seems barely awake, his hair and sideburns dyed a lifeless white, his pupils moving sightlessly in the slits of his eyes.

The man's face suddenly appears on-screen, six stories high, staring right at Bobby. He wears mascara and green eye shadow. He seems to have deliberately made himself ugly, a zodiac glyph traced in ash on his forehead. He starts to dance in a slow shimmy, his arms extended, the wand still in his hand, his chest heaving in and out, eyes defiantly fixed straight ahead. Every time the body on the stage moves, the body on-screen moves in the same way.

The music gets louder, more insistent. It's a ca-cophony of noise — a tank's engine, a helicopter's blades, a satellite's bleep, a missile's thrust. The man takes off his hat, throws it into the seats. He puts his hands on his hips and rotates them back and forth, angrily staring straight ahead. He cups one hand be-hind his ear and one down by his waist, vamping,

jutting his pelvis, then switches hands in rhythm.
The credits roll.
   A film by Anger.
   Invocation of My Demon Brother.

THE EMPRESS, 1928–1947

HIS MOTHER CARRIED KENNETH past the olive trees, the backyard sprig of bougainvillea. The colors blurred and seared. His last name was Anglemyer. Later he would change it to Anger. Even in those years of the Depression, his mother spoiled him, buying him drawing paper, movie magazines, comic books, cutout paper dolls.

While his father saved, they lived in his grandmother's house in Santa Monica. Hollywood wasn't far. His mother and his grandmother talked about movie stars, Hollywood stories Kenneth could only partly understand. Once, his grandmother took a sugar cube, soaked it in bitters, placed it at the bottom of a glass, then filled the glass with champagne. "It's called a champagne cocktail," she said, letting Kenneth taste. It was only a few months later that she left. In one of the first painful mysteries of his life, she moved in with a thin, dark-haired woman named Meg, who worked in the production department of MGM Pictures.

It became his father's house after that. His older siblings—terse, industrious—were already in his father's sway. He was a silent man who worked as a mechanical engineer. When he wasn't at the office, he made things on a lathe in the garage: tables, chairs, wooden stools. Amid the carpenter's benches and the table saw, the utility lamps with their dangling cords, the three children would sometimes watch him work, and he would explain each step of what he was doing, tapering the spindles for a chair back or molding the hinges of a drawer. Sometimes he would allow them to hammer in dowels or turn the drill axle, peering with a surgeon's gravity over their shoulders at the instrument they held in their hands. "Watch it from the side," he would say. "The angle. You're about to come in at an angle."

Kenneth daydreamed. His grandmother and her companion, Meg, showed a special interest in him that they could only feign toward his older siblings. They took him to the movies, the theater adorned with African designs, its walls broken up by enormous pillars carved with conga drums and crossed spears. There they watched epics from the Bible: bare-chested men, their muscles accentuated with grime and sweat, struggling with hard, implacable women who wore coiled bracelets in the shape of serpents. In science-fiction movies, men in skin-tight suits wandered Mars, stalked to the edge of madness by sentient beings who took form as blurs of light. There was a film set in Mexico, on the Day of the Dead, in which peasants ate candy skeletons and danced ecstatically under glowing torches. Skeletons in shrouds moved in carts beneath flames, while the living exulted in their own bodies, or suffered agonies of religious grief, or strutted clownishly in the abject shamelessness of their poverty.

Even as a child, he suspected that there was another world being concealed from him by a mother and father who had conspired to lead lives of convention and disguise. The movies gave him clues about lives they had chosen to disown, or perhaps lived out at night when he was not there to see them.

At dinner, there would be a pot roast surrounded by potatoes, which sat directly before the father. Nearer the children were bowls of beets and beet greens, white bread and butter. His mother would talk about the neighborhood women, the book club, the chatter at the bridge game. The father would interject terse commands: *Kenneth, fork. Napkins.* Sometimes he would strike the table. Sometimes the meal would be interrupted for a round of spankings.

It was a ritual that started in dread and then accrued a kind of hysterical momentum. Each warning would lead to more noise, more pinching under the table, more desperate squealing and giggling. Kenneth would howl and grin, his legs twitching beneath the table, leering eyes fixed on his father. It was always as if the father would single out only one of them. The game was to plead helplessness, giddy innocence, as if innocence had a meaning or a value once the game began.

He would send them all to their rooms, where he would make them wait until he finished his meal. Kenneth would sit on the edge of his bed and bury his face between his knees, breathing. In this self-imposed darkness the fear would become an unwelcome kind of yearning, guilty and hopeless. His hands would grip the backs of his legs through the fabric of his jeans. He would imagine himself in a rough cave lit by a fire, a vision from the movies. On the cave's back wall, a man struggled in chains, a few narrow cuts across his chest. Then he would see himself and his brother wrestling in the driveway, their hands joined in struggle, Kenneth's head buried in his brother's armpit. It would end with Kenneth grinding a rock into his brother's knuckles.

His father smelled like alcohol and cloves, the scent of aftershave. There was something almost shy about the way he entered the room, adjusting his glasses and clearing his throat, then telling Kenneth to take down his pants. Kenneth could not look at him. He felt detached from himself as he unbuttoned his jeans and pulled them down around his ankles, covering himself with his hands. Without speaking, his father removed his belt, then he bent Kenneth over his knee and beat him methodically with a small length of the doubled-over leather, breathing through his nose. He did it without emotion or even interest. Perhaps worse than the pain itself was the sullen intimacy of his lap, his rigid grip on Kenneth's back, the idea that Kenneth couldn't see his father's face.

Kenneth thought of the dinner table: the plates a dull white that showed their scratches in the bright light, the tablecloth olive green and mustard yellow. He saw the jelly glasses that he and his siblings used, the faceted garnet-colored goblets for his parents. It was a kind of ceremony: that was why his mother pinned up her hair and put on a clean dress, but also why his father was allowed to unbutton and roll up his sleeves.

The blows came in a slow, precise rhythm that made Kenneth buck and kick. He became smaller and less aware of himself, reduced finally to the smallest pinpoint of whoever he was. When it was over, he lay curled up in the corner of his bed, wheezing and lost. His jeans were still down around his ankles, his warm skin exposed to the air.

"Relax," his father said. "Let's try to calm down now. Let's try to settle down and get some sleep."

When he left, Kenneth opened his eyes to the room he lived in. There were his careful drawings of Japanese scholars, of geishas with piled hair held in place by lacquered sticks. There were the cutouts of Flash Gordon and Aquaman, the illustrations from *The Wizard of Oz*. He turned to look at the marks on his buttocks, nursing them with his fingers. In the bronze light of his bedroom lamp, the pictures on his wall had been transformed. They were witnesses to this secret bond he shared with his father.

It was his grandmother's friend Meg who got him a small part in a movie adaptation of *A Midsummer Night's Dream*. At first, he and some other kids in different costumes ran up and down a cellophane-wrapped staircase, reaching up for girls in cellophane dresses who were lifted away on guy wires. Next, they frolicked aimlessly in a forest of artificial trees. There was an odd stop-start quality to it all, a vacant pause between brief snatches of play. They ran with their hands at right angles to their hips, crouched or fell to the ground in laughter, teased one another in smiling pairs. The play began to feel important. They became immersed in it, aware of themselves as children. It was as if they each had unique talents that it was now their duty to exaggerate. Kenneth found himself running around the trees, faster and faster, waving his hands like wings above his head until he was shouting. By then, he was dizzy from the fumes, the acrid smell of shellac, the bright reflections of the lights.

Afterward, in the costume room, they chose him for a special role: the Changeling Prince. He didn't know what this role involved or even what the story was about. He stood in a shiny plastic suit with three strands of pearls over his chest, a thicker strand around his neck, and two rhinestone earrings that dangled to his chin line. On his head was a turban that culminated in a spray of white ostrich feathers.

He would watch it a half-dozen times in the theater with his grandmother and Meg. Here was the important moment: the woman who played Titania lifting him onto her knee, her body softened by a fill light so that there was no distinction between the beaded fringes of her sleeves and the silver spray of hair that descended like a shawl to her waist. She and Kenneth were in close-up, his dark hair and small features nearly as Asiatic as his rounded turban. The plastic trees and flowers radiated a light that had nothing to do with any actual season or time of day. On-screen, his body and the woman's body were hardly bodies at all, more like figments. Gone was any vestige of the actual soundstage: no smell of shellac or hairspray, no visible trace of his own anxious joy.

It affected him like the first manic vision of a would-be saint: his first Hollywood role. Afterward, there would be much struggling and compromise, an endless effort to return to that original moment.

When he was ten, he began begging his father for the left-over ends of film from the home movies they made on their vacations. He examined the black Bolex camera, the riddles of apertures and shutter speeds, the light meter, the different filters for indoors and outdoors. He shot little fragments that evoked unexpected emotions: a few seconds of his sister brushing her hair with her fingers, or stepping out of a car in a long dress. He worked out scenarios in his mind, fairy tales involving kings and sorcerers and princesses, power struggles that ended not with a plot twist but an image: a candle burning on his parents' dresser, a potted hyacinth on the kitchen table, a patch of sky between cypress trees. He found by accident that if he spliced together snippets from the family's home movies—group poses at Yosemite or Big Sur—the images took on a different meaning, a lonely, distant quality, as if his family were strangers or dead. The images seemed more real than the moments they recorded. They made everything suggestive and strange, as if highlighted or outlined.

He filmed the family Christmas tree, bestrewn with silver tinsel and colored glass balls. A few weeks later, he filmed its undressing, the ornaments packed away in boxes. Then he filmed the bare, broken tree on the grill inside the fireplace, the flames slowly reaching up to its limbs until it had withered to a charred skeleton. It was only after watching it in his room on the bare wall that he realized what the film was about. It was about the holiday's actual meaning, the story of Christ told in some strange new language that only he seemed to be aware of.

It was a lot of knowledge to carry around by himself. Sometimes he spent time with his sister, Jean, playing Chutes and Ladders in her bedroom, listening to Frank Sinatra records, watching her try on makeup. He kept going to the movies with his grandmother and Meg. He fell in love with actresses who were elegant and strong, brought down in the end by loneliness or jealousy or age, but always wittier and dressed with more flair than their rivals. He daydreamed that he was a girl himself, leaving home for an uncertain career, embarking on a life of struggle and tribulation.

What it amounted to at first was a certain preoccupation he had with photographs of men, particularly well-dressed, capable men who seemed at ease in their own skin. The sight of their faces would strike him in the center of his chest with a feeling of both menace and safety, as if they could see inside him but were somehow protective of what they found there. Executives who carried briefcases, combat pilots standing before their airplanes, their eyes screened by sunglasses—for a long time, he wasn't aware of what drew him to these men, only that they made him alert and still. He found them in movie magazines, in fashion ads, in recruitment propaganda for the armed services. They hailed cabs in raincoats, or twisted at the waist to meet his gaze. When he finally understood how important they were to him, how much they cost him in guilt, it was like discovering a new birthmark in the crook of his leg, a stain that had to be studied carefully in order to be assimilated. It was like the feeling of spying or eavesdropping, a practice that became harder to resist once you had started doing it, no matter how appalled you were, until the loathing itself became a part of the fascination.

In dreams, a hive of bees would push itself slowly through the skin of his mother's face. The family would appear as monkeys, crashing over the dinner table with inflamed genitals, their hands full of food. In the blue glow of a city covered in ice, a young girl with a dog's slender body would drag a cart full of glowing coals through empty streets. The dreams were full of irrational feelings—a sudden urge to eat rotten fruit, a calm fascination with snipping off the ends of his own fingers—fears that modulated into a cocooned sense of safety. His father would appear as a fat man with a few strands of oily hair and an old-fashioned pin-striped suit. When Kenneth began unbuttoning his father's vest, he nestled Kenneth's face against his chest, and Kenneth felt two long rows of nipples beneath his undershirt.

One night, he came downstairs to find his father still awake, reading the newspaper in his armchair. He looked at Kenneth for a moment in openmouthed uncertainty, as if on the verge of sleep. His glasses were slightly crooked on the bridge of his nose, his hair a disheveled spray of dark fronds.

"I want you to look at something," his father said. Then he rested his paper on the ottoman before him and stood up slowly in his slippers and robe. "I want you to see if there's anything over here that you can salvage."

He was indicating a neat pile of his own clothes, which he had stacked on the side table by the door. They were old trousers and work shirts, a pile of laundered garments that had been reserved for work in the garage.

"They would have to be taken in," he went on. "The pants anyway. Do me a favor, Kenneth. Stop wincing."

Kenneth looked at him, annoyed not so much at his father's words but at his own transparent discomfort.

"Tomorrow, go through the pile," his father said. "What you don't want, I'll take to the Salvation Army. There's no sense wasting it."

Kenneth went absently back up the staircase, creasing his brow in feigned consideration. He had forgotten why he'd come down. His father was always urging him to go outside, to do something physical, always perplexed by the solemn stacks of books he brought home. But the books gave him documentation, proof of other places, other times, that had nothing to do with this one.

Before long, he no longer wanted to stop, or no longer believed that he would stop. The simple word "men" began to signify a hidden world of smells and sensations: men shaving, men perspiring, men tucking in shirts and buckling belts. Eventually, he sent away for a bodybuilding course through the mail. When it arrived, he had a few nights of guilty ministrations before a series of tiny black-and-white images of a muscleman in dark briefs, lifting chairs or squatting in front of a mirror with rigid thighs.

There was no way to think about any of it except as a developing illness. It was not that it was evil to give up control over your own body, or to have a mind so weak that you could not restrain its thoughts for even half a day. What was evil was when you stopped resisting, when you began to take a secret pride in the foreign places your body could take you.

He wanted to make movies, not just short films on a 16mm Bolex, but lavish epics dense with atmosphere and color. His bedroom was festooned with dream figures: Isis, Apollo, Bacchus, Orpheus, and also Valentino, Lex Luthor, the Cobra Lady, Plasticman.

His mother tilted her head back in the lounge chair, eyes closed in feigned magnificence. "The magic of Hollywood," she said. "But it's such a nuisance, isn't it? All the other people you'd have to work with?"

He was angry without knowing why. Then he realized that it was because she was trying to form an alliance with him, an alliance based on his own weakness.

In the fall of 1944, his sister, Jean, joined the WAVES, following his brother, Bob, who had enlisted in the air force. The country was still embroiled in the same abstract war, a distant operation conducted by airplanes and tanks and battleships. He knew of it only through newsreels: deployments of troops, diagrammed tactics, men in barracks posing in their undershirts. It was a struggle of machines and haircuts and uniforms, all of which held for him an implicit, personal threat. He was sixteen now, a dark, handsome impostor, thin and broadshouldered, with a serious cast to his eyebrows, but the effect was ruined by his effeminate walk and the high lisp of his voice. The world could see what kind of person he was, could tell just by looking at him what his future held. People like him wound up living in residence hotels. They worked as floorwalkers in department stores, cooked their meals on a hot plate, spent their nights alone in a bathrobe making up their faces or getting brutalized in public toilets. He could not summon up any humor to neutralize these stereotypes, nor was he seduced by fantasies of self-pity: the mental ward, the empty pill bottle, the melodramatic farewell note. What made it worse for him was that he had the same masculine pride as his father, but with no easy way of expressing it. He would stare at his face in the mirror, the stern face of a matinee idol, dark-eyed and gaunt. He wanted to live inside that body, not just to inhabit it awkwardly, without awareness or intention. It led to all kinds of affected postures, placements of the hands, exercises in carriage and comportment that only made things worse.

He had to go to out-of-the-way places to find what he needed now, rare-book stores in downtown L.A. where he bought pictures of musclemen, their brows shadowed by sailor caps, their groins covered by dark G-strings called "posing straps." At night, he would sometimes sneak out of the house to walk the pier, never approaching the men there but watching from a distance, looking for the secret signals of canted wristwatches or lit cigarettes. After a while it became an exercise in hopelessness, until finally he was surprised by a sudden craving for the initial feeling of wrongness, a feeling that no longer existed.

He made a film of himself in his grandmother's apartment one weekend when she and Meg were on vacation. He sneaked into the closet in Meg's bedroom, where she kept a collection of old costumes she had taken from the MGM lot, castaway gowns once worn by actresses. There were only a few that he could get himself into: a red-and-white-sequined gown and an aqua silk dress with silver panels above the hips. It was important to get them all the way on, carefully working his arms into the tight sleeves and then feeling the fragile zipper between his shoulder blades as he painfully edged it up his back. Encased in these second skins, he filmed himself before the full-length bedroom mirror, not preening or posing, but glaring at himself with solemn incomprehension. He did not look feminine at all. He looked like an angry boy, someone completely other and apart.

It was that winter that he discovered a rare book in one of the stores downtown, a worn black volume kept under glass. Its cover showed no title or author; instead it bore a thin line drawing of an Egyptian eye at the center of a triangle that radiated shafts of light. There was something about its spare design, its aura of secrecy and contraband, that made him walk around the store for a few minutes, pretending to browse, until at last he brought himself to ask the man behind the counter for a closer look.

It was called *The Sephiroth,* though there was no author mentioned anywhere. He found the title on the frontispiece, above three symbols and an invocation to an Egyptian god called Horus. What followed was a kind of mock sermon, written in biblical cadences, laced with odd, sometimes contemptuous asides to the reader. A good deal of its initial attraction was this anonymous voice, propounding its information through a scrim of knowing, private humor.

> Thy Will Be Done! The proposition is bald, even basic—as bracing as the gusts of Flatus, or as boring as last week's beans: Thy Will Be Done! For who shall chooseth, if not the hand that grasps? And who shall see, if not the eye that yearns? Think of one thing only, O heedful one, as ye walketh the wide way: Thy Will Be Done! For is not thy yearning like unto a column of jasper, or the rich scent of hyssop? Is it not as the darkest jewel of Hamman, or the farthest star over Nor? Nay, it is as the lust of the goat, the blood of doves, the fire in the virgin's loins! For who shall chooseth, if not thine own hand? And how shalt thou see, if not through thine own eye?

It was not just the words but the austerity of their presentation—the book's dilapidated binding, its ugly type, all of it reminiscent of a student dissertation. It was destined for only the smallest clique of readers, its boastful voice muted by the fact of its utter obscurity. There was a faintly intimidating allure in its symbols and diagrams, the feeling that just by looking at the figures—the pentacle, the zodiac, the tarot, the sephiroth—he was exposing himself to secrets. There was the sense that the author or authors, unnamed and so impossible to imagine, could somehow guess that he was looking at it, not only the book in general but the specific copy he held in his hands.

He bought it for twelve dollars, a fortune in 1944, when even the bus schedules bore the words "Don't waste time-tables; paper is a vital war material." The man at the counter told him casually, almost skeptically, that the author was a drug addict and famous satanist. He knew before he'd even got it home that he had at last stumbled upon the secret door into that parallel world he had always hoped was there.

According to *The Sephiroth,* the world was a shifting fabric of reality and dream. There were people who without knowing it took on the attributes of certain mythological figures or gods. This could make them purposeful and bold, like Prometheus or Cain, or could render them passive and wounded, like Vulcan, the archetype of the artist. There were cold, solitary spirits like the huntress Diana, and tricksters like Hermes and Pan, and communers with the dead, like Hecate and Persephone. There were stern, paternal figures, like Shiva or the risen Christ, and there were law-abiding slaves like Mary or Job. You had little choice as to which of these spirits inhabited you personally. Indeed, most people spent their whole lives in a futile effort to become someone they were not meant to be: powerful when they were born weak, wise when they were born to take commands. All unhappiness stemmed from just this misperception: the failure to know one's true nature or the obstinate refusal to embrace it. Your date of birth, the letters of your name, the color of your eyes, the lines on the palms of your hands—everything in the world was encrypted with the secret and conflicting information that determined the kind of life you were meant to lead.

There were a few rare souls who saw through to this pattern in things and could change it according to their wills. These people were called magi, bringers of the age of Horus, the old Egyptian sun god, who would put an end to the submissive, feminine sway of Isis and the prohibitive, masculine sway of Osiris. They were the children of Lucifer, the bringer of light, who signified the end of all opposites and dualities.

Male and female, self and other, reality and dream. At the meeting point of these opposites was a zone of energy and pain where the spirit of Lucifer burned in isolation. It was the wild chaos of orgasm, the music of war, the entranced stupor of hallucination. Only a few could even perceive this zone. To penetrate it was to negate any difference between good and evil, life and death, desire and fear.

He kept reading *The Sephiroth* even when he could no longer think about its words with any acuity. He kept looking at it even when he knew it was not going to give him any more pleasure, but only fatigue and hollowness. It was something he had to keep struggling with, like his body, even when its mystery was no longer interesting but blurred and tangled and exasperating.

He had a dream one night of a mob chasing after him: the soldiers from the newsreels, the students at his high school, the cruising men on the piers, all of them chasing him down, tearing at his clothes. They forced him to the pavement and began to kick him and scratch his face. When he woke up, he was unable to recognize his bedroom for a moment. Then, as always, the pictures of gods and heroes on his walls appeared to regard him with a solemn, knowing complicity. For a moment, they were more real than he was — they were the hidden movers inside him. It was in this way that he had his first visceral understanding of what was meant by the word "magick."

For a brief period that fall, a boy named Ted Drake had attended his school. He was a tall, hawk-nosed kid who in some misguided effort to make a place for himself would pick fights in the parking lot. Kenneth had seen him in the hall one day with a dark cut over his eye and a broken hand wrapped in bandages and tape. He wore work clothes: chinos and thin cotton shirts and black engineer's boots. A few weeks after school had started, he stole a car and forged some checks and tried to run away from home, after which they sent him to a juvenile detention facility outside Sacramento.

According to *The Sephiroth,* there was a difference between the "self" and the "soul." The self was a set of conventions, an outer garment that the soul was forced to weave out of its various encounters with the world. It was in the delinquent Ted Drake that Kenneth saw his real soul, the true essence hidden inside him. He saw that to be true to that soul—to escape the fraud of his self—he had to somehow find a way to live inside Ted Drake's skin.

He had something like this in mind when he entered the small rotunda at Palisades Park where they housed the camera obscura, a dark box fixed with a lens that took in images of the park outside. It was a concrete room with a white table at its center. On this table, the camera projected a surprisingly sharp rendering of the palm trees and the pathways and the beach beyond its walls, an image you could rotate by means of a large metal wheel. It was the kind of place (like the pier, or certain bars downtown) that you knew about if you were someone like Kenneth.

He waited for nearly an hour that afternoon, moving back and forth from the rotunda to the bright sidewalk outside. Finally the right kind of man approached, a middle-aged man with the last bits of an ice cream sandwich pinched in his fingers. He wore a faded gray work shirt and dark trousers with loose, fallen cuffs. When he took the last bite of his ice cream sandwich, he threw the wrapper to the ground behind his heel and wiped his hand on his hip. He eyed Kenneth indifferently as he stepped inside the building, then stood for a moment at the metal wheel, his back turned, one hand in the back pocket of his pants.

On the nape of the man's neck, above the collar, were thick creases that looked almost like scars. Kenneth stood watching while the man casually spun the wheel, watching the rotating images, then moved farther back into the rotunda. It was only when he had reached the far wall that he looked over his shoulder at Kenneth, then turned again, his hands crossed in front of his waist so that his elbows could be seen beneath his rolled-up sleeves. He said nothing, which was the only clue Kenneth had to go on.

To the right, against the back wall, there was a small alcove that led to the toilets. That was where the man went next. Kenneth stood outside the beige door for a moment, no longer knowing what he expected. His mouth was dry and he put his hand flat on the dimpled surface of the door and stared for a moment at the shifting cloud of red light behind his closed eyelids.

Inside, the man was leaning with his back against the sink,

his ankles crossed. He was examining his curled fingertips, then he looked up at Kenneth, his image flattened by the dim brownish light.

His hair was a reddish gray bristle. He had a narrow face with close-set eyes, two arched dimples between the brows. He started nodding his head, his tongue poking at the side of his mouth. Then he stood away from the sink and moved back toward the stalls, and Kenneth followed him, his face unconsciously mimicking the clipped purposefulness of the man's.

"I thought so," the man said, turning.

Kenneth raised his chin, his nostrils flaring.

"Right away, I thought so," said the man.

In one sudden motion, he grabbed Kenneth by the shoulder and with his other hand gripped his waist. Kenneth couldn't see his face now, could only smell the tang of his perspiration. The man held him upright and pressed his body against his own. He held him with a kind of paternal restraint, breathing a little heavily through his nose, as if carefully choosing his moment. Kenneth's eyes were closed. All he could see was the vague red light, faintly throbbing like the membrane of a cell illuminated on the stage of a microscope.

"Go ahead," the man said. "What did you come here for?"

He took Kenneth's hand and placed it on the inside of his thigh. Through the coarse fabric, Kenneth's fingers gathered in the length and presence of the man's erection, the delicately curved head poking up at an angle above the elastic band of his underpants. Then the man put his hand on top of Kenneth's and pulled it away.

"Go ahead now," he said. "Kneel. Get down on your knees."

His belt buckle jangled at his waist. Kenneth pulled the

man's stiff briefs down to reveal the muscles of his upper thighs. He was almost hairless, only a tight clump of red fuzz above the bland shock of his erection. It was pale and smooth, almost colorless. When he guided it carefully into Kenneth's mouth, cupping Kenneth's chin in his hand, it tasted faintly of milk, or like the faintly sour smell of milk when you first open the carton. It probed his mouth like a bodiless thumb.

The man took a step back for some reason. He inhaled deeply through his nose, his eyes half-shut. His cock jutted out to the left, faintly glistening with the thin coating of Kenneth's saliva. He shook his head as if to clear it.

He wedged his stiff penis back beneath the waistband of his underpants. Then he hoisted up his pants, working them from side to side over his hips, softly grunting with the effort. "That's what I thought," he said, looking down at Kenneth. He buckled his belt. Then he told Kenneth that he was under arrest.

The creases between his close-set eyes were almost sarcastic. Kenneth was still kneeling, then he sat back on the floor, his eyes on the row of urinals to his left. The man's taste was still in his mouth, stale like the pages of a long unopened book. Then the man said, "Let's go," and Kenneth felt the jagged grip just above his elbow, pulling him upright, and he moved sightlessly forward, letting out little rabbity breaths of something like laughter.

There was another cop—in uniform—waiting up the road in a marked sedan pulled up to the sidewalk, the same path Kenneth had seen in mirror image on the white table of the camera obscura. It was chalk-bright in the sunlight now. The second cop cuffed Kenneth's hands behind his back. A pair of teenage girls rode by on a tandem bicycle, a smear of yellow and green that gave way to the raised, violet-budded arms of a coral tree.

They took him to jail. There were actual bars, like in the movies, but nothing had prepared him for the full-color gloom of the chipped tile floor, stained and crusted with lime, and the dented black drain with its orange scabs of rust. When his father arrived, distracted and out of context, the office was still in his face. He stood up in the precinct lounge with his hat on, his hands in the pockets of his baggy suit, as they led Kenneth in from the cell with the cuffs still on. His voice was flat, faintly sardonic, as he spoke to the cop. "All right," he said. "That's fine." Then he looked at Kenneth, his mouth tight, and without saying a word turned toward the door.

They didn't speak on the ride home. His father drove aggressively, then absentmindedly, refusing to look at Kenneth, whose wrists were scored pink from the handcuffs. His father would only nod his head occasionally, as if working his way back through the past to the various clues.

At dinner, he was still wearing his suit and tie, though he had spent the intervening hours working in the garage. He helped himself to bread, setting three slices on his plate and methodically smearing them with butter, then making a stack. He asked Kenneth's mother how her bridge game was. Then he asked Kenneth if the food was all right, if it was refined enough for his delicate tastes.

"Will," said Kenneth's mother.

"Well, we can't help coddling him now, can we?" he went on.

"Will, please."

"I understand," he said. "You don't want to embarrass him. Kenneth, would you like some cottage cheese? A salad?"

He imagined an appropriate response: violently overturning the table, or slamming down his fork and knife and storming out the door. But he wasn't doing any of these things. He wondered why he was just sitting there, eyes averted, slowly breathing.

The war had ended. In Santa Monica, there was a new coalescence of gay life, infused by the hordes of returned sailors, newly freed. There were vague farm boys willing to experiment, and aesthetes who hosted parties by the pool, but it wasn't what interested Kenneth. He was the sparrowlike boy who seemed to be starving himself, who could sometimes be seen lurking outside of bars in black jeans, his unwashed hair falling in blades over his forehead. He was silent to the point of hostility. Everyone wanted to save him.

He spent most of that next year in a tiny basement apartment in West Hollywood. Its barred windows looked out on a neglected patio where the landlady grew herbs and fed a pack of cats with cubes of stale bread. On the bare wall, he would project his films. He would gather old newspapers and food wrappers and catalogues and tear out the words and pictures and paste them to sheets of butcher paper, then at night carefully burn their edges over the flame on the kitchen range. He made a kind of shrine out of one of these collages, which he preserved on the wall above his bed. At its center was a picture of a bare-chested sailor flexing his biceps. Then there were images of cars, particularly German cars, one of them a long black Mercedes with Nazi regalia on the hood and above the headlights. In the background, a kind of two-dimensional altarpiece was constructed out of flowers, guns, superheroes, the mushroom cloud over Hiroshima. Over this, he painted a pentagram

in red fingernail polish, smearing it thinly with an edge of cardboard. Then he wrote the words "Ted Drake" in tiny cursive
script, over and over again, filling in each blank space with the
letters of his name.

One night in Hollywood he met a boy. It was at an art gallery
where they showed films on Thursday nights. That particular
night, the film was Maya Deren's *Meshes of the Afternoon,* an
evocation of trance states and shifting identities—the realm of
The Sephiroth, where everyday objects became talismans and
an ordinary living room took on the disquieting normalcy of
a nightmare.

When he left the foyer, after the film was over, he saw the
boy outside, standing in profile with one foot against the wall.
He was smoking a cigarette in a convoluted way, examining it
like a specimen between his thumb and the tip of his middle
finger. In the darkness, he appeared almost as thin as Kenneth,
almost as frail, with short, dark bangs. With a slow-blooming
swell of unease, Kenneth somehow knew, by the way the stranger
wouldn't look at him, that he was in fact waiting for him to
approach.

"The mirrored sunglasses," the boy said.

Kenneth turned to him suspiciously. Then he remembered:
the moment when a pair of mirrored sunglasses, more like gog-
gles, appeared on Maya Deren's face, just as she raised a long
knife that would finally be the instrument of her death.

The boy looked at him for the first time then, his eyes hazy,
abstracted. He was older than Kenneth had thought, maybe
twenty-five. Up close, he had a faintly unpleasant shading of facial hair in little patches below his ears and on his chin.

"When she stands up with those glasses on," he said. "And

then you see her in that field. The bright sunlight. The way she crouches with the knife." He shook his head solemnly, then raised his shoulders and pretended to shiver.

He said his name was Francis, Francis Coogan. He was a film student at UCLA. He and his fellow students helped the armed services make training films, which was how the film school stayed afloat.

He had smoked his cigarette down to the nub, so that he'd almost burned his thumb, and now he stubbed it out on the pavement with his shoe. "You drink coffee, don't you?" he said. "Why don't we go get some coffee?"

Kenneth had only partly emerged from the film's trance. The boy before him was still half-real, half-apparition. He followed him to the diner across the street, a brightly lit place with a glass display case full of cigars and chewing gum and a poster for war bonds taped to the aluminum hood above the griddle. There was hardly anyone else there: a couple in a far booth, two men eating separately at the bar, where plates of doughnuts and pie sat under greasy bell jars. By now, Kenneth felt oddly large, as if he were somehow emanating from beyond the framework of his body. Coogan regarded him with a kind of patient fraternalism, as if he already knew everything he would say. He wore an ill-fitting dark suit and a blue shirt with no tie. His knowingness accentuated the sense of their similarity. Kenneth knew perfectly well that no one was looking at them, but still he felt their eyes. It was as if his own wrongness had been redoubled by Coogan's, as if they were sitting there in that booth holding hands.

"You're so solemn," Coogan said. "How old are you?"

Kenneth let out a penurious sniff of laughter, his head bowed. "A hundred and five. Eighteen. What difference does it make?"

He looked at Coogan: his boyish dark bangs, his wrinkled bohemian clothes. He was hardly sexual at all, which made his interest in Kenneth a glaring, confusing thing.

"I have to tell you something," Coogan said. He leaned closer over the table, making a show of conspiracy. "I noticed you a few weeks ago," he said. "It was at the Cocteau film, I think. That was where I saw you. And so tonight I thought I'd wait around for you, find out who you were, but before I did that, I went into the toilet and smoked a number. Do you know what that is?"

Kenneth looked away, holding his coffee cup between his hands. "Yes," he said. "I know what that is."

Coogan smiled, then rolled his eyes up and to the side. "You're so serious," he said. "Don't you know by now that nothing ever happens to people who are so serious?"

He found himself trying to imagine Coogan's father—Irish and rough, a broad man in an undershirt—trying to find some vestige of that image in Coogan's own boyish face.

They went to an alleyway behind the diner. Coogan reached his long fingers into the side pocket of his jacket and brought out a thin, wrinkled cigarette, tapered at both ends. The rich smoke made Kenneth cough. He looked up into the lit window at the rear of the diner's kitchen, a yellow oblong smudged with grease. Then he closed his eyes and hacked again until Coogan put his arm around him and then with his other hand gripped his shoulder blade. Then he put his lips to Kenneth's ear and reached his hand down the back of his jeans.

He saw a flash of pictures from the film: Maya Deren's sandaled foot tramping on grass, then sand, then concrete, then the carpet on the living room floor. Everything was happening so suddenly that he could only react and try to comply. They were standing near a pair of garbage cans, and then Coogan was down on his knees, unbuttoning Kenneth's fly. It was oddly shaming until it became something else. He looked down at Coogan's hair and experimentally touched it. He felt vividly for the first time that they were both boys. It sent a wave of stiffness up his spine, a barely perceptible tingling around the heft of his scrotum. He closed his eyes, feeling the atmosphere on his skin—the cool air, the wedge of sky above the alleyway, the resonant hum of distant cicadas, Coogan's mouth almost indiscernible around him. Then he began to swell and dissolve, merging into Coogan's warmth, until his mind could register only the light on his skin, the expanding air, the sweet reek of the garbage rising from the cans. He swallowed and breathed and stretched his fingers out beside his waist. Then he came into Coogan's mouth.

"I bet you always thought about that," said Coogan. He was looking up at Kenneth, grinning as he wiped his lips with the back of his wrist. "I used to always think about it too, when I was serious."

A boy is sleeping on the living room couch, troubled by dreams, surrounded by photographs of sailors. When he wakes, he steps through a white door on the wall beside the fireplace. The door is marked MEN. On the other side he finds a highway blurred in darkness, the cars' distant headlights like smears from a grease pencil. Now he is in a kind of saloon, except that it is obviously only a paper backdrop. A sailor appears, takes off his shirt, flexes his muscles in a showy array of poses. The boy knows what to do, or knows the conventions of the game. He takes out a cigarette and asks for a light. The first onset of violence is mostly comical, vaudevillian: it happens as a kind of slow-motion punch that sends the boy falling lamely to the ground, as if both he and the sailor are acting. But then in the darkness and fog, a group of other sailors emerge, a few of them tall and menacing, most of them scrappy and small, carrying chains and hammers and pounding their fists. Their faces gloat and then grimace with the effort of what ensues, knocking the boy to the ground, flat on his back where they can prod him like a dying bird. Someone jabs his thumbs into the boy's nostrils and they burst forth with blood. He is screaming now; he mouths words, but there is no sound. He screams harder when they tear off his shirt, his chin and neck spattered with blood. Someone probes his nipple with the point of a knife. Before long, they have torn through the skin, their fingers stripping away at the gleaming viscera, until they find the boy's heart in a tangle of meat. It is a machine, a light meter with an oscillating dial. Somewhere far away, against the gray sky, an abstract shape looms like a pair of plaster dunes or a polished white stone. It begins to quiver slightly as a thin flow of milk bathes it from above. It reveals itself to be the boy's chin. The milk covers the ridges of his lips and slowly spreads over his cheeks and his eyes and finally drips like paint over his bloody chest until it is covered in white. He finds himself alone on the floor of a tiled bathroom, completely naked, lying on his side near a row of urinals. His groin emits shards of light. He has a sailor's cap on his head; his body is intact and clean. The door opens, and then another sailor, this one blandly handsome, lifts him in his arms. They form a kind of pietà in the humid darkness by the highway, the sailor distantly smiling, his face like a face from a recruitment poster. They lie together on a bed in a living room, bodies half-covered by white sheets. Above the fireplace is a faux Renaissance painting of a cherub on a bed of clouds: the boy Lucifer, extending his hand in a blaze of light. The sailor stands above the bed with a firecracker jutting out from his fly. He strikes a match and the long tube explodes in a shower of sparks. It causes the boy to writhe, bare-chested, in the living room, with a tinseled Christmas tree on his head. Its pronged branches rise from his skull like metastatic silver antlers. Some combination of boy and Gorgon, he dances out a frenzy that is equal parts pleasure and pain. It is in this state of rapture that he aims the point of the tree at the fireplace, beneath the portrait of the cherub, where the photographs of sailors burn in the flames.

He called the film *Fireworks*. It starred Kenneth as himself, along with a dozen amateur actors dressed in sailor whites, recruited by Francis Coogan. No one, apart from pornographers, had ever made a film so candidly gay. Eventually, it would make its way to Biarritz, France, where it would take first prize at an underground film festival. The judge would be one of Kenneth's idols, Jean Cocteau, who would find it disturbing and dub it a masterpiece.

SWAY

It was possible to find antecedents in Picasso's *Demoiselles d'Avignon,* or Stravinsky's *Rite of Spring,* or so it seemed to Kenneth, who was about to leave America for a new life in France.

His first sight of Paris was obscured by darkness, a vague impression of identical wedges of slate-roofed, six-story buildings. It was damp outside, the streetlights glowing like orbs through the fog. His taxi let him off just before dawn in the sixth arrondissement, outside his hotel, which he found locked for the night.

He took his duffel bag and walked for a while down the old broken sidewalks, looking up at the balcony windows and dark mansard roofs. The city seemed fictitious at that hour, its buildings emptied of people, left to crumble beneath a low oyster-colored sky.

He sat on a bench in the Jardin du Luxembourg and looked out on the empty urns and the white basin of the drained fountain. He had in his front pocket the fan letter he'd received from Jean Cocteau.

> *Your work astonished me. It comes from that vast*
> *darkness from which all true poems emerge.*

The sky was whitely dissolving, less blue each time he looked, and the distant roofs, once black, were now dark gray, stained green in places from the runoff of countless rains. The first pigeons cooed and batted their wings. It was easy to forget that his mother had given him the hundred francs and the thin sheaf of traveler's checks that were in his wallet. He was thinking about his father, how he wished his father could see him in this place, its stone palace and geometric park the furthest thing imaginable from the garage with its table saw and lathe. The leaves of the trees were tinted silver at the edges. They looked as if they'd been requisitioned and carefully altered for the making of a film.

The theater shakes. It feels as if it's being bombed now — the flickering lights, the dust and sudden calm. Bobby can feel and hear the girders above him shaking, giving way, water pouring down through the ceiling in rivulets, white and blue mist illuminated in the projector light.

A film by Anger

Invocation of My Demon Brother

The next image on-screen is of Bobby himself, his long hair coming down to his shoulders beneath the crown of a black top hat. In the background, someone is holding a noose. Bobby sees himself smoking a skull-shaped pipe. He and a few of his friends — Ron, Carol, Sharon — sit in a circle in the dark, surrounded by candles. One of the girls has painted on her jacket the words LOVE, EVOL, LOVE, EVOL. *He sees himself from some earlier time, his arms raised in the green light, his bare torso all muscles and ribs. He sees his face in hallucination, mirrored eight times in a shadowed whirl.*

Over the speakers, there is a sound of revving motorcycles. There are pictures of motorcycles in neat rows, motorcycles on mud tracks in the desert, motorcycles being ridden through a crowd of fans on a lawn. The singer, Mick, gestures with his fingers as if to pull an invisible veil over his face, then crouches and stares out into the crowd. Keith leans forward and swings his arm up in a roundhouse, lashing at the strings of his guitar. The film cuts away, and for a moment there is only a red tableau of helicopters, soldiers disembarking in Vietnam, the silhouetted figure of Kenneth Anger dancing in front of them on the stage, shouting. It had been such a long time since Bobby had seen Kenneth that he hadn't even recognized him at first. It occurs to Bobby that this theater is nothing more than a looping repetition of his own past, a room of caged and suspended time. It occurs to him that this is the kind of place you end up in when you are no longer alive, the space that is not a space at all, the moment that is not a moment because it has no beginning or end.

PART TWO

thanatomania *n.* **1** condition of homicidal or suicidal mania **2** belief that one has been affected by death magic, the resulting illness.

... Kenneth became friends with them maybe a year before Brian died. The band were always pushing their luck, and Kenneth would have already seen where that was leading because of this boy he knew in San Francisco, Bobby Beausoleil, who's now spending the rest of his life in prison. It becomes a kind of craziness, the things Kenneth's so attracted to. I don't know if it's his curse or just the way things are.

—**WILL TENNET,** filmmaker, interviewed in
Dream Plays: A History of Underground Film

MARRAKECH, 1967

MAYBE MONEY AND FAME would change everything. Brian had not been home in almost three years. He stood with his girlfriend, Anita, outside his parents' house now, his blond hair cut in bangs just like hers, their long fur coats falling almost to their ankles. They had gotten high in the back of the limousine, and there was an intensity of recognition he hadn't counted on: the evergreen shrub inside the iron gate, the white wooden box with its empty milk bottles. He held a cellophane-wrapped gift basket from Harrods behind his back.

His mother answered the door, smiling at him, a little breathless. "Come in," she said. "I was just getting everything ready."

In the living room, the windows were covered with lace curtains and framed by heavy, wine-colored drapes. There was an electric fire, two dressers displaying plates and books. His father slowly closed his newspaper above his crossed legs, then folded it in his lap, clearing his throat. Already there was the vague hesitation, the swirl of fear and goodwill.

He put the gift basket on the floor and kissed his mother on the cheek. "Mum," he said, taking her hand, "this is Anita."

Jokingly, he held the two women's hands in his own, as if to join them in marriage. Beneath her coat, Anita wore a paisley minidress. Gold earrings hung just above the ridges of her collarbone and her eyes were outlined in black kohl. She seemed to grow taller and thinner as his mother appraised her.

"We had a lovely drive," she finally said. "The countryside. You must enjoy living here."

His mother led them farther into the living room. "Yes, it must make quite a change from London," she said. "Though to us Cheltenham is rather a large town."

On the television, there was a formation of Stuka bombers flying through gray banks of clouds. Then a fire brigade trained its hoses on a smoking building whose roof and upper windows were luminous white flashes in a grid of black.

"We've just got back from Rome," said Brian. He was standing near his father's chair now. His father was looking down at his newspaper as if he'd forgotten something important.

"You drove down from London, did you?" his father said.

Brian looked at the TV. "Yes. Nice drive. A little rain."

"We've brought all sorts of things," said Anita. "I think I could live for a month on all the things we have here."

She had picked the basket off the floor and now they all looked at it in her hands. Its little pots and tins of food were obscured by the green cellophane, the basket's handle crested with a dark green bow.

"Anita's from Switzerland," Brian said. "She's been teaching me German, haven't you?"

His mother handed his father a cup of tea on a saucer. Then she turned to Anita, whose hair was so much like Brian's that they seemed to be impersonating each other. "Do you take yours with sugar?"

"Yes," said Anita. "I'll just go and put this in the kitchen, if that's all right."

She turned in a purposeful way, a robotic smile on her face, and walked out of the room. Brian sat down in a seat angled toward the window. Through the lace curtains, he could see the silent street outside. He could see the silhouette of the white limousine that was waiting for them. He was trying to remember how this had all played out in his mind beforehand—a couple of jokes, a little comic nervousness as his parents tried some caviar from the gift basket, holding up one of the little tins in curiosity to read the label.

He stared out the window of the limousine, his face rigid, watching the neighborhood pass by. There were ranks of iron fences, hedges whose leaves had turned a muddy brownish green. He held Anita's hand absently, his wrist on the leather seat.

"They never told me their names," she said.

"Lewis and Louisa. Very droll. They met at a jumble sale."

"They never asked me any questions. Nothing."

"They know everything they needed to know about you."

"They were afraid, I think."

"No. They weren't afraid. They were glad that everything went the way they expected it to."

She lit a cigarette. In her lap was a magazine she had brought over to amuse his parents but had never taken out of her purse. Inside it was a picture of Brian and her that could have been an advertisement for "Swinging London." He was standing with his back to her, holding her hands behind his waist, turning to the camera with a faintly mischievous grin. She was falling away from him in a sudden fit of laughter, her mouth open to reveal a white ridge of teeth. They looked like twins, that's what everyone said, Brian in a finely tailored suit, Anita's long legs seeking purchase on the slick white floor.

She rested her head on his shoulder and took his arm. "Do you have anything left?" she said.

He looked at her from out of the corner of his eye. "No. That's the worst part."

But then he reached his fingers into his jacket pocket and smiled, pulling her closer with his other hand. When she caught his eye, sitting up a little, their life together came back in a sudden blur of color. On their last night in Rome, her friend had come back with them to the hotel and all three of them had ended up on the bed, kneeling and kissing and touching one another's hair, laughing. Whatever they'd smoked had made the room brighter, outlined in a haze of yellow and violet. They were both smiling at him as they took off his clothes, admiring him as if he were their creation.

He handed her a canister and a tiny silver spoon. She leaned against him as she brought them carefully to her nose. Then she tilted her face up to his and he put his finger on the ridge of her cheekbone, staring into her upside-down eyes.

"I wish we were back in Rome," he said.

"No. Someplace else."

"Where?"

"I don't know. Morocco. I've always wanted to go to Morocco."

Their flat was in Earl's Court. It was made of sooty red brick, with tall windows whose wooden frames were covered in flaking white paint. When they got back that night, Keith called them from his house on the Sussex coast. It had just been raided by the police. They'd found drugs everywhere — drugs on Mick and on their art dealer friend, Robert Fraser—and when they went upstairs, they'd found Mick's girlfriend, Marianne, curled up in bed with no clothes on. They were all coming down from an LSD trip: a walk in the woods, an hour or so of wandering on the beach, looking at the stones and the remnants of the wooden piers. For the half hour that the police were there, it had never fully sunk in that the raid was real.

Keith's voice was almost inaudible, more solemn than Anita had ever heard it. She hunched on the edge of the bed, shielding her eyes with the flat of her hand in an effort to concentrate.

"Are you all right?" she said.

"I'm fine. Surprisingly fine."

"I'm sorry. We're a little out of it. We've just been lying here, sort of strung out."

"Well, whatever you've got left, you'd better chuck it. Brian's going to be next."

"You think so?"

"I don't know. It wouldn't surprise me."

"Everything's gone."

"Well, just tell him to cool it. You know how he is. That's the last thing we need."

"I'll tell him."

"I've got to hang round here for a while. Are you all right?"

"Yes, I'm fine. Are you?"

"I'm not too worried right now. I'll see you as soon as I can."

She hung up the phone. Then she closed her eyes, inexplicably lonely.

"They were busted," she said.

"Who?"

"Everyone. Keith, Mick, Marianne, Robert. Keith is out on bail."

He stood up from the bed. The air in the room, clouded by candle smoke, moved in circular waves.

"They would have come by now if they were going to come, don't you think?" she said.

"I don't know."

He felt dizzy and sluggish at the same time. He looked at the Moroccan rugs on the floor, the religious icons, the pop-art painting of a 7UP ad on the far wall. His sinuses burned and his mouth was dry, but he knew that they were down now to just booze.

"What did Keith say?" he asked.

"He said he was all right. He seemed calm."

He went over to the window and pushed aside the curtain. His heart pumped in a strange, disjointed rhythm, and he closed his eyes and then opened them until it stopped.

"They could come in here and plant something if they wanted," he said. "We should go through the drawers."

He looked at her, her face tinged yellow in the light from the candles. She wouldn't look back. She sat with the distant, sullen concentration of a child, one foot in her hand, crossed over her knee.

"What else did he say?" he asked.

"He said he was worried about you."

He turned. "He said that or you said that?"

"Don't. You're acting like it happened to you. Like you're at the center of it all."

He grabbed her by the arm, but she twisted away. She

closed her eyes and shook her head, as if too exhausted to say anything else.

He walked out of the room. He felt awkward, unwieldy, more drunk than he'd thought. Every movement he made now reminded him of his father.

She could hear him banging around the flat, knocking things off the bookshelves, moving the furniture. When she finally got up, the lamps in the living room were all burning. He was standing in nothing but his underpants and the white dress shirt he had worn to lunch.

"You're not going to keep it together, are you?" she said.

"No. Not if you're like this."

"I'm sorry. I'm not getting started with all that. I'm not going through the drawers."

He shook his head, smiling. "I never should have taken you there. That was all very funny to you, wasn't it?"

"I don't know what you're talking about."

"My parents. What else would I be talking about?"

She brushed her hair out of her eyes, then rubbed her cheek with her hand. "They were just two people. A little ordinary. I don't see why it matters."

He grabbed her by the shoulders. When she freed herself, she stubbed her toe on the edge of the carpet and they both fell to the floor. They rolled and struggled, their hands grappling and their elbows cocked. They didn't stop until they were both curled up in their separate numbnesses, unable to look at each other.

The heat went on with a banging in the pipes. She heard cars passing in the street. She looked at the dim bedroom, lit by the streetlight through the thin curtains: the Moroccan tapestries, their clothes in piles on the floor, the mirror on its stand at the foot of the bed. He was stroking her shoulder beneath the sheet now, saying her name, his face burrowed against her back. She lay there with an impassive stare. He was emptied now, a boy seeking his mother. The more they stayed alone in this room, the more they seemed to merge.

Before he hit her, he sometimes looked wild, as if a spirit had entered his body. Afterward, she would see the old confusion in his eyes, the babyish rage, and the wildness would disappear. But before it disappeared, there was a glimpse of someone he never could be for very long: the blended image of themselves that they used to look for in the bedroom mirror. He would look like she'd imagined him the first time she'd seen him onstage.

The next day, all the papers printed front-page layouts of the band's captioned photographs, all of which now looked like mug shots. Their disembodied heads stared out stupidly between blocks of text: "POP STAR ORGY. NAKED GIRL FOUND UPSTAIRS. FUTURE UNCERTAIN FOR MICK, OTHERS." It was more serious than Keith had made it sound. According to the papers, he and Mick were both facing ten years in prison.

———————

They had never stopped wondering when it would end. Until recently, for the last four years, they had done almost nothing but work, struggling to keep their luck going. They had written songs, recorded songs, promoted songs, toured behind songs, and it had turned out to be a kind of endless tantalization, a way of traveling the world without ever really seeing it. What they'd seen was duty-free shops, swimming pools, parking lots, ashtrays. They'd seen themselves, always at a remove, made increasingly strange by the scrutiny of cameras and the remoteness of crowds. They'd get jumbled together, speaking phrases and jokes that originated with one of the others, then seeing themselves in the others' faces, a warped and disjointed reflection. In interviews, they didn't have to be funny to make people laugh, or interesting to provoke their scorn. They became a set of pictures in magazines: pouting young men in lavender and rust, oddly tailored suits made of suede. As if cities were moods, each stop seemed to bring out in them some new kind of flamboyance, the ceaselessly changing backdrops — Sydney, Tokyo, Munich, Rome — triggering an urge to live out another aspect of the total freedom that was the compensation for having given up their identities. They wore white suits, white shoes, acrylic blue shirts with polka dots, sideburns and tinted sunglasses, and the girls never mentioned the sweat on their backs or the corn oil stench of their hair. They were all in their early twenties. They moved through everything in an increasingly arrogant fog, aware of secret jokes and ironies, except for Brian, who sometimes moved through it like someone already dead, standing onstage with a Vox guitar and bangs that covered his eyes.

It was no longer his band. It was Mick and Keith's band. They wrote all the songs. The music they made was rhythm and blues with a jaded edge, the music of being young and famous and still dissatisfied, and onstage, in a French fisherman's shirt and red jeans, Brian still seemed to somehow embody what the music said. He seemed to have gone past the point of wanting anything at all, and the fans, more and more of them male, could feel vicariously that they had gone past it too. They knew perfectly well about dissatisfaction, but now they could experience it as a consequence of fame, which they could imagine was theirs, and which turned out to be another, more glamorous form of isolation.

Onstage, as a "joke," Brian would sometimes play the wrong parts to songs, especially the big hits, all of them originals, no longer covers, all of them written by Mick and Keith. The shows consisted of twenty or thirty minutes of violence. It was as if the prettier the band got, the more rivalrous they became, the more the crowd needed to feel the nightsticks. After the pressing of records, the stamping out of cardboard sleeves, the distribution of identical disks to thousands of distant stores, perhaps it was no wonder that when the fans at last heard the music live, in its pure form, they rioted.

Brian could not write original songs; his attempts were intricate and stiff, like formal exercises. In the studio, he would ornament the songs Mick and Keith came up with, adding color and instrumentation. As he did with his clothes, he would make striking collages out of different, seemingly incompatible styles. Marimba, saxophone, organ, piano, dulcimer, sitar—it became a strange kind of trap after a while. It was so easy. He began to think that Mick and Keith were providing him with simple frameworks, three-minute pop songs that would be nothing more than that unless he was there to transform them. It was a little boring for him sometimes, a little silly.

He would start with speed and liquor, then take a tranquilizer to calm himself down, then more speed to give him energy, then more liquor to relax. It would usually take several hours of these arduous switchbacks before he finally reached the summit of clarity, the buoyant sense of who he was, high above the petty, nagging fears of his isolation.

At the beginning of 1966, he met in Munich a nineteen-year-old girl with straight blond hair just like his. She had been traveling around Europe for more than a year, working in films and on model shoots. She was sophisticated in a way he knew nothing about and so would never understand.

"What is the matter?" she said.

He stared at her, unsurprised, vacant, the only color in his face in his lips. In the light of the dressing room, his hair was not so much blond as white. Onstage, in a turtleneck sweater and plaid slacks, he had looked otherworldly, almost albino, and now the impression was even stronger because he appeared to be on the verge of collapsing.

"They sent you in here, didn't they?" he said.

"Who?"

He smirked a little, as if to echo her question. As if she were a spy.

She decided it couldn't be real. One of the things Anita liked to do was to insist on contradicting other people's emotions, particularly when they were self-indulgent. "I have a hotel room," she said. "Do you speak German? *Kannst du Deutsch? Ich habe ein Zimmer auf dem Bayerplatz.*"

The dressing room had mirrors and lights, and the lights made his hair look like a wig and his face like a mask. Perhaps what made her stay was that he was so abstracted and strange and yet looked so much like her.

Three days later, when his house was still besieged by photographers, Keith drove to their flat in Earl's Court. He had been practically living there when he wasn't at his house in Sussex. It was Anita's flat, and she had made it a kind of group headquarters. Keith had brought a stack of the tabloids with him in his car. He was trying to think of it all as a joke, and this was easier in the company of others. Perhaps the worst part of the bust was when everyone had gone home, retreating to their private lives, and for the first time, by way of memory, he'd had to experience in full the blunt stupidity of his hours alone in the police station: the deliberately pointless waiting, the detectives' neutral voices, the drab ceremony of showing his driving license and having his fingerprints taken in the dim room.

He had changed in the last few months. Even his body looked different now, lean instead of scrawny, his black hair hacked off at different lengths so that it stuck up on the top of his head and fell down over his ears and the back of his neck. He was still quiet and sarcastic, but he was also the one who could be serious without it seeming like an affectation. He could see the others emulating him sometimes, stepping back from the world to process it in their minds. Even Anita, who mostly teased him, had started to do this. There was some secret attentiveness between them now that made him feel an odd generosity toward Brian.

He knocked on their door, then he let himself in with his

own key. The floor in the living room was piled with clothes, the rug at a slant from the sofa. Anita was standing in the kitchen in a silk kimono, brewing something on the stove.

"You're home," she said.

The ironic glint in her eyes and her faint German accent still made whatever attention she paid him seem rare and empathic, a gift he somehow deserved without knowing why.

He shut the door behind him. Upstairs in the loft, he saw Brian wrestling with some woman he had never seen before, both of them laughing. The woman had nothing on but a pair of black panties, her breasts hanging sideways above Brian's hands. Her lipstick, when she turned to him, was as dark as the skin of a plum.

Anita put her arm around him. She held him for a long time and he could feel her breathing behind his ear. "We've hardly left," she said. "There were photographers everywhere. Are they still out there?"

"I didn't see any."

"They've just been waiting for us. But they seem to have kept the cops away. That's the theory anyway."

He looked up at Brian, who was making a face at him, turning up his nostrils with two fingers.

"I thought you were going to tell him to cool it," he said.

"I did."

He looked at the mess on the floor, the ashtray full of cigarettes butts and the twisted ends of joints. "Right," he said. "Well, then do you have anything to smoke?"

He watched them from the couch as they made a show of helping the other woman find her clothes. Brian threw a shirt at him over the railing of the loft. He brushed it off, dragging from his joint, then went over to pick up the guitar that was leaning on the wall. He wasn't sure anymore why he'd come here. There was something between them all that went back to childhood, the part of childhood that no one remembered, the secrecy and plotting and divisiveness. When he got stoned with them in the loft upstairs, surrounded by candles and tapestries and religious trinkets, there was sometimes a strange suspense in watching things go right instead of wrong. It was easy to think that they were all just friends. In the glow of their flattery, which was constantly aimed at him, it was easy to dismiss all the times he'd seen them screaming at each other, slapping each other, grappling spastically in hallways like two people struggling over a gun.

A little later, Mick showed up with Robert Fraser. He frowned down at Keith and brushed his silk scarf with his fingers, as if testing its quality. There was a tension in the room now that no one wanted to acknowledge, as if they'd all been caught acting foolish.

"Where are the cops?" Mick said, turning toward Brian and Anita.

She stood by Brian's side, sharing his cigarette. "You just missed them," she said. "We were all fucking on the floor when they came in. You missed that too."

He licked his lips. "Ah, but someday," he said, raising his chin. "Someday there'll be that special someday."

"Is that a new song?" said Fraser, sitting on the floor.

"Lovely to see you, Mick," said Brian. It was as if he'd just noticed his entrance, as if they were the only two in the room.

He had put on a strange kind of costume: pajama bottoms and a T-shirt, a woman's white hat and a flouncy velvet jacket. He looked good even in that. In a way it was like a challenge or a threat to everyone else. But when he glanced up into the light, his eyes were alarmingly vague, as if you were seeing him through a slightly unfocused lens.

Keith drew a map on the side of a brown paper bag. He scratched out the geography of the U.K. in green blobs with a felt-tip pen, then parts of Europe, then the coastline of North Africa. He made sure not to look at Anita while he was doing this. He was being reckless—he was being himself—but if he thought about her watching him, then he would feel he was performing.

He wanted to get out of England, he said, away from the scandal. His idea was that they all go to Morocco. They could drive there, in a kind of motorcade. It would be more fun to drive than to fly. In the process they could make a spectacle of their limousines, acting like the spoiled pop stars they were about to be put on trial for being.

"You get the ferry to what is it, Calais? Then it's a straight shot through France to Spain. You get a look at the scenery, see the change. Valencia, Almería—that's where they film the cowboy movies. Then there's another ferry at Málaga, and you're in Tangier."

It seemed fanciful and unlikely. No one knew how seriously to take it, except Mick, who was studying the map.

"I don't know if Marianne will go for it," he said.

He looked down at the floor. If what he really meant was that he didn't want to go, he would have been smiling at them. Instead, it now sank in with everybody that Marianne wasn't there.

"It's been bad for her," Mick said. "It's been bad for all of us, but now it's like she's at the center of it all."

Though her actual name had been kept out of the papers, there was no question that Marianne was the "NAKED GIRL FOUND UPSTAIRS." She was a pop star herself, a singer of love ballads and folk songs, but unlike them she was a woman. Her career was almost certainly over.

"We'll fly," said Mick. "We'll meet you over there somewhere."

Keith raised his chin at him. "So you're doing it. You're coming."

"Of course we're coming."

Later, Fraser took a photograph of them all. It shows the room littered with clothes and newspapers, a message scrawled on the wall in felt-tip pen in Keith's handwriting: CALL YOU *tomorrow*. On the left, Anita is reclining in a chair with a cigarette held near her ear. Across from her, Keith is sitting on the arm of the couch reading one of the tabloids. Anita's crossed legs are resting on his knee. From the other side of the couch, Mick is looking at her with bored aversion. Large paper sunflowers droop from the wall behind him. On the right, Brian is standing in front of the couch, drinking a mug of beer. He's still dressed in his odd, clownish array of clothes. Whatever is going on in this picture, he is oblivious to it, unable to see it from behind his upturned glass.

Three weeks later, they met up in Marrakech. Nothing had gone as planned. The only people who ended up going by car were Brian, Anita, and Keith, chauffeured by the band's assistant, Tom Keylock, in Keith's Bentley. On the first day, Brian started coughing in the back of the car, a wheezing asthmatic gasp that got worse and worse, until he couldn't breathe. It was much worse than his usual attacks—they had to check him into a hospital in the south of France when he started coughing blood. When the doctors insisted he stay there for five days, to be safe, there was an awkward few hours by his bedside, no one sure what to say. Eventually, he was so ashamed that he told Anita and Keith to go ahead without him, that he'd meet them in Morocco.

They were staying at a modern hotel outside the old city of Marrakech, its beige front hidden by palm trees. He arrived at night and took a cab from the airport. In the room, Anita's bags were opened on the foldout stand and there was a candle burning on the dresser, casting a bronze glow on the bedsheets that had been neatly turned down by the maid. They had five rooms on the tenth floor, all in a row, but he hadn't heard any sound coming from down the hall. The more he thought about it, the more difficult it was to reason with himself that they were just in town, enjoying their holiday.

He went out onto the balcony and breathed in the strange, thick air. Then he saw a few small lanterns burning on tables by the pool. He could just barely make out their forms in the darkness and hear the timbres of their different laughs: Anita and

Mick and possibly Robert Fraser. He heard the muffled, out-of-phase sound of an acoustic guitar.

He went inside and poured some whiskey into a glass. On the bathroom mirror, he now discovered, there was a message scrawled in red lipstick, written in Keith's handwriting: COME DOWN *to the pool!* His face looked absurd behind the lipsticked words, tired and pale from a day of traveling. It was his asthma, his weak, ridiculous body, that had kept him away these five days, and now he told himself to be buoyant and relaxed, but the letters on the mirror were garish and somehow overexcited and he took a Mandrax tablet with the rest of the whiskey before going downstairs.

It was cooler by the pool, and the air felt good on his face, along with the first flush from the drink. In the darkness, Anita was sitting next to Keith on a lounge chair, smoking a cigarette while she watched him leaning over his guitar. Across from them, Mick and Marianne were sitting in a similar arrangement, wrapped up in a blanket. When she saw Brian, Anita gave him the wry smile of a hostess, embracing her knees in her arms. She seemed weirdly proud of him, or proud of herself for arranging this poolside greeting, but it was Marianne who stood up and gave him a kiss, asking him how his trip was.

"Look at the sky," she said. "The moon. It's perfect."

He looked up and saw what she meant. In the dark sky was a crescent moon that sat high above the silhouettes of distant minarets. It was a view you couldn't look at without admiring the fact that you were in Morocco.

"Come here," said Anita.

She wore a man's purple caftan and a single bead on a leather thong around her neck. She reached her hands out to him, lean-ing into her knees and almost falling forward out of the lounge chair. He grabbed her by the fingertips and held her up.

"Was it all right?" she said, looking up at him.

"What?"

"The flight. Everything. We've been worried about you."

"Yes. Fine."

She leaned into Keith and he barely moved. He was playing a B7 chord, filling in the bass line with his little finger, a diffi-cult maneuver he kept attempting without getting it to come out cleanly.

"I'm feeling much better," Brian said.

"Good."

Mick rearranged the blanket around his feet as Marianne sat down beside him. "There's a pack of journalists arriving tomor-row for a press conference," he said.

He let go of Anita's hands and folded his arms across his chest. "Are you kidding?"

Keith finished with his chord and smirked up at him in wel-come. "Why don't you have something to smoke?" he said.

Brian scratched at the corner of his eyebrow with his fore-finger. "A little joke," he said.

"Yeah, right, a little joke," said Mick. "Just catching you up, sweetheart. Anyway, I thought you liked talking to the press. Rambling to the press."

"I like it when you stop poncing around long enough that I can get a word in."

There were bottles of wine on the pool deck. He picked one up and took a sip and then held it in his hands. Anita watched him, then burst out laughing. She put her hand on

Keith's shoulder and pressed her face to his sleeve. Keith turned his head toward her and put his hand in her hair.

"I'm glad you're having fun," said Brian.

She smiled at him from behind her bangs. "I am having fun."

"I'm sorry I've been away for five days missing all this fun."

He took another sip of the wine and licked his lips. No one said anything. Finally Tom Keylock leaned forward in his chair and tossed him a joint. He caught it awkwardly in his cupped hand and looked down to make sure that it was there, then he took another sip of the wine and reached into his hip pocket for the lighter.

He lit the joint and took a long, slow drag. There was nowhere obvious to sit, so he took the wine bottle and found a seat at one of the tables where a lantern burned beneath the folded-up umbrella. Keith had gone back to playing his guitar. Anita leaned her shoulder against the chair back, holding her knees to her chest, looking thoughtfully out at the swimming pool.

In their room, she sat on the edge of the bed and spoke calmly, reasonably, with the self-assurance of someone who took pleasure in confrontation. They were just having fun, she said. He knew that they were friends, and he and Keith were friends, so why was he making things up in his mind? They weren't old people who based their whole lives on appearances. She wanted them to get along, like they did before, but he kept making it harder and harder when he was so jealous and paranoid and strange.

He poured himself another glass of whiskey and went into the bathroom. There was the lipsticked message — COME DOWN *to the pool!* — the letters slanted and thick in the light from the yellow bulb. He added some bottled water to his glass and now he could picture the two of them laughing together, Keith fumbling in her bag for the lipstick, the two of them exaggerating their enthusiasm, or maybe not exaggerating it at all because he wasn't there.

"You're not telling me what's really going on," he said.

She turned to him, exasperated. "What do you want to believe is going on?"

"I want to know whether or not you're fucking him."

She stood up from the bed. She crossed her arms over her chest, slowly massaging her elbow.

"You're making accusations, but you're not thinking about what they mean. You've been away for five days and then you come back and expect everything to be exactly the same as it was."

He put his glass of whiskey down on the dresser. "I was sick."

"You were sick and it's not easy. I know. I know it's not your fault. But you're always sick and then you're always wasted and now you want to make rules for me that I don't believe in and that you would never follow yourself."

He hit her so hard that she stayed on the floor, her leg bent strangely at the knee, as if she had broken it. When she finally breathed, it was with a sudden high-pitched wheeze, as if she had just then caught her breath. She didn't move. Her head hung down from her shoulders, her purple caftan twisted around her back. He grabbed her arm and hit her again, leaning over her body, unable to get a response. It was the first time he'd ever been afraid of what he'd done.

It was overcast and hot the next morning. On the pool deck, some of the band's entourage read newspapers or sipped drinks from tall, narrow glasses like tubes. The sky was a diffuse silver haze that seemed to rise higher than the sky in London. In the shade of an umbrella, Brian was sitting with Tom Keylock while a photographer circled around him, crouched in the sunlight, taking his picture.

The air had a faint sourness, an edge of yeast. It brought on a brief shallowness of breath, a slow flipping-over sensation in his heart. For a moment, his heart seemed to be sputtering to a stop, weighted down with blood, and with its last lazy thud came a sense of abandonment, then of release.

Anita was at the far corner of the pool, moving slowly through the water, her hands sweeping in front of her half-submerged chin. She was looking ahead at Keith, who was on the other side of the deck, his shirt off and his eyes closed.

The water sparkled around her like a swirl of giant fish scales, pale green and white. A few palm fronds, yellowed and sere, floated on the surface behind her. The photographer took Brian's picture, and he pretended to ignore him, or assumed the pose of ignoring him, going back to the newspaper that he had spread in front of him.

She kept looking at Keith. Brian knew that everyone around the pool could sense what was going on inside him.

The elevator had mirrored walls that were mostly obscured by intricate sandalwood screens. When Keith came out into the hallway, he found Mick quietly closing his door. He was pale and hadn't showered and his face looked pressed together toward the center.

"What happened last night?" Mick said, flipping his key in his hand.

Keith kept walking down the hallway. His T-shirt hung over his bare shoulders like a scarf and he tugged at the twisted ends. "That's the big mystery, isn't it?"

"I told Tom to keep an eye on him. Make sure he keeps it together."

"Sort of like sending the dealer out to mind the junkie, isn't it?"

"This is brilliant timing. We're going to need him. You keep forgetting that. Unless we're just going to pack it in."

Keith scratched his shoulder. "Well, that's up to Brian, isn't it? I mean, either he'll look after himself or he won't."

Keith went into his room and tossed his shirt on the bed. Lined up against the walls was the equipment that had been brought up for him on the day they'd arrived—the microphones, the tape machine, the acoustic and electric guitars, all the tangled gray cords. He stared at it for a moment, then went out on the balcony and looked down at the pool.

He could see her moving through the water, her brown arms pushing down toward her sides. She kicked her legs so that her back and shoulders rose up above the surface, her wet hair seeping down her neck.

He went back inside and switched on the TV without any sound and lit up a joint. He could feel it starting to gather in the back of his mind, but it had been almost a month since he'd written a new song and he also felt lethargic. It would either come in a flash, which was rare, or it would come out of trial and error. Either way it wouldn't be a song until it went through hours of plodding and revision, drudgery and repetition, the exact opposite of the sound that only sometimes, inexplicably, emerged.

The last time they'd recorded, he'd spent five days in the studio with just Brian, working out the song. They'd added piano, cello, flute, recorder—small harmonic lines that pushed the song slowly outward until it was something you could listen to many times and still want to hear again. He'd watched Brian pick up instruments he'd never played before and just start playing them, doing it while he was so stoned he seemed hardly awake. Without Brian, the song would have been nothing more than some Baroque guitar studies he'd been tinkering around with by himself—Bach, Vivaldi—but together they'd managed to smooth away the worst part of that and fuse it to the simple, three-chord music they were known for. The song was about Anita—even Brian must have realized it. It was about the runaway girl who couldn't be tamed, the girl you would have to share if you wanted to be with her at all.

What was amazing then was that it seemed as if Brian were going to pull it together, be a true part of the band again. That's what she had done for him at first. But on the drive down to France, it was obvious what was happening, and Brian hadn't even noticed. He'd just made it easier and easier for Anita to forget about him when he finally broke down. He kept changing the music and insisting that this was the way the band should go, back to the blues, the old songs they used to cover when it was still fun to play and everyone got along. He would be sentimental, then angry, then half-asleep, vague with liquor and pills, and he had been like that so often that it was not upsetting, just irritating, familiar. Still, they had never seen him cough up blood before: thin red drips that spotted his chin and a darker kind that rimmed one of his nostrils. Suddenly they were speeding through Toulouse, looking for a hospital, thinking he might die. He'd wanted Anita to stay there at his bedside, but she'd felt worn down by then. He had stopped coughing. It had already started to seem like another one of his games.

They left him there after the first night. It was a cold thing to do, but he'd told them to go. They got back in the Bentley with Tom Keylock and headed south toward the border town of Port-Bou. It was a sunny day and they crossed the Pyrenees into Spain, where they could see cactuses and yuccas growing between the rocks on the sides of the road. They smoked some hash and listened to the reel-to-reel tape player, and their lives—even Brian's—suddenly seemed funny in a way they hadn't seemed since leaving London. She was laughing the first time she kissed him, and he could hardly concentrate on her body, her tan thighs spread across his hips, her breasts, which he felt for the first time through the thin fabric of her acrylic shirt. It had happened so fast that only afterward did it really sink in, the reality of this girl who was so beautiful he used to keep sneaking glances at her to make sure he wasn't exaggerating it.

Brian stood up and walked over to the edge of the pool. She looked up at him, wiping some water off the side of her face.

"We're going to go hear some music," he said. He turned back toward the table, where Tom Keylock was still sitting. "He's going to take me into town."

She rested her arm on the glazed tile, looking down at her fingers. "I think it's a good idea," she said.

"I'd like to find some instruments to bring back to London. Something different."

"I think we should just cool off for a while, don't you? I mean, just for the day. I think it will be good for us."

He looked away. For a moment, everything that had happened last night—the calmness of her voice, the tight soreness in the bones of his hand—came back, jumbled together with the sunlight on the patio, the green and white reflections on the swimming pool, the coarse gray bark of the palm trees.

"You should go and hear the music," she said. "Try not to think about everything so much."

He nodded. Across the pool, there was a waiter in a white jacket and a white fez clearing glasses from one of the empty tables. Anita smiled, touching his bare ankle with her wet hand.

"It's just for one day," she said. "Not even a whole day. Everything's going to be fine."

He had never felt like this. Jealousy, fear, hopeless anticipation—these were familiar feelings, but he had never felt them with such claustrophobic intensity. It made his pulse thick and prolonged, worse the more he tried not to think about it. Everything he didn't want to believe about himself was once again suddenly, explicitly true. Could he go for one day—not even a whole day—knowing that she was out of his control? It was like deciding that nothing between them had ever mattered.

An hour later, she and the others were in a tiny carpet shop owned by a man named Hassan, sampling different kinds of hash while they listened to Moroccan music on the radio. The walls were an even, vibrant blue that made it difficult to remember what time of day it was. Keith leaned back against the wall on a pile of carpets, his eyes closed. She was curled up beside him, her arm entwined with his. She wore white boots, her legs bare and tan, and beneath her straight blond hair she had a feather boa wrapped tightly around her neck like a scarf. Mick and Marianne and Robert Fraser were on their right, looking at a book of Arabic calligraphy. As usual, someone was taking pictures, and so the last hour had been full of vivid reactions to minor events, canny smiles and thoughtful stares and a minimum of talk.

"It's better now, isn't it?" she said.

"Yes. It's always good to have a smoke."

"I want to go for a walk later in the market. I want to buy something for Brian. Something to cheer him up." Her smile was the smile of someone who never felt any difference between acting and being herself. "Don't be solemn," she said.

"I wouldn't dream of being solemn."

"We're all friends. It's a simple idea, but no one seems to understand it anymore."

"We are friends."

"Not if everyone's going to be so solemn about it."

Someone took their picture. Keith closed his eyes, nodding off slightly to the music. It was trancelike and insistent, a syncopated weave of oboes and violins backed by drums. Each note pointed to a shape without making it too obvious, each note a surprise but also a logical next step. It was like looking at a dark sky and gradually making out constellations in what had been a scrim of random stars.

Her hand felt embarrassingly alive in his. It was long and firm with a pair of rings beneath the first knuckle of her middle finger. He knew that the rings had nothing to do with him and that her hand in his meant nothing, but it made him not care about Brian, or about the band, or about the possibility of spending ten years in jail. It made him want to see what would happen. He kept noticing the faint, greenish bruise on the edge of her cheekbone.

Above the big open square called the Jemaa el Fna, the sun was starting to open up a gap in the mild cloud cover. It lit up the long folding counters of the food stands, where plates of raw ground lamb, diced tomatoes, olives, rice, sausages, and kebabs sat atop thick beds of wilting greens. Brian was just coming out of the darkness of the clothing souks with Tom Keylock when the light on the buildings changed from a muddy brown to a bright pink, all of it suffused with a saffron yellow that was like a second dawn in the middle of the afternoon.

"The acid's starting to come on," he said.

"Yes."

"There's that sort of humming you always feel in your teeth."

"We have money. Cigarettes. Nothing can go too badly for us now."

There was a persistent drone of horns. From the food stalls came the bitter smell of burning charcoal and the dry, organ-meat smell of grilled lamb. A thin man in chef's whites and a toque was ladling a brown liqueur over a wide pan full of stone-colored snails.

"You knew, didn't you?" said Brian.

"Knew what?" Keylock took him by the arm and guided him out of the way of a man walking by with a stack of crates on a dolly. Keylock was tall and round-shouldered with sideburns and horn-rimmed glasses. "It's too much to talk about," he said.

"It doesn't matter," said Brian. "I should have finished with that bitch a long time ago. It's really starting to kick in, isn't it?"

"Yes. We'll just need to cool out for a while somewhere."

There were three old men in brilliantly colored robes standing on the other side of the square. Their shoulders were slung with leather pouches and several strings of bells and brass cups. Their hats were like enormous tasseled lampshades woven from brightly colored yarn, reds and blues and yellows and greens.

"Perfect," Brian said. "They're brilliant, right?"

"Those men? Yes, fine, they're brilliant."

"I may take some more in a little while. I'd like to buy some of those hats. Or maybe just buy the men themselves, take them back to England."

A man in a dark sport coat and a dingy woolen vest approached them, whispering something in French and fanning out some tattered business cards. Keylock brushed him aside with a rise of his chin. He turned to Brian, steadying him again with a hand placed lightly on his shoulder.

"Now you see what I was talking about," he said, and suddenly each moment was so densely packed with situations that Brian couldn't begin to take them all in. Bicycles and animals and carts moved in strange diagonals through the alleyways at the corners of the square. The sunlight gleamed on the hundreds of numbered plaques above the food tables, turning them into row after row of toylike moons. A group of men in white robes and turbans were dancing in a crowd, rattling a set of square metal tambourines in their hands. Translucent doves fled from the folds of their clothes.

When they got back to the hotel, they were all so high that each moment arrived in its own frame, like a set of projected slides — the revolving glass doors, the tiled lobby, the carved rosewood screens behind the fountain, the bellman in his white jacket and fez. The sun had come out, so they decided to spend the rest of the afternoon by the pool. Anita went upstairs to change, still feeling the bluster she always felt when she was with Keith. Walking back through the medina, he had been so stoned that he could hardly move his feet, his white fur coat slung over his back like a dead dog. Packs of boys had hovered around them, solemn and staring, only the youngest ones daring to come up close. One of them, about eight years old, followed them up a set of stone steps, his hands laced behind his back, as suspicious as an old man, mimicking every one of Keith's clumsy movements as if learning the steps to a dance.

It was only when she got upstairs to the tenth floor and opened the door to her room that she remembered what was really happening that day. There were all the clothes scattered on the beds and the chairs and the tiled floor: Brian's clothes and her clothes, all of them mixed together, just like at their flat in Earl's Court.

In the bathroom, she picked up a book she'd been reading called *The Sephiroth*. She opened it at random to a page somewhere near the middle.

> Speak to me of desire. Of the endless, coiling desire
> of the Self. Of how the Self, goaded by desire, be-

comes like an animal, compelled by need, caught in its sway. Now speak to me of the Soul, whom we see only in glimpses of others, in the blur of music, in the senselessness of dreams. Not who we are or what we believe, but the blinding shimmer from the void.

Figure 3. Trump XV, The Devil, Lucifer in his aged and corrupted form. As the Father of Fear, he has horns and batlike wings. Below him, two Lovers, Adam and Eve (Trump VI), are chained in darkness at his feet. Note how comfortable they appear in their chains, so loose around their wrists that they could free themselves at any time if they so desired.

THANATOMANIA, 1963–1964

KENNETH ANGER WAS WALKING by the boardwalk on Coney Island one afternoon when he came across a group of boys working on their motorcycles. They were working-class kids, mostly Italian and Irish, their hair greased back in the manner of James Dean or Marlon Brando. From a distance at first, then closer, Anger watched them as they ratcheted and stared at their engines, their triceps shifting in the broken light, shaded by the board-walk's wooden planking.

He didn't approach them that first day. Even on that hot afternoon, he was dressed entirely in black, except for a pale lime silk scarf around his neck. Surely the boys would see what he was, but then again what was he? The boys would never have guessed that a person like him would have tattoos on his forearms and wrists. A pentagram, an Eye of Horus, a scorpion—his rising sign, a sign associated with trickery and deceit. They would never have guessed that among other things, Anger thought of them as brothers in arms.

He was living in Brooklyn Heights now, penniless, sleeping on the roof of an apartment building in what could only be described as a shanty. It was a small metal shed without windows. Inside, he had a mattress and a kerosene lantern and an assortment of mugs. The shed and the apartment below it belonged to a film professor and his wife, Eliot and Beverly Gance, whose hatred for each other was like a cunning distraction from the doom that seemed to thicken the air around them: their sagging thoraxes, their nicotine breath, the haunted, midday fatigue that permeated their rooms. The Gances would start drinking on a Friday afternoon and not stop until Monday morning, during which time Anger would witness their brawls — broken dishes, humiliating sexual accusations, suicide threats, then a shoving match with drinks and cigarettes in hand along the raised brick edge of the roof where Anger had his shed. His presence seemed to reassure both of them into further flights of aggression. He didn't have to pay the Gances rent, but he seemed to be paying them instead through a steady depletion of his own vitality.

More and more, both he and the world around him seemed on the verge of a breaking point. He could feel suppressed hostility running like an invisible current through the city's televisions and the flickering lights of its subway cars. If it wasn't the fear of Communists, it was the fear of Negroes. If it wasn't the race to blow up the world, it was the race to send dogs or monkeys to the moon.

There were nights when it was too hot to sleep in the metal shed, and so he would spread one of his sheets out over the asphalt roof and look across the moonlit river to the speckled towers of Manhattan. He had friends there, and there were circles of people who knew his work and screened his films and had him over to their apartments for dinner. Afterward, he would sometimes go in search of boys, lost drifters in denim jackets or mechanic's clothes, Lucifers, he called them, like so many avatars of his teenage crush, Ted Drake. They were mostly straight kids, hungry for a steak dinner, young enough to think of him as old, not fooled for a minute into thinking he was anything like them. When he got them alone, they were often as passive as ghosts, but sometimes there was a muscular scorn that brought him into contact with the real thing—a clenched fist at the end of a forearm, the edges of a ring abrading the bones of his back. What mattered was the first flash of desire, that almost nonexistent few moments when you could confront someone purely as a body and perhaps be confronted yourself in the same way, divorced from the dull facts of who you were. After that, things could only be tedious—two men talking to each other like ironic girls.

He believed that his films were lasting works of art, but perhaps this idea was evasive. Perhaps it was a way to justify being thirty-five and living in a metal shed on someone else's roof.

He presented himself to the boys with the motorcycles as a camera enthusiast, a solemn man in his thirties who despite his whispery voice seemed to know something about tools. He bought them beer, and over the course of the next few days he filmed them as they moved in a crouch around the concrete floors of their garages, smoking cigarettes as they turned the wrench on a crankshaft or fitted a gas tank back into its slot. He filmed their gearboxes and sprockets, the pages of their repair manuals, the red taillights and chains and batteries laid out on the gray tarpaulin in the garage's dark corner. None of them did well under the camera's gaze for more than a minute or two. Being watched changed them, made them self-conscious. It got him thinking about the wavering line between fakery and authenticity, the way a dangerous pose sets up the expectation for actual danger.

Because what was a motorcycle for, if not to flirt with the

crash? And what was the point of all that tangible speed, if not to outrace age and move directly to the end?

He didn't remember where he'd come across the word "thanatomania." When he looked it up in the Gances' dictionary it wasn't there, but he couldn't help thinking that this word held the key to whatever it was he was sensing all around him. The vague restlessness seemed to have its source in some unspoken, half-yearning fascination with death. It didn't escape him that those boys with their motorcycles made a perfect tableau of aggression and indifference. Their bikes, fitted with neat round mirrors on either side of the crossbars, were just like the spartan racing bikes that Jean Cocteau had chosen for the minions of the underworld in his film *Orpheus*.

About a week after he'd filmed the bikers, he met a thirty-one-year-old hustler named Bruce Byron outside a movie theater in Times Square. Byron wore a cowboy hat and a denim jacket that made him look rangier and younger than he was. He was good-looking in a blue-collar way. But it didn't matter, since Anger was in that state of obsession now where everything he saw or heard became related to what he was working on and immediately found its rightful place. When he mentioned the biker movie, the response was silence: Bruce Byron squinting off into the distance, his eyes shadowed by the bent brim of his hat, his cheap boots creaking above the hot sheen of the sidewalk.

"I don't have a lot of time," said Anger.

"Maybe I'd be interested," said Byron. He was still looking off down the street, lightly drumming his fingers on the edge of his thigh.

"Why don't you give me your phone number?" said Anger. "I'll call you later."

"I don't know about the phone."

Perhaps part of the problem was that Anger had a mild crush on him. Perhaps he couldn't quite forgive Bruce Byron for the matter-of-fact perfection of his ears, the stubbled contours of his chin, the way his small eyes focused so tightly on whatever they were trying to decipher.

A few days later, they met at Byron's apartment, a walk-up on Tenth Avenue with red curtains patterned with silver snow-flakes that were somehow strangely futuristic. Atop the television was a picture of a woman who might have been Byron's sister, a comb in her brown bouffant, rheumy eyes that peeled down a little too far at the bottoms, like certain dogs'. Anger began setting up lights in the corners of the apartment's only room, training them on a sagging bed with a loud scarlet cover-let. He had brought along two shopping bags full of props: leather jackets, engineer's boots, a plastic skull, several posters, ashtrays, doilies, and commemorative plates emblazoned with the faces of Marlon Brando and James Dean. He arranged this paraphernalia around the room, replacing the decorative prints of Hawaiian beach scenes and the Golden Gate Bridge. This décor suddenly made more sense when Byron picked up the photograph of the woman on the TV and mentioned that she was his wife.

"I didn't know you were married," said Anger.

"No, there's a lot you don't know."

"She's at work?"

"She stays with her mother sometimes. In Queens. Debbie's

all right, except when she's not all right, you know what I mean?"

They had both taken a hit of speed. Anger was already prepared to start, his light meter in his hand, but Byron was standing contemplatively in his denim jacket and cowboy hat, stretching his arms in a bridge before his chest. He seemed to be getting himself into character, which made no sense as Anger had given him no indication at all about what his role involved. He asked Byron to take off his hat. Then he asked him to strip down to his undershirt and lie on the bed in front of the TV, maybe with a pair of sunglasses on, maybe with a cigarette behind his ear.

"I don't see what that has to do with the motorcycle idea," said Byron.

"We're not there yet. Just wait."

"You want me to watch television?"

"Just for a minute. Everyone does it differently. I want to see how you do it."

"You're going to film this?"

"I think you should take off your jacket at least. Obviously the hat."

Byron frowned and lit a cigarette. "I've always considered it an idiot box," he said. "If I was bored I might put it on. While I was reading."

"Look," said Anger. "You need to relax. You need to stop thinking about everything so much."

There was something like suppressed sarcasm in the sullen way Byron finally started unbuttoning his denim jacket. He gave a kind of silent chuckle, squinting as the smoke rose from the cigarette in his mouth. It seemed possible that this was the look he gave everyone just before he finally gave them what they wanted.

"She watches that thing day and night sometimes," he said, raising his chin at the television.

"Who?" said Anger.

"My wife. Debbie. If it was up to me, I'd smash it. Throw it out the window."

"Maybe put the sunglasses on. The big ones. The green ones."

"You want me to lie down?"

"Yes, lie down."

"Bedroom scenes. I usually get paid for this kind of thing."

"I'm here to make a film. I'm not here for that."

He had seen it happen many times. Almost as soon as the camera was on its tripod, a person like Bruce Byron would start to imagine himself as the Star. At the same time, he would second-guess everything Anger said, because he'd never heard of him, and yet he still imagined that the film could somehow make him famous. It was a consequence of Anger not being famous enough himself, not being a Hollywood director who could bark commands instead of working through trickery and deceit.

"It's not working out," Eliot Gance said to Anger the next morning, standing just outside the stairwell that led up to the roof. The collar of his Cuban shirt was spread to reveal his veined throat and the top of his pink chest.

"I may go to Mexico," he said. "Perhaps the Far East. Can you have your things cleared out by the end of this month?"

"Your life, Eliot. None of it makes any sense."

"If she thinks she can just finish me off, she'll find it's not so easy. I've got different elements in play now. Different strategies."

"I'll speak to Beverly about this."

"Stay out of it."

"Let's not forget that other people exist, Eliot. I have a film I'm trying to finish."

"A film. That must be difficult. Will you stay in town, do you think, or will you go back to Europe?"

"I'll speak to Beverly."

"Leave her out of this."

"We'll see about this Mexico trip. The Far East."

"Good-bye, Kenneth."

"Wait a minute."

"Good-bye."

On the last night of filming, he took Byron to the bikers' club-house, along with four cases of beer and a box of props. In some secret part of their minds, the bikers must have known what kind of person Anger was, but there was something about Byron—he was dressed all in black leather, like a mannequin or a doll—that let them know for sure. They staggered through the cases of beer and then they went wild, the radio on, form-ing conga lines, sloppy cancan routines that got more and more sexual, miming sodomy, their faces hidden by Halloween masks. They ended up jumping on one another's backs, wrestling each other to the floor, gibbering like apes with their pants down. Byron had never met them before. His only instructions were to try to blend in. All he could do was stand off to the side, drinking beer. The refreshment table was knocked over on its side. People rode their motorcycles through the clubhouse. They had one of the younger kids on the ground and were squirting a bottle of mustard on him, his pants around his ankles, and though it was happening right in front of him, Byron just stood there by the wall, his hand in his pocket, so aloof that it was impossible to tell what he was thinking.

"That's what you wanted, I guess," he said when it was over. "A big ridiculous scene."

They were in Anger's rented station wagon. Byron was slouched back in his seat with a beer on his knee, his sunglasses on in the darkness.

"I thought you would get more involved," said Anger.

"They were just kids. I was asking them about their bikes. I know more about bikes than they do."

"What's the matter?"

Byron stared ahead through the windshield, his face hidden in shadow.

"What?" Anger persisted.

"You want me to eat shit, that's fine," he said. "I've been eating shit my whole life."

They were on their way to the next location. It was an abandoned church, its windows smashed, rainwater pooled on the plastic sheeting that covered the pews. It was there that Byron's character would erupt in a last frenzy of rage, climbing up on the altar in a fit of desecration. It would be the best part of his performance. In the church it would be dark, and he would gesture and pose for almost an hour, acting out a sermon that in its senseless, dictatorial lunges would be a perfect ending for the film.

"Are you all right?" said Anger.

"I'm fine. Let's just get it done."

"We'll do it your way this time. You tell me what you want to do and I'll film it."

"I want it to be real. I'm the only one putting anything real into this. Every time it gets serious, you start smirking, playing your games."

After all his recent failures, Anger hardly expected that this would be the film to have so much success. Even as he raced to finish it, he didn't foresee how confusing it would be to most of the audience that eventually came to see it, nor could he know that the word it invoked so strongly, "thanatomania," would end up sounding like a diagnosis of the next six years. He called it *Scorpio Rising*. He didn't realize that this little film he'd made with Bruce Byron would prefigure so much madness, nor did he anticipate that Byron would be so obtuse that he would entirely miss its mockery and believe that it flattered him, made him a star.

It ended with Byron marching off to the abandoned church, wearing a leather mask and an infantryman's helmet. The sound of bikers followed him, the revving of their engines, the dream minions of some private army in his mind. With a sudden flourish, he turned and barked commands from the ruined altar. He paced like Hitler, raising his arms to the sky. Outside, the bikers massed in darkness, idling on wet roads, waiting for his signal. There was a crash—a pileup of bodies, flesh, machines—then the empty cry of sirens. The ambulances stood in the rain. Byron was all alone. It was getting light out. That was the year four Klansmen bombed a church in Alabama.

The year a lone gunman shot JFK as he passed by in his open car. Always the television started as a white pinprick, gathering width until it filled the screen, bringing its different kinds of news. Day after day, the subway lights flickered with the unseen clues about death magic, thanatomania.

The state of California banned the film in 1964, and in doing so elevated it to an importance it might never have achieved if it had been simply left alone. After that, Anger kept bumping into different aspects of some newly distorted idea he had of who he was. Strangers sent him letters. They wrote to him as the pornographer, the fascist, the sadist, the necrophiliac. He was whatever they needed him to be. Handsome, intense boys would introduce themselves after screenings, and their interest in his every rambling word made him garrulous. He became a character, a talker, an opinionated fool.

At the film's premiere in New York, Bruce Byron had shown up dressed in full biker regalia, down to a leather cap and a black leather jacket with a scorpion painted on the back. He stood by himself, a figure of embarrassment that nobody wanted to look at. Anger ignored him (he himself was never alone that night), but sometimes when he looked back on the scene he would imagine it through Byron's eyes: the smugness, the utter conviction of his own centrality, the injustice of Anger being treated as the film's star.

At night, an image would appear behind Anger's closed eyes: a lithe boy with dark hair that fringed his forehead. He would arrive on a motorcycle in a fog of yellow light, making reckless circles in some vast hangar, his arms flexing as they wielded the silver handlebars. At top speed, he would mount a flight of red stairs that led to an altar adorned by a giant silver eagle. Airborne, he would crash through a pane of glass and tumble onto a concrete floor lit by klieg lights. His motorcycle would be bent and smoking. He would lie spread-eagled on the ground, his arms tattooed with anchors and skulls, blood in his hair. Then he would open his eyes and Anger would enter the boy's mind, where there was nothing but images: a red curtain over still water, a blue gas flame reflected on chrome, a black sky pocked with green specks of light. It was now that the dreams of Lucifer began to proliferate.

MARRAKECH, 1967

IT WAS EIGHT O'CLOCK in the evening, though it felt to Brian like midnight or afternoon. He had lost Tom Keylock somewhere in the fabric souks a few hours ago and now he was looking through the window of the cab, at the dense wedges of buildings, earth-colored or eggshell-colored, which appeared as if they'd been scraped together out of sand. A few electric lights burned like flares along the busier streets, bright orange or neon green. They made the city of Marrakech look more and not less ancient.

In the elevator up to the tenth floor of the hotel, he became aware of someone else's presence looming just behind his shoulder. It was a middle-aged man in a wrinkled suit, a closed umbrella at his side. Brian knew this without having to turn around, just as he knew who the man was without being able to remember his name. He hunched forward with an impatient smile on his face, hands fisted at his sides, not looking. When he closed his eyes, he saw numerals, first chiseled into gray stone, then colorful and stylized, like numerals on a Victorian signboard. Not more than three seconds passed before he was waiting in anticipation of the man's seizing him by the arms.

The elevator's doors opened with a brutal series of lurches. He walked down the hallway, listing slightly in response to the faint undulations in the walls. There were animal shapes moving in the plaster, hooves and hindquarters that seemed to press against the surface from the other side. Faint music was seeping out from the farthest suite down the hall.

He matched the key in his hand to the number on the door. All the doors were an identical dark brown.

Next door, there was a crowd in Keith's suite. He and Mick were working on a song, ignoring the others, Keith with one heel resting on the edge of his chair, his guitar's body wedged awkwardly between his thighs. He hit the strings hard, then lightly, then harder, the process a kind of math, or like trying to coax a flame out of a few smoldering sticks. Mick was sitting on a little tapestried stool before him, trying to follow along on his guitar, watching Keith's fretboard. In the room with them were more than a dozen people, some of whose names they didn't even know. They were talking and playing Moroccan music on the radio and someone was setting up a movie projector on a table. He told everyone to turn out the lights. There was a confused grumbling, a cackle of laughter, then the room went dark. Keith and Mick kept playing, their guitars out of sync, a nonsense of rhythm that no one else in the room had any patience even to watch.

"Mortify the spirit in order to more purely inhabit the body," a voice said in the darkness. "Enter the nightmare until it loses the veneer of credibility."

A film started in the projector. On the wall, there was a rectangle of saturated black, almost purple, and then a slow upward pan of words written in gold ink: *A Film by Anger. Inauguration of the Pleasure Dome.*

Anita was still grinning at something when she looked up to see him. The room was lit by only a few candles and Brian felt the man in the wrinkled suit behind him, mocking him. They were all sitting on the bed—Anita, Marianne, Robert—sifting through a large opened box full of bracelets and rings.

"Brian," she said. "You've been gone for so long. We were worried about you."

There were clothes all over the room. Robert had something on his head that looked like a stocking cap that had melted and blackened into a fine wisp. Beside him, Marianne was wearing a green sari and sunglasses, smoking a cigarette.

"I was in the square," he said. "I've just been checking it out. The Jemaa el Fna."

He had forgotten all the specifics of how Anita looked, forgotten her wide mouth, the comic insistence of her eyes. Everything he said or did now created the exact opposite impression of what he intended. He could see small hooves pressing against the wet plaster of the walls.

She took a long, heavy necklace from the box and held it out to him. "Look," she said. "I thought this would be perfect."

"Sacred magical necklace," said Robert. "We stole it." He pulled the strange cap down over his face. It turned out to be a black nylon stocking. It made his face look angry and Mongoloid. "We stole everything in town."

She held the necklace out to him, standing up and throwing her scarf back around her neck. It was a strand of mirror chips and colored beads and between them were a dozen or more jagged shapes that turned out to be human teeth.

"We're all very high," said Anita. "Are you all right?"

"I'm just very high."

"Put it on. We want to see you with it on."

"We need to talk for a while."

"I can't talk now. You know that I can't talk right now."

He looked into her eyes and she was smiling at him with the bland approval of a big sister. He saw now that they'd been playing a game in which Anita and Marianne were humiliating Robert with different kinds of jewelry and Robert was pretending to be him. The goats started scraping at the walls with their horns, others were kicking at the walls with their hooves. He wished that Anita would stop acting as though she couldn't read his mind.

In the darkness, Keith could feel the beginnings of a vague shape starting to emerge beneath the surface of what he was playing. He leaned forward in his chair, slowly nodding his head at Mick, adding a little ornament on the D chord, a bright suspended fourth that he played with his pinkie. Projected on the wall behind him was an image of a man in false eyelashes and black lipstick who reclined on a lavish bed. He was surrounded by pictures of dragons and Chinese gods, and on the bed's velvet coverlet was a large opened box full of rings.

Robert Fraser stuck his head into the suite's barely open door, the black nylon stocking on top of his head. Then Marianne came in behind him, taking his arm as she stepped inside. She was still wearing sunglasses, like a blind person. She had the kind of lips that made their own separate expression, reticent lips that curled mischievously upward at the corners. Mick looked over at her, but she was deliberately not looking back. On their way back from the medina that afternoon, he had noticed something that he'd seen happen several times now: for no reason at all, her eyes had started welling up with tears. She'd pretended it wasn't happening, but the effort had made her so distant it was like self-hypnosis. When he asked her if she was all right, she looked at him as if he were being deliberately confusing.

On the wall, the man in the film was twining a long silver necklace around his fingers. Then he dangled it above his face and began to coil it slowly into his mouth.

Keith nodded his head in that absent but emphatic way he had, which made Mick settle down into the music, forgetting himself. It made his face change into a near replica of what Keith's face had been just a moment before. He closed his eyes, his lower lip jutting slightly forward. The sounds they were making had no meaning yet, they were just a set of tones, but part of what was making the song take shape now was the sense that they were doing it in front of Marianne, that she was within earshot but had no idea what he was thinking.

Brian was on his knees in the bathroom. His hair was scattered across his neck in such a way that Anita could see the pale skin beneath it. The fractured light came from a single yellow bulb screwed into the ceiling and when she closed her eyes the yellowness flashed like a chain of miniature suns in the veins of her temples.

"It's all right," she said. "Let me help you."

He turned and his eyes were so distant, looking into hers, that he seemed to be seeing her though a thickness of glass. She rested her hand on the side of his face and with the other hand she smoothed the hair over the back of his head. He kept staring at her, his nostrils glistening, and for a brief moment he seemed to recognize her with more clarity and she almost thought they were going to smile at each other.

"You think it's funny," he said.

"No, I don't think it's funny."

"It is. It's funny if you think about it long enough. Keith, of all people."

He started coughing and turned around. It made his head shake, the fringes of his hair rising and then coiling against his shoulders. She crouched beside him, waves of nausea moving in her throat and stomach.

"Get out," he said.

"Brian."

"I just wish that Keith could have stayed the way he was. That you could have left him alone."

She stood up. "I don't know what to say to you."

"He was my friend. And you were this massive thing. Terrifying."

"He's still your friend."

"I don't want him to be my friend. Are you out of your mind?"

"Then you're a bastard."

"Just get out. Get out, and I'll leave you alone."

She left him there. When she walked back into the bedroom, she glimpsed herself in the mirror. Her eyes were all black pupil and the bruise on her cheekbone was a purplish green against pale skin.

They were all standing around in the dark when she came into the room next door, still stunned from the sudden quiet of the hallway outside. There was a movie being projected on the wall, casting a green and red glow on the dim standing figures. She saw Mick moving through the dark, his walk loose-jointed and balletic like his walk onstage, a walk that had nothing to do with anyone else in the room.

She saw Keith, mixing himself a drink at the impromptu bar in a far corner. He had his back to her, and Tom Keylock was gripping his shoulder and reaching for the bottle of Scotch.

Projected on the wall was the middle-aged man in false eyelashes, examining himself in a mirror. He was standing in a narrow red hallway, looking at himself with such concentration that eventually the hallway dissolved and he emerged as a different person, a woman, standing by herself in darkness, wearing a black sequined gown.

"You would like this film," said a voice behind her.

It was Robert Fraser. He passed something into her hand, a clumsy, furtive exchange. It was the black nylon stocking.

"The Scarlet Woman," he said. "Jezebel. The Whore of Babylon."

The woman's short hair was dyed a lurid red. She was lit by a pink light in the otherwise endless expanse of darkness. She was beautiful in a cold, androgynous way that was either extremely sexual or not sexual at all.

Anita put her arm around Fraser's waist and leaned her head against his shoulder.

"Brian's lost it," she said.

"Of course he has. But there's nothing you can do about it now, is there?"

Keith saw her from across the room. He raised his glass and gave her a sardonic grin, his craggy teeth glinting in the dim light. Tom Keylock was whispering something into his ear.

. . .

When Brian opened the door, the room was dark except for a beam of white light that spread across to the far wall, flickering and occasionally dimming so that the standing figures were sometimes lit up in neon tones of green or red. He looked at it too directly and for a moment all he saw was a whirling field of white. The music was loud, a syncopated weave of drums and ouds and violins. Then the curtains billowed and glowed like burnt sails against the high windows that gave out onto the balcony, and he felt the strange man's presence behind him, leaning forward on his rolled-up umbrella.

A woman's face was projected on the wall, her bright red hair cut like a Roman emperor's. In the palm of her hand she held a tiny, horned figure made of clay. She extended it before her face, her long eyelashes casting a fine, softening shadow over her rapt gaze. The figurine burst into flames.

In the darkness, the first people he made out were Keith and Anita. She was walking toward Keith, her fringed scarf trailing off her shoulder.

Keith took her in his clumsy arms. Her eyes started to burn with a strange desire to laugh and she let her head fall back so that she could smile at him. She pressed her cheek against his and kissed his earlobe. She could feel the muscles moving in his shoulders through his thin cotton T-shirt, and she knew that behind her head he was sipping his drink, could sense him rattling it slightly, crushing an ice cube with his molars.

"Everyone so smashingly divine," he said. "Just a lovely gathering of the loveliest people."

She took the drink out of his hand and took a sip. Then she

turned to find Brian striding across the room, small-eyed and pale.

He was dressed in a long blue velvet coat with a fake ermine collar. He also wore the necklace made of human teeth. The hair around his face was strung together in damp tendrils that fell into his eyes.

Keith stepped forward, head slightly bowed. He draped his long arm around Brian's neck, so that the three of them were gathered for a moment in the same embrace.

"We're going up into the mountains," he said. "You must come with us, man. We'll catch the sunrise, bring along the Kodaks."

Brian grabbed Anita roughly by the shoulder of her jacket. "We have to leave," he said.

"Brian, don't."

"I'm not fucking around. Let's go."

The film on the wall showed people in strange costumes drinking from long silver chalices. Then a woman in fishnet stockings removed an African mask from her face and started laughing.

Anita walked away, out of the room.

"Cool it," said Keith.

"Let go of my arm."

"If you want to blow it, this is the way, man," said Keith. "Follow her, and it's just going to make it a million times worse."

Brian looked at him blankly, then watched the door close behind her.

On the wall, a blond man in red boots was being clawed at by several hands with painted fingernails. He fell to the ground in a swoon that seemed equal parts pleasure and pain.

. . .

"You're a cunt, Brian," she said flatly. "I'm taking a sleeping pill and going to bed. You can do whatever you please."

She held her palms out by her waist. Then she looked at him impatiently, shaking her head. "I don't think we can talk right now, do you? Or do you want to just hit me? Is that what you want? Or do you just want to leave?"

"I want you to think about what you're doing," he said, raising his chin. "This is really it."

She closed her eyes, disgusted. He couldn't look at her after that. He heard her sorting through the luggage, rattling the plastic bottles of pills. He was remembering that afternoon in the Jemaa el Fna, the sight of the water sellers, standing there in their tasseled colored hats. He was remembering how in that place where everything was foreign and brightly colored, his life had suddenly seemed benignly distant and unreal.

She got into bed and covered her face with the pillows, and he stood there in the flickering beige light of the candles, looking at the shapes in the walls.

In the Jemaa el Fna, the girl stood beside him against a wall in the darkness and counted out the foreign money he offered her in his clumsy opened hands. There were lanterns set up on the tables, kerosene torches lighting up the food stalls. There were young, blank-faced men scanning the crowd, cigarettes cupped in their hands. There were fire-eaters and musicians, and there was a man in a black robe and a black headdress who gesticulated with a pair of painted sticks, his eyes hidden by mirrored sunglasses.

On the street, Brian raised his chin at the first cabdriver he made eye contact with, his hand on the girl's shoulder. The drivers were all clustered beside their cars, smoking or eating food from the stalls. In his mind, they had become an admiring audience whose stares he now ignored, helping the girl into the cab.

He imagined Anita in the souks, picking out the necklace of teeth, Keith at her side, his fingers moving from her back to her shoulder and down the length of her feather boa. Then he saw an image of himself in the Jemaa el Fna with Tom Keylock, his hand lingering at midchest before his scraggly shirt with a dangling, forgotten cigarette.

There was no point in talking now. He should have known that from the moment in the bathroom, when she'd looked at him and wanted to laugh.

Back in the elevator of the hotel, his lips were tight with determination, like a priest with some difficult truth to impart. The girl beside him looked straight ahead at the sandalwood screen above the panel of buttons. She wore a striped cape and a headscarf and had a tattoo on her chin like a stylized trident. Everything was luridly bright, as if on display.

There were no more hooves in the walls. There was no more imaginary man behind him. In the hallway, there was the clarity of rectangular doorways and hotel carpeting beneath artificial light.

"Anita," he said.

She rolled over in bed to see the two figures in the darkness. He switched on the lamp and stood in the yellow light, raising his chin, the necklace of teeth hanging from his neck. He was taking off his long velvet coat, shaking the hair out of his eyes, and she could feel the adrenaline coming off him like a wall.

"What's going on?" she said.

"A little surprise."

He gestured toward the girl, who was standing by the door, leaning her head on her shoulder like a sleepy child.

"Come on now," he said. "Who do you think I am? Did you think I was just going to disappear? That I'm just some tosspot with no balls?"

He snapped his fingers and moved toward the bed. Then he grabbed her arm, just above the biceps. She jerked her body backward and fell sideways, clutching the pillows to her chest.

"Get up," he said.

Diamond-shaped patterns of blue and red bloomed behind her eyes. She could feel the light in the room radiating into her skull like a sun. She dove for the foot of the bed, but he grabbed her by the ankle and she fell onto the floor. She put her hands over her face, covering her eyes, but he was on top of her then.

On the wall of the room next door, the Hindu gods Shiva and Kali were laughing beneath superimposed flames. It was the second time they had played the film, and no one was watching it anymore. They had ordered food that sat untouched on the dressers and the tables: couscous and ground lamb and a large pie made of phyllo dough covered in cinnamon and powdered sugar.

Green-faced Shiva brought his hands together in blessing, raising his joined fingertips to his lips, saluting the goddess Kali. Then there was an overlay of orange above a yellow Egyptian eye inside a triangle. Then the single word "End" appeared in gold letters on a saturated black background.

Brian was on the balcony, looking down at the pool, remembering a dream he'd had in the hospital in France. In the dream, he'd been walking through a kind of rice paddy, a pool full of tall green reeds that he pushed aside with the tips of his fingers. He had waded in up to his chest before he realized that there were hundreds of spotted deer on either side of him, almost submerged, raising their snouts just barely above the surface.

He could see now that she had been right all along and that none of it had had to matter. He had chosen to make it matter. He could see that clearly, now that it was over and she had no reason not to leave him.

When he came back inside, the girl was sitting on the bed, her hands clasped over her closed knees, looking at the mess of clothes on the floor without interest or intent. He lit a cigarette and it fell out of his mouth, then all the cigarettes came shaking out of the box and he picked the lit one off the floor and rose up out of his crouch with it smoking between his lips.

He saw the necklace on the floor, the beads and bits of mirror and human teeth. He saw his long blue coat with the fake ermine collar.

He sat down on the bed beside the girl and told her to lie down. Her legs were smooth and thin and gleamed as if they'd been rubbed in oil. He lay on top of her and closed his eyes and felt her face and lips against his throat. He held her like a limp thing in his arms and started coughing.

Anita was in the bathroom, holding a warm wet towel to her face, her chest heaving with some desolate mix of sobbing and mortified laughter. When she closed her eyes, green stars pulsed through her eyes back into her skull, where they swelled to a searing brightness. The pain ran from her shoulder up her neck, then twisted like a screw through the long ridge of her jaw. She sat on the floor and wiped the mucus from her nose. She was thinking that she couldn't leave the bathroom, she couldn't let them see her like this.

On the floor, *The Sephiroth* was still lying where she'd left it that afternoon. On the cover, the Eye of Horus gazed back at her with an almost gleeful indifference.

When he woke up, the girl was gone. There was a smell of sandalwood, of incense. There was a bar of light coming from between the curtains and on the nightstand was Anita's glass half-filled with soda and limes. She wasn't there. Her clothes and her suitcase were gone.

It was clear and warm that day. The patio in back of the hotel was a white glare, like light off glass, and the water in the pool was a bright, complicated green. There were only a few guests swimming or sipping drinks on the blue lounge chairs. Beneath the awning, on the patio, Tom Keylock sat by himself with a cup of tea. He was waiting for Brian, who wasn't answering his door. Brian didn't know yet that he was the only one who hadn't checked out of the hotel.

A short cab ride away, in the medina, the others were in the blue shop owned by the man named Hassan, filling in the last few hours before their flight home. They had just booked tickets that morning; they had left it to Keylock to break the news to Brian. Marianne was dancing to the Moroccan music on the radio now, her eyes closed, rolling her head, her long blond hair falling almost to her waist. Gold bangles slid down her forearms; the folds of her green sari loosened around her shoulders. She started spinning around faster and faster, unfolding her hands in the air. There was something defiant about how fast

Zachary Lazar

she was moving, a rebuke to the others for just sitting there, being calm. Hassan called out, clapping his hands. Robert Fraser started clapping too, raising himself erect. Mick brushed something off his sleeve, incredulous, then annoyed. He looked over at Anita and Keith in their corner, then back at Marianne, and something about her dancing reminded him of Brian: a helpless, unsuccessful gesture. She was the "Naked Girl Found Upstairs," and she seemed to feel obliged to play out the role now.

Mick walked out the door, frowning, faking a cough. He saw a newspaper image of himself dancing on the set of a TV studio, his arms dangling from his shoulders like a scarecrow's arms, a moment taken out of context and so made ridiculous. He didn't know where to go now that he had separated himself from the group. He strolled with his hands in his pockets, lips set in a posture of grim appraisal, passing the row of whitewashed storefronts.

He had never liked Anita, had always thought she was poisonous, but now he had to come to terms with what she had done. He saw that in a way she had become the center of the band.

The walls of the buildings were pasted with hypersexual movie posters and Fanta orange soda ads in Arabic. He tried to imagine that he was amused by the teeming life before him—the men lugging broken stones in a wheelbarrow, the little barefoot boy in a wool shawl smoking a cigarette, the walls stenciled with black letters: DÉFENSE D'AFFICHER.

When they got back to England, the band would either go on or it wouldn't. Brian would either look after himself or he wouldn't. He and Keith would either spend ten years in prison

146

or they would make another record. When he was onstage, things went fast and he solved each problem in the same moment that it arose, building momentum, forgetting himself. But in ordinary life, even with the others around, there were times when there was nothing to say or do and everyone looked aimless and false.

He remembered the morning before the bust at Keith's house, the way the bare trees had started to shine like aluminum, the way the rocky beach had aligned itself all at once into endless ranks of perfectly situated debris. It was strange how the past was still there, even after all this time of pretending that it didn't matter. He realized that Keith was the only person he trusted.

They were walking through the Jemaa el Fna, Keith and Anita, buoyant and laughing and stoned, feeling free of everything that had happened the night before. Her hair was disheveled and greasy, and her mascara was smudged. Both of her eyes were bruised, but they were holding hands, determined to push things further, if only for the sake of pushing things further. He had no idea how long this was going to last and he didn't care.

A band of *gnaoua* musicians were shaking their iron castanets in the center of a circled crowd. They leered and stuck out their tongues, or suddenly froze in a suspicious, sideways glare, but it was daytime and there was no menace in their poses. They wore bright silk tunics and high-crowned, tasseled fezzes studded with cowrie shells.

"Lovely country," Keith said.

He reached down for the cheap Kodak camera that dangled

from his neck. At the last second, Anita leaned into the picture from the side, almost stumbling, smiling at her own clumsiness as she pressed her hand to the crown of her floppy white hat.

"Greetings from Morocco," she said.

"Right. I'll send it home to Mum."

"Dear Mum, this is my friend, the Whore of Babylon. Note the damaged look in her eyes."

"Yes, please send money. Care of Scotland Yard."

In four months, Keith would appear in court for his drug trial, and some remnant of the feeling he had now would come back to him then. He would tell the court what he thought of five policemen invading his house, peering into his privacy. He would wear one of Anita's scarves around his neck. During the recesses, he would order expensive lunches from his cell and get drunk on wine. When they asked him about the naked girl in the upstairs bedroom, he would say that he was not an old man and did not share their petty moral outrage, that the girl had just been taking a nap and that in any case she was his friend. When it was over, he would emerge from the trial transformed, a swaggering outlaw figure, no longer a lone misfit, no longer the shy dreamer who had been preyed upon at school by older boys who called him a faggot and a girl. He didn't know that the next night the police would raid Brian's flat, the flat in Earl's Court he had shared with Anita, and frame him for possession of cocaine. When he thought of Brian now—leaving Brian by himself in the hotel—he couldn't picture Brian himself, only the empty room.

LUV N' HAIGHT, 1966-1967

THE BOY'S NAME was Bobby Beausoleil. His last name meant "Beautiful Sun," he'd told Anger. He had the kind of cheekbones that formed triangular shadows beneath his eyes, and the eyes themselves were an unlikely, almost violet shade of blue.

"This is like a test," Anger said, crouching behind the camera. "I just need to see what you look like on film."

Bobby was looking not above Anger's head, as some people would have, but right into the lens, his hands clasped behind his back. He wore a kind of swashbuckler's shirt with puffy sleeves and a set of crossed laces at the collar.

"I've never seen your films," he said.

"No. But this has nothing to do with my other films."

"I was just saying, I'd like to see them."

Anger moved around him with the light meter in his hand, checking the levels near his face. It was a slightly intrusive process, but Bobby did not seem bothered by it. He tilted his head a little, determined not to falter, determined to make the most of what he was already thinking of as his chance.

"My last film was very black," said Anger. "Motorcycles. People falling in love with death, that sort of thing. I'm trying to make the opposite of that now. What I was talking to you about before."

"The Lucifer idea."

"Something about San Francisco. The whole thing of peace and flowers. I want to understand what that's about."

They were in the bedroom of Anger's new apartment, on the ground floor of a crumbling Victorian house in the Haight-Ashbury district. He had painted the walls purple, and with black and silver paint he had transformed the egg-and-dart molding into what looked like a runner of studded leather. The result was calming, occult, dreamlike. The windows were recessed in high alcoves, and at the top of each, still intact, were frescoes of women's faces, windblown and ethereal.

"People falling in love with death," said Bobby. He gave a little sniff of something like laughter, then looked at the purple wall. "I've known some people like that."

"I suppose there were lots of them in high school," Anger joked.

"I was kicked out of high school."

"So what does that mean? Reform school? Juvenile hall?"

"Are you filming this?"

"What?"

"I'm just wondering if you're filming all this. How much of this anyone is going to see."

It was spring, 1966. Anger would go for walks in his new neighborhood, a slum taken over by young people, and try to make sense of the odd mishmash of deterioration and adornment: broken stairways with freshly painted railings, run-down porches crawling with morning glories or draped with a faded American flag. He saw young people holding hands and whispering to each other, or sitting on the sidewalk playing guitars, barefoot, the muscles moving solemnly in their shoulders and arms. In Golden Gate Park, he saw streams of soap bubbles drifting over the lawn, flashing prisms of light, and in the distance behind them there might be anything: a group of truant schoolkids, a girl with a German shepherd, a cross-eyed boy in black body paint juggling a set of knives. Everyone under thirty had decided to be an exception: a musician, a runaway, an artist, a star. They seemed unaware of any past that was not as safe or malleable as this present.

He had met Bobby last week at a concert in an old church that was now a community center. LSD was still legal, and it sent tight cords of tension up Anger's legs and his spine, his skull nothing more than a diaphanous veil. In the darkened building, Bobby's band was playing in front of a movie screen that showed otherworldly scenes from nature: the blue and red membranes of dividing cells, the pink torrent of corpuscles rushing through a vein, the solar glow of an embryo in the black ink of its amniotic sac. Onstage were conga players, trumpeters, guitarists, violinists, five girls dressed only in harem pants, circling their naked breasts with their outstretched fingers. At the side of the stage was Bobby, playing guitar in front of one of these girls, dressed in a purple cape and a black top hat that shone in alternating bands of white and blue. The song he played had no chorus, no verse, no recognizable structure at all. Perhaps it was a new kind of music, or perhaps it was just noise. It didn't matter. What mattered was the way his hair fell all the way down to his shoulders, beneath his top hat, like a woman's hair. He went into a gradual crouch before the girl, bending the knees of his fringed buckskin pants, and she trailed her silk scarf over his shoulders. For a brief moment they both appeared to be framed inside the red and gold border of an antique playing card that buckled and threw off motes of light. Then the image melted into a neon impression of Times Square. Anger could see the revolving red lights as Bobby tilted his head and, in another aspect of his showmanship, ran the tip of his tongue over the girl's sweat-glistening breast.

Afterward, Anger tracked him down in the parking lot, where he and his girlfriend were loading equipment into a van. He was a filmmaker, he said, he was making a film, would the boy have any interest in playing a part in his next film?

His girlfriend put her fingers on Bobby's cheek and whispered something into his ear. He turned to her and whispered something back. Then the girl looked at Anger with a furtive smile, a smile that echoed and expanded and gleamed.

He was eighteen, Bobby told Anger that afternoon. Most people thought he was older because he'd been living on his own for the past year and a half, first in L.A, then in San Francisco. His parents in Santa Barbara had kicked him out, because he was out of their control. He would disappear for a couple of days, sometimes more, not even realizing it, just forgetting to call home, forgetting why it mattered. It was his dreaminess that his father never understood. It was what they fought about day after day, for as long as he could remember.

When he was sixteen, they'd sent him to a reform school north of Sacramento, where he'd lived in a barracks with thirty other boys, digging ditches, moving rocks, cleaning bathrooms, loading sacks of potatoes onto flatbed trucks and then riding with the trucks to the grader to unload them. For a year, he'd worn the same uniform as everyone else. Like everyone else's, his hair had been shorn with an electric clipper, so that the curve of his skull shone like a knob beneath the taut gray skin. Eventually he lost his real name and was called by a nickname chosen by the others, a way of being told all over again that he would be perceived in a way that had nothing to do with who he was. There were fights almost every day — fights behind the mess hall, fights in the showers, fights with bare fists or with plungers or with brooms or with knives from the kitchen. He learned to fight with a joyless focus that made his opponents lose interest, until eventually his friendship became coveted and he didn't have to fight at all anymore.

When he got out of reform school, he was seventeen. He lived with his parents for an abortive month, then he lived for a while in a trailer with a thirty-six-year-old woman. In the meantime, he'd started playing with a rock band in L.A., a band who had a recording contract now — who were on their way to becoming famous — but who had told Bobby he was too young, too pretty-looking, that they were serious musicians and he had to leave.

Anger couldn't stop looking at him that afternoon. He could feel the faint tension as Bobby paced the room, wondering perhaps if Anger was even listening. At times, it was like looking at a beautiful girl, a diffuse desire that he wasn't quite sure what to do with. At other times, the desire was so blatant that he could feel his face burn.

"There's this thing about women," Bobby told him. "You get to a point with them where they can't say no without hurting themselves, some idea they have about themselves. I used to go to nightclubs in this very straight outfit, suit and tie, my hair all combed and watered. I would have a Coke or a ginger ale. It was like, 'Oh, I'm just this lost little boy. So shy I can barely talk to you. Maybe you could take me home.'"

"A good act," said Anger.

"But it wasn't an act. I never thought it was an act. If I did, I never would have been able to do it."

He was making a film about Lucifer, yes, but it was not the devil he was talking about, not the pitchfork and the horns, not the spooky thing from the movies. Lucifer was a god of light, a child god, the fallen angel who after two thousand years of repression was finally coming back. He was the god of desire, illicit desire, the liberator, the revelator. How could he explain it to someone like Bobby, whom Anger could not look at without seeing the angel's wholly unknowing embodiment? He'd said that it was just a way of naming or looking at things that were happening in the world right now, a kind of mythology he liked to play around with sometimes, a way of describing how the world was changing, opening it up to deeper meanings. Yes, he'd told Bobby, Lucifer was the role he would play in the film, but it wasn't worth thinking about very much. All he would really be doing was just playing himself. At first, it would just be a matter of watching him, watching him and seeing what happened.

They started by making little films around town: at Golden Gate Park, in front of the Diggers' "free store" on Frederick Street. One day they went for a drive north of the city toward Bolinas, the camera and the equipment in the back of the station wagon, Bobby at the wheel, Anger in the passenger seat. Through the windows, the hills were a pale brown, like wheat, and the ocean, when they glimpsed it, was gray beneath the fog.

"I'm going down to L.A. for a while," Bobby said.

Anger looked down at his hands on his legs.

"We have to get something going," Bobby said. "The band. All the record companies are down there." The road flattened and rose into a gradual incline, and he gripped the lever on the steering column, forcing it into lower gear.

"I thought we were making a film," said Anger.

"Well, there's that too. That's obviously a priority. But the band is about to go somewhere. I can feel that."

Anger nodded slowly. At the end of the hill, on their left, they saw the beginnings of the event they were about to attend. Beyond a row of picnic tables and a pair of outhouses, someone had erected a kind of pavilion made of different-colored bed-sheets. Around it were people in costume—a boy with a flute and a leather vest, a boy in a painted cape and a wizard's hat. It was a style that mostly eluded Anger, an irreverent humor that never settled on innocence or sarcasm but wavered between them. Bobby was already smiling in the strange, coded way that Anger had learned to recognize, the smile of people who were younger than he was.

"How long will you be gone?" he asked.

"I don't know. Maybe a few months? It's up in the air."

"A few months."

"Like I said, it's not set in stone. We're going to be lining things up once we get there. Showcases and things."

"It sounds like maybe it's not set at all."

Bobby stared straight ahead through the windshield. "We won't know until we get there," he said. "That's all I know for now. I told you from the very beginning that the band was what I was about. I would think that you of all people would understand that."

Anger immersed himself in work, just like his father, who had spent all his spare time in his garage, fixated on his machines. After Bobby left, he did an elaborate reediting of a film he now saw could be called "psychedelic," a film called *Inauguration of the Pleasure Dome*. He added superimpositions, doubling and tripling the images so that the action seemed to take place in a vast, floating darkness. He synced each cut to the music, jumbling the separate tableaux until they began to build a rhythm, finessing tension and drama out of nothing but images. Outside it was June. The streets were lined with sycamores whose leaves were yellow-green and full of the strange, quasi-tropical succulence that reminded him of the trees of his childhood in Santa Monica. He stayed inside the editing room; he tried not to think about why he was there. The work was time-consuming, and for ten or twelve hours he would lose himself in its intricacies.

It was fine, until a package arrived, three days after Bobby left. It was an overstuffed manila envelope containing a motorcycle T-shirt and an anonymous note, a quotation from *The Sephiroth:* "Look into the sightless Eye of the Moon and see what Light glows there. There is no Life without Death. You have been sleepwalking. Now go back to bed and dream of the Sun."

The T-shirt was ripped and covered with brownish stains, obviously bloodstains. It was silk-screened with a picture of a BSA motorcycle. Anger guessed right away who it was from, because a month ago Bruce Byron had sent a telegram, the latest in a series, congratulating him on the success of *Scorpio*

Rising, its interesting ideas, and leaving the implication that he was somehow owed money.

Bobby was gone for six days when there was a phone call. Less than an hour later, he showed up in front of the crumbling Victorian house with his guitar wrapped in an army blanket against the rain. His hair was wet and his white buccaneer's shirt hung from his body like a soaked, transparent rag. Someone had stolen his money, or he had lost his money—it would never be clear when Bobby talked about money. From what he'd told Anger on the phone, he had slept the night before in an abandoned car.

The two of them stood in the front hall, Bobby in a puddle of water that was absolutely clear, like new varnish on the pine floor.

"He just turned on me," he said. "That's how it is with people like that."

"Who?" said Anger.

"I don't know. This spade cat, Donald, it's not important."

Anger bowed his head as Bobby came farther inside, hugging his guitar to his chest.

"I'll have to go back later," he said. "I just need to cool out for a while. They have my clothes, everything."

They went past the kitchen and into the apartment's extra bedroom. It was an old ballroom with molded ceilings and high windows that looked out on the sycamores below. It was cluttered with boxes. Bobby peeled off his shirt, dropping it on the floor, his back to Anger. He roughed up his hair with his fingers. He bent over and let its ends fall to his knees, then stood up straight and flipped his head up so that the wet black strands shot back over his shoulders.

"I appreciate this," he said, looking into Anger's eyes.

"Don't be ridiculous."

"No, really. I appreciate it."

His face was younger and plainer without all of his hair falling over his forehead. Bare-chested, his white skin taut with goose pimples, he looked like a high school boy damp from the shower after gym.

Anger moved some of his boxes and trunks into the closet and stacked some others against the two far walls. He plugged a desk lamp into the socket by the window, trying not to look at him.

An hour later, they were in Anger's room—the only room in the apartment resembling a common room—where they sat on the couch and shared a joint. Through the leaded windows, the leaves on the trees were a shiny green, sagging from their branches. The rain had stopped, but the sky was still gray, making every color stand out like something permanent.

"You're not telling me what really happened," said Anger.

Bobby shook his head in a bored way, his eyes closed. Anger watched the smoke come out of his nostrils.

"Some things went wrong," he finally said. "On the way to L.A., it didn't happen the way I thought it would. There are people—some people don't care about themselves. So then they can't care about anything. That's the way it happens sometimes."

"You never made it to L.A."

Bobby wiped the corners of his eyes with his thumb and forefinger. "That's all I can say," he said. "I'll leave, if you want me to leave."

There was a newspaper on the floor. It brought word of Vietnam—Saigon, Haiphong, Da Nang—the names by now somehow remote without being exotic. Anger looked at the words without quite seeing them, and for some reason he thought of Bobby's band, the tuneless, naively serious band that he thought was going to make him a star. He thought of the foolish scheme—a drug deal, he supposed—that had failed to facilitate that plan.

He brought his fingers to Bobby's still-damp hair. He had touched him like this before, while filming, but there was no camera now, and Bobby went still, calibrating his response. He didn't stand up or push Anger away, but only sat there with an abstracted expression in his eyes, as if this were happening to someone else.

"You're having a strange day," said Anger.

"Everything is strange."

"No, not everything is strange. Some things are ordinary."

When he reached for Bobby's thigh, Bobby didn't move, he just looked down at the hand, his lips parted slightly. Anger loomed over him for a moment, watching, then he shifted himself onto the floor. Bobby's eyes were fixed on his now, his forgotten joint still burning between his thumb and forefinger. Then he looked down at Anger's hand, his Adam's apple shifting drily in his throat.

Bobby's damp skin smelled faintly, oddly, like kerosene. Anger pressed his thumbs to where his abdomen met his hips, feeling it expand and contract with his breaths. He had unzipped Bobby's pants, but it was Bobby, not Anger, who had pushed them farther down over his knees. After he came, he kept his eyes closed, breathing heavily through his nostrils. His face was peaceful then, as if in sleep, except at the corner of his mouth, where there was the faintest shadow of a grimace.

"I just think you should know," Bobby said. "I'm not like that."

"You're not like that."

"You know . . . I'm not that way. I don't mind it sometimes, if it's there. I'm not uptight. But it's no big deal either way."

Bobby moved into the extra bedroom that week. Anger bought him a mattress and a blanket and some pillows, and he stacked the rest of the boxes as well as he could in the closet. He bought Bobby groceries: white bread, potato chips, beer. It happened gradually, without much discussion. The mention of all these practicalities was not something either of them believed in.

Late at night, through the half-opened door, he would sometimes see Bobby on the floor of his new room, smoking pot with his friends, listening to music or playing music on their guitars. They would lean their heads back toward the ceiling in neutral contemplation, as if the world had just been created for their benign explorations. There would be girlfriends, an endless succession, in jeans or flowered skirts, long hair falling into their eyes. One or two of them would always end up in Bobby's bed by the end of the night, lying beside him in the dim light of a few candles, Bobby with one of Anger's effects in his hands — a toy motorcycle, a deck of tarot cards — anything he could absently study while the girls waited and watched.

Anger never felt that he was being taken advantage of. He saw their arrangement through Bobby's eyes: the sense of justice that would come from having his own room in the apartment, a private place to take his girlfriends, a sink in which to leave his dirty dishes. When Anger had his own guests over — filmmakers, artists, theater people — there was a cachet in having so many young people around. It made him feel like Bobby's accomplice, younger than he really was, young enough to be Bobby himself.

He had only the vaguest idea of what the film they were making was actually going to consist of. So far, he was just filming Bobby's life: playing his guitar, smoking a joint, standing in front of the house where they had painted the door purple and scrawled the words THY WILL BE DONE! What happened between them, when the day's filming was over and there were no more guests around, was a secret that Bobby seemed to keep even from himself. His ambivalence—his obstinate, closed eyes—never resolved into a refusal or an invitation. He had threatened to kill Anger if he ever told anyone.

If you took away the nails and the cross, then the god would be only a naked boy, extending his arms in calm recognition. Removed from his post, he would be free to go where you'd always wanted to follow, stepping down into that fiery zone where there was no meaning for words like "self" and "other," "reality" and "dream," "desire" and "fear." Lucifer, the morning star. His paleness would cast a green reflection in the night sky. In the secret darkness, he would be as glad as you were to see that the stupid pretense of his chastity had finally come to an end. But he could be as distant and elusive as any other god. Like his counterpart, the god on the cross, he came to bring not peace but a sword.

"That's how the cable cars work," Anger explained one afternoon that fall, pointing out three enormous cogs connected to chains and engines, the city's powerhouse. Bobby was standing in front of him in a brown leather overcoat, looking at the cogs, painted bright green, bright red, and bright yellow. He couldn't help moving toward them—Anger could see from the way he'd forgotten his posture that he had never considered the cable cars, or the electric current that pulled them, or anything else about the city's mysterious infrastructure.

He turned around then, hands in his front pockets so that his coat hung behind him like a cape. "I forgot to tell you," he said. "There was a phone call the other night. I forget his name."

Anger stared at him.

"The one who helped you direct the last film," Bobby said. "In New York."

Anger bowed his head, then raised it abjectly at the sky. He'd been waiting for a phone call from a film society in Germany, a potential source of funding, but now he knew who had called.

"Bruce Byron," he said. "Was that his name?"

"That's right. Bruce Byron. He wanted to talk to you about the next film. He said he has a new idea. Something about motorcycles." He was looking at Anger through the orange lenses of his sunglasses, something almost accusatory in his gaze, as if he knew more about Bruce Byron than he was letting on. He seemed to be always surprising Anger with some disappointing news that he only pretended to not know was disappointing.

"I'm not speaking to him," Anger said.

"You're not speaking to him."

"No, I'm serious. If he wants something, he can call my lawyer."

Bobby nodded to himself, his head bowed. Lawyers — Anger could tell that that's what he was thinking. They were absurd to him in the same way that Anger was absurd.

When they got home that afternoon, there was more news of Vietnam. The Vietcong had shelled Saigon: they were growing stronger, not weaker, and the war had spread from the jungle villages to the capital city. It was no longer something you could even pretend to ignore. It was, Anger realized, another reason for someone like Bobby to keep out of sight, to have no fixed address.

That night, they stayed up talking. Bobby was looking at the images on the bedroom walls, the gods and occult signs: the pentacle, the zodiac, the sephiroth with its Hebrew letters designating each of the ten emanations of God. Anger offered him a few explanations, casual and brief, but would not make it clear what was a game to him and what was serious. "You don't need to know all that," he said.

Bobby turned.

"You already know about it in some ways," said Anger. "This is just part of the game."

"What game?"

"Thinking that you don't know what I'm talking about. That we have less in common than we do." He sat down in a chair by the window and looked down at the floor. "I don't want to talk about this," he said. "It's not going to be helpful. But I think you feel the same way. You're here for yourself, not for me. I understand that. That's one of the things we have in common."

They smoked a joint. He watched Bobby go thoughtful and

quiet, reclining in his chair, his fingertips touching, as the angular music made dim shapes in the air. He told Bobby a little bit about Bruce Byron then. He said that Bruce Byron was a kind of Frankenstein's monster he had created by filming him in bad faith. He said that filmmaking could have real consequences, that it was more than just a game, that it could be like an act of aggression if director and actor didn't understand each other deeply. He said that understanding each other had nothing to do with words, that words could be a hindrance to knowing another person. He said that New York had been a dead city and a dead culture and that was why he had come west, in search of fresh ideas. He didn't mention the tin shed he'd lived in on the Gances' roof, or the mix of arousal and scorn he'd felt in the presence of Bruce Byron's body. He didn't mention that on the night of Byron's phone call he'd been in a dark basement off Castro Street, prostrating himself on the floor for five anonymous men. He knew that Bobby—this boy he'd cast as Lucifer—would see it only as an image of degradation. He didn't try to explain how it had been transcendent in its brutality, how for a few moments it had reconfigured the surface of everything around him. Instead, he said that the point of art, like magick, was to undercut the rational mind, to remind us of how difficult it was to know what was real and what had merely been created to appear real.

He went into the kitchen and made some tea, bringing it back in two stained cups that he carried on a plate. As a way of changing the subject, he took out some photographs of Paris. He talked about his time there, about the artists he'd known. He talked about his former mentor, Jean Cocteau (dropping another name that Bobby had never heard), letting it all come gushing out, all that feminine talk.

Sometimes Byron would call, usually in the middle of the night, usually without saying a word. Anger would pick up the receiver to stop it ringing—Byron could wait for several minutes—and hear nothing but the faint static that conjured the distance between them, the miles of wire tense and responsive in the darkness.

He would see Byron's face, unshaven, somehow off-kilter behind the large green sunglasses he had made him wear for all those bedroom scenes. *I want it to be real. I'm the only one putting anything real into this. Every time it gets serious, you start smirking, playing your games.*

In the bathroom, he would find Bobby's jeans lying in a pile by the toilet. Through the cracked door of the extra bedroom, he would see the bare shoulders of the girl who moved slowly above him in the dark.

"I don't really see where this is going," Bobby said.

He was sitting naked on a wooden crate, cross-legged, raising his arms up in the darkness. With Anger's watching presence invisible behind the camera—with the music on, the jagged meanderings of Sun Ra—Bobby had been stoned enough to enter into the role, aroused by his own nakedness, holding the pose, but now the moment was over and he was ashamed.

"The band is playing tomorrow," he said, getting down off the crate. "Light show, everything. You could film that, help us out for once."

Anger looked down at the camera. "I can't always film the band, Bobby. You know that. It's expensive."

"Right."

"I'm not going to talk about this anymore."

"But that's what it always comes down to, isn't it? Money."

"I don't know what you think that means. Like I'm trying to rip you off or something."

"There's no script, no anything."

"This is the script."

"I'm making a bunch of gestures in front of a camera."

"Why are you getting angry?"

"I'm just saying who has the money? That's all I'm saying."

He bent over to pull his pants on, clumsy on one foot, then the other. The strobe light was still on. It made everything hysterical, exaggerated, prolonged.

"I don't have any money," said Anger. "That's the truth. It won't change anything, getting angry."

"I'm not getting angry. You're always making more out of this than there is. The truth is I really don't give a shit anymore."

That December, Anger went on a business trip to New York. *Scorpio Rising* was having an almost permanent run there. He was going to meet an art dealer uptown, Robert Fraser, from London, who had sold some prints of *Scorpio* and *Inauguration of the Pleasure Dome* to a few of his private clients. Among them was a famous rock band. Anger had seen them before, but he had never paid much attention. While he was in New York that week, he saw a clip of them on TV. They were playing a song about a young man's fantasies of blackness, a throbbing, hypnotic song with an Arabic melody played at first on an Indian sitar. It was more aggressive than any pop song Anger had ever heard. Like his own work, it was dark, but also shot through with exotic colors that had as little to do with darkness as a stained-glass window.

It came first from the blond one, Brian, who sat cross-legged on a white disk suspended onstage in purple-tinged darkness. He was the one playing the sitar, dressed in white Indian pajamas, his facial expression switching from a studied aloofness to an embarrassingly complicit, head-nodding smile. He looked very stoned. He looked alternately glad to be a part of the band on its latest televised appearance and less convincingly intent on the music, always on the verge of breaking into laughter.

The singer, Mick, wore a green military jacket with epaulets and a brass star. It was a hint of fascism that, along with his purple mascara and silk tie, made him look uncannily like a character in one of Anger's own films. He moved and leered like an epileptic, contorting his arms and fixing the audience with a judgmental stare. His hair was cropped short on top and longer in the back—an awkward haircut, reminiscent of prison—and when he pointed at the crowd, the glare in his eyes was like the glare of two chips of mirror.

At his side, the guitar player, Keith, was like his henchman, dressed all in black, with a black guitar, looking at his leader with open, self-conscious joy.

There was nothing about the band that wasn't outwardly camp, but somehow they'd reversed the meaning of it all so that they looked more aggressively, even violently, straight than they would have if they were dressed in business suits. They made Anger feel oddly embarrassed for Bobby, who would never have dreamed of such a simple, compressed, and utterly sexual song.

When he got back to San Francisco, Bobby wasn't home and the apartment was a shambles. There were bedrolls and piles of clothes in both bedrooms, even in Anger's, where someone had left a pair of hiking boots and a suitcase and a shopping bag full of groceries. There were dirty plates left not just in the kitchen but on the floor of Bobby's bedroom and on the sheets of his unmade bed. *The Sephiroth* was lying there on the floor, its pages held open by metal clips. Someone had been tracing some of its diagrams. There were sheets of these copies on the floor, some of them colored in with pencil, some of them lettered with the name of Bobby's band. From where he stood, Anger could not read the legend beneath the diagram, but he knew what it said: "Look into the sightless Eye of the Moon and see what Light glows there. There is no Life without Death. You have been sleepwalking. Now go back to bed and dream of the Sun."

In the kitchen, on the stove, there was a pot of ruined noodles, charred black at the center where they were stuck in a resinous clump to the aluminum surface. Everything smelled like American cheese and smoke.

He took *The Sephiroth* back to his bedroom and returned it to its shelf. That was when he noticed that although the other books there were neatly arrayed, they were not in their proper order. There was something particularly irritating about this, just as there was something irritating about the way someone had pushed his boots and suitcase into one corner of the room, as if this tiny effort at neatness could make the general intrusion any less offensive.

He took a more careful look at the bookshelves. It was only now that it occurred to him that something had been stolen. Why had all the books been taken down, and why had they been rearranged? Perhaps because whoever did it knew that Anger would never remember everything that was supposed to be there.

Bobby came back at around seven o'clock, carrying his guitar case. The two girls he brought with him were unusually ragged. One of them wore a lumberjack shirt over a stiff, synthetic dress. The other was freckled and auburn-haired, her eyelashes very fair, almost invisible, so that her face looked stripped or as if it had recovered from a mild burn. All three of them were so stoned that their cheeks were stiff and their eyes swollen, their gestures a parody of three people acting surprised, anticipating a greeting.

"I thought you were coming back tomorrow," Bobby said.

Anger was bent over the kitchen trash, scraping at the pot of burnt noodles. "I came back today," he said.

"Shit."

"What's been going on?"

"Shit. I thought you were coming back tomorrow. We were going to clean everything up tonight."

Something about his stoned eyes revealed several shifting layers of falseness. They would change in an instant from rational self-assurance to befuddlement, blankness, and then become for an even briefer moment panicky, apologetic, as if they could read Anger's suspicions, but only for an instant before they resumed their rational self-assurance.

"Here," he said, reaching for the pot in Anger's hands. "Let me clean that up."

"I don't think it's worth either of our time, Bobby. Why don't you go relax? We don't have to make a ceremony out of this."

Bobby's eyes were simply confused now. It was as if whatever he was trying to conceal from Anger had at last been concealed from himself. He didn't know what any of this was about anymore. He was trying to grin knowingly, to acknowledge Anger's sarcasm, but in his eyes there was also some helpless appeal for sympathy.

They were calling them the Love Generation now: these kids who didn't doubt themselves even when they were wrong, who would try anything, who acted as though life was an idea and not a block of time with a beginning and an end. It was impossible to disagree with them — they were what Anger believed in — but he saw that they were lost, and so a part of him wanted them to get into trouble, to find out how serious their rebellion might actually be. Later, when Bobby had disappeared, making off with his camera and almost all of the footage they had shot that year, he would wonder how he could have ever been so credulous about the Haight-Ashbury, about the whole thing of peace and flowers, about whatever he'd thought of as the opposite of thanatomania.

That evening, some more people came by in a van. The two girls were still there, as was their returned friend, the boy who had left his boots and suitcase in Anger's bedroom. Bobby was sitting on the floor of his room, playing one of his exotic instruments, a Greek bouzouki that made a thin, percussive plinking sound. The others sat with their bare feet curled beneath them, passing around a skull-shaped pipe, inhaling its smoke with tight-lipped frowns, then turning a silent gaze on the next member of the circle. On the ceiling, a mirror ball—one more gift from Anger to his protégé—threw pinprick stars on their faces and on the frescoed walls. The girls' bushy hair hid their foreheads and obscured their eyes. There was something darkly sexual to Anger about their hair. It hung not in tresses or curls but in hanks, as raw as the hair on their bodies.

He stepped over their circle, ignoring them, aware of himself as a stranger in his own apartment. He began rifling through some of the trunks he kept in Bobby's closet. It occurred to him that even if he found something missing, some proof that Bobby had stolen from him, it wouldn't matter. Bobby would just lie, it would just be one more fight he couldn't afford to have. What mattered was the suspicion itself, the feeling that Bobby had been stealing from him all along.

There in its yellow envelope was the ripped and bloodstained T-shirt that Bruce Byron had sent him in the mail almost a year ago.

It was wrinkled and dry, as soft as a dustcloth. When he shook out its folds, it gave off a thin dust of dried, rust-colored blood. He held it in his hands, a tight shrewdness in his lips. The tastelessness of what he was about to do now was so extreme that he failed to acknowledge it.

"This is what happened to the boy in my last film," he said, turning around, offering it up like an artifact to whoever would look.

The girl he leaned over reached out her fingers. Beside her, the girl in the lumberjack shirt was looking at him mischievously, as if waiting for the punch line. Anger looked at Bobby, gravely convinced of the threat he was making, but the look on Bobby's face was blank, his skin gray, his eyes two black pupils that seemed blind.

There was no way for Anger to play this remark off now as some risqué joke that the others were too tense to laugh at. There was no way to make any sense of the situation at all.

In the vestibule outside the front door, Anger had to step around a clutter of shoes and boots that had been left there by the upstairs neighbors. It was too cold outside for the clothes he was wearing—a sweater but no jacket—but he kept walking, past the huddled group of kids outside the corner grocery with its dim brown light. He walked all the way to Golden Gate Park before he realized he had forgotten his keys.

He hurried back at a half jog, then a self-recriminating walk, then a half jog. There was the same group of kids, witnesses now to his absurdity. In the vestibule, he stared at the lock for a long moment and rattled the door, but there was no point, it wasn't going to yield, and Bobby wasn't going to let him back in.

PART THREE

"You never know what is enough unless you know what is more than enough."

—WILLIAM BLAKE, from *The Marriage of Heaven and Hell*

THE DEVIL, 1968-1969

ANGER HAD BEEN THERE for close to two hours now, waiting for them to get started. He was watching them from the control room, not filming yet, just standing behind the sound engineers on their stools, dressed in the same flared black pants and purple acrylic shirt he'd been wearing every other day for more than a week. Through the soundproof glass, he could see Mick trying to teach the new song to Brian. Brian was very stoned and Mick seemed almost embarrassed by his perseverance, humoring him, smiling and shrugging his shoulders as he demonstrated the simple beat on his acoustic guitar. "That's the other one," he said. "You're thinking of that other bit."

It was disappointing to watch them tonight, in spite of the other times he'd seen them drain the air from a room just by stepping into it. They were struggling—he had always thought the whole point of them was their effortlessness. It was clear that if Mick was going to rouse himself out of mediocrity tonight, he was going to have to be far more ruthless with Brian.

The studio was like a concrete bunker, with a shabby red carpet on the floor. Styrofoam cups and beer bottles rested on the amplifiers and the soundproof panels, which were orange or brown or green. Finally Keith arrived, coming into the control room, wearing dark sunglasses and a torn white shirt.

"Keep taping," he said to the sound engineers. "Just keep it rolling. Let's not miss it this time."

The engineers did not look up from their panel of dials. Keith was looking at Anger now.

"Did you come over with Mick?" he said.

"No, they sent me a car."

"Right, good. The star treatment." He turned and looked at the others through the soundproof glass. Brian was looking steadily into Mick's eyes as he played something on his guitar, the two of them working their way into further and further complications, further from any possible song. "You should ring up Anita sometime," Keith said. "She gets bored. She keeps asking about you."

He walked into the booth then, with his sunglasses still on. As he passed a pair of carpeted sound buffers, he picked up his guitar with such fluid indifference that it might have been a jacket or a set of keys. Without a word, he sat down in the chair next to Mick and started playing, not even looking at Brian. He looked at Mick, nodding his head, taking up the song in a completely different style, as if he'd been there all along, sifting through the variations.

It was a folk ballad, minor-keyed and slow. It was more English-sounding than American, almost mournful, like a dirge. The words, Anger knew, were a monologue in the voice of the Devil. They spoke of the evils wrought by humanity in the sway of a sly, sophisticated con man who in the end was just a bewildering reflection of themselves.

Mick looked up at Anger through the panel of soundproof glass. He was always flirting, always putting his hand on Anger's arm or leaning forward to state his opinion. The way he spoke, at least around Anger, was arch, camp, blasé, as if he were imitating some idea he had of how an heiress might speak. They had met at a party at Robert Fraser's gallery, all mirrors and pink light, and immediately Mick had shown an interest in the Lucifer film, more interest than Anger would ever have thought possible.

"I should show you what I get in the mail sometimes," Mick had said. "Death threats, curses, hexes. That's the mood now, it's very dark. You start to wonder what it means. It's too easy to just write it off as nonsense."

His new songs were all Devil songs in one way or another. Perhaps the Lucifer film was something to help him fill out this new role, the role of Mick—the Prince of Darkness, the Angel of Light, it wasn't easy to tell the difference anymore. It was a role Mick had stumbled into, not exactly chosen, but it was also a role that practically nobody else could have even attempted. Brian had been preparing for it his whole life, and you could see it eating him from the inside, the dream that had come true but not in any of the ways he'd expected.

"It's just music, but they want us to be revolutionaries now," Mick had said. "So fine, let's tear everything down, start over, what we have now makes no sense anyway. When they busted us last year, it was like the whole country was pressing up against you, trying to shove you down into a hole. But then you realized they were just shoving themselves into the hole, that you were just getting bigger and bigger. They'd made you into these myths."

It was 1968. The press was calling it the Year of the Barricades. In France, there had almost been a revolution that May, fueled by dadaist slogans and students throwing stones. It was not hard to see the band as emblematic of the desire you could feel all around you now, not for peace and love, but for something militant, perhaps chaos for the sake of chaos.

The drummer was practicing drumrolls in his corner. Then he leaned back his head and shook it, loosening up the muscles in his neck, his face as blankly patient as a horse's. Brian was beckoning to Keith from across the length of the room now, spreading his opened hands for a cigarette. He waited for Keith to throw him the pack, then he waited even longer before Keith noticed him again, then he dropped the lighter when Keith finally threw it to him and he stood for a long moment looking at the floor.

It would take them three nights to put the song into its finished form. In those three nights, it would change from a folk song to a psychedelic song to a soul song, and then emerge as something raw and percussive, like the voodoo music of Haiti. It would end up the exact opposite of a mournful dirge or an English folk song. It would start with a yelp, a monkey screech, and a flat patter of bongos, a resonant thud of conga drums, a locust-like hiss of maracas. It would become a wild celebration of everything it had started out lamenting.

But for now it was just a song with three chords for the verse, one more for the chorus, and they couldn't even play it through. They were lost, as tentative as beginners. The bass player sat absolutely still on a straight-backed chair, dressed in a red velour outfit with matching red boots, smoking a cigarette he held with the straightened tips of his first two fingers. Brian sat inside an enclosure of soundproof panels, his eyes half-closed. He seemed to be propping himself up by gripping the strings of his guitar, not so much an instrument as a beautifully painted wooden object he cradled half-consciously in his lap.

For the next four hours, as far as Anger could tell, there was not a single joke or a word of casual conversation. They kept

Brian off to the side—silent, obedient, lost. They all knew not to look at him, though every time they turned around they must have seen him.

———————

It was almost five AM when the driver dropped Anger back at his flat. It was a small, badly heated set of rooms in Notting Hill Gate, a slum neighborhood where he and a few hippies were the only whites. He'd been careful not to let the band see it very often or for very long. A boy he'd met recently, Will Tennet, had helped him decorate it with stills from *Inauguration of the Pleasure Dome* and some other odd touches—a jeweled box, a green glass toad—that gave it the usual occult ambience, but the fact that he was gay, that he lived with boys, was something the band never seemed fully to acknowledge. They were drawn by something else, an aura they maybe half believed in, maybe wanted to believe in: the occult filmmaker in his vaguely dangerous world.

Will had left a note: "Gone to Kilburn. Don't expect me." Anger put his things down and looked at the half-lit room: the couch, the afghan, the coffee table with its battered, tasseled lamp. There was a strange, penitential feeling, the particular emptiness of being alone after four in the morning. An unexpected sight was waiting for him on the table, a package wrapped in brown paper. Inside he found a bird's nest of shredded newsprint and another note: "Dear Kenneth, I saw this book of pictures and I thought of you. Anita."

It was a book of black-and-white pictures of musclemen in dark briefs, lifting chairs or squatting before a mirror with rigid thighs. Some of them even featured men in sailor caps, as in his film *Fireworks*. He had no idea where Anita would have found such a book or how she would have known it had such significance for him. It made him feel fraudulent for some reason. He didn't know if she was trying to mock him, or if she had left it there with some friendly anticipation of his nostalgia.

In the tiny bathroom, the water was so cold that his fingers started to go numb beneath the tap. He dabbed some of it on his face, his hands shaking. He looked in the mirror and saw that one of his eyes was opened slightly more than the other. His lips stretched across his mouth like two strips of bloodless rubber. He forced himself to stare at it until it wasn't a face at all but just an image, something gray made out of stone.

He switched on the TV, knowing that there would be nothing on at this hour but the static of dormant channels. There was only the one light on in the doorway, and it was hypnotic with the TV on, the sound turned off, a field of swarming particles that never coalesced into any shape. The worry had become a repetitive fugue now, a scrim between himself and the things in front of him. It had become a narrowing tunnel of fear. He had had a nervous breakdown last year, after Bobby had disappeared. For almost a month, he had lain in bed, sleeping or just lying there when he couldn't sleep, cocooned like a child in the warmth of his sheets. The walls of the Haight room were purplish and muddled. Everything became the same: the empty apartment, the stolen Lucifer film, the mindless antagonism of his checkbook. He'd had no money, no film, no reason to believe there would ever be a film, not even a job history or a set of skills he might use to start some other, more predictable way of life. He would see Bobby in his leather overcoat, standing in front of the city's powerhouse, the brightly colored cogs behind him, the orange lenses of his sunglasses. He knew that Bobby was never coming back, but the wish, or the fear, had rooted itself so deeply in his mind that it became a kind of false memory, disorienting when he realized all over again that it hadn't happened.

It was still with him now, the pendulum of embarrassed recollection and the fear that he was out of control. He thought of being in the studio with the band and it was hard to believe that it had really happened. The walls of the room before him were still in place, but everything was made transient by the blue light from the TV.

He thought of Bruce Byron, all those afternoons of filming him in his tiny apartment, lying in bed in front of what he'd called the "idiot box." *Everyone does it differently. I want to see how you do it.* He'd heard that Byron was driving a cab in New York now, every inch of its interior covered with pictures of James Dean and Marlon Brando and stills of his own face from *Scorpio Rising.* He was still showing up at the screenings, still dressed in biker clothes. The film had somehow become his life: a collage assembled by a total stranger who had included him in it almost by accident. But that was how life in the world could be sometimes. Sometimes you were the stranger, sometimes you were Bruce Byron. Who would have thought that it would happen to him, that at his age, forty-one, the same boy, Bobby, would still be appearing almost nightly in his dreams?

Notice how comfortable they appear in their chains, so loose around their wrists that they could free themselves at any time if they so desired.

He went to bed, but as soon as he had drawn the curtains, the phone rang. On the other end of the line was the kind of sound that comes out of a doll when you pull the string on its back, a recording of a man's boisterous laughter.

"Hello," he said.

It was the laugh of a villain in a superhero comic.

"Hello."

There was no answer. There was the pop and then the sudden staticky boom of a TV. Then whoever it was hung up, the sound of the dial tone as dreamlike and accusatory as the sound of the doll's toy laughter.

———

"We're going on tour," said Mick. "That's what Keith is trying to say. This summer we're going back to America."

They'd driven out to Brian's new house, the former residence of A. A. Milne, the children's writer. Statues of Pooh Bear and Christopher Robin stood in an informal garden beyond the pool. Brian wore a cape that looked more like a tapestry, flowers in a tangled design. One of the things they would remember was that he was completely sober that afternoon.

"It's nothing surprising," he said. "I mean, I haven't been a part of it in a long time."

Keith blew out a cloud of smoke. "It's not necessarily a permanent thing," he said. "It's just that right now, fuck, you're in no condition. It's three months on the road."

Brian nodded, bowing his head. "Such a serious business," he said. "I never would have thought it would go like this. Or what I should say, I never thought it would be so much like working at a firm."

Mick uncrossed his legs. "You've been fucking about for the last five years. Been getting paid pretty well while doing it."

"You always had it in for me. Why is that?"

"The fuck I did, Brian."

"No, I'm not going to fight with you. I understand that it's over. I don't have much interest anymore in being in a rock group."

Keith stood up, twisting a little, looking down at his boots. "All right, then," he said. "Well, maybe that's that."

"You going to shake my hand?" said Brian.

"Why don't we leave it?"

Mick leaned forward in his chair. "We'll have the press release tomorrow. Just a simple statement, nothing big."

Keith turned. "Come on."

"What," said Mick.

"Just cool it."

Brian stood up. "I'll be seeing you around. Is that it?"

Keith cocked his head a little to one side. "You know, you pushed me every step of the way. You're still pushing now."

There was a crew of workers that summer renovating Brian's house. They were restoring beams, sanding down floors, rebuilding staircases, glazing windows. It was an unusual job, Brian an unusual client. Any small resentment would have been intensified by the fact that the men doing the work would have been unable to respect him. Sometimes he would be lucid around them, sometimes he would be out of his head. Sometimes he would treat them with a lisping courtesy, and sometimes he would walk by without saying a word, or he would criticize some detail of their work. He was a pop star with a series of Scandinavian models for girlfriends. They were tradesmen who saw a boy in his twenties with a Rolls-Royce in the driveway. They double-billed him for their supplies. Even the caretaker double-ordered groceries and liquor and kept the second batch for himself.

One night there was a party. Brian was swimming, the latest girlfriend was swimming. Everyone had been drinking, taking pills, diving off the low board into the blue-lit pool. The workers were there — they were swimming too, in borrowed trunks. One of them splashed water in Brian's face. He didn't retaliate. Perhaps that was the reason it didn't stop, because he just wiped his eyes and shook his head a few times. Someone dunked him underwater a few minutes later. After that, there was a lot of splashing. The girlfriend turned and saw it from the porch: a thrashing in the water, the swirling blue surface broken at one end. She turned and continued toward the house, looking for cigarettes. When she came back out, they were all standing around the pool except for Brian, who at first looked like just a shadow beneath the surface of the water.

No one ever said what happened. He was a strong swimmer, there were plenty of people there with him. Either they drowned him or they let him drown.

THE HANGED MAN, 1969

IT WAS JULY 5. In the center of London, in Hyde Park, five hundred thousand people were waiting for the band to arrive in his honor. The past year had already been full of vivid catastrophes: the assassinations of Robert Kennedy and Martin Luther King, the Soviet invasion of Prague, half a million troops in Vietnam, the Cuyahoga River going up in flames. Now Brian had died, and half a million people were spread out from a large black stage with towers of black scaffolding to make a dense rectangle of tiny flesh-colored blips, mostly faces and hair. They wore the somber, utilitarian clothes of that year: jeans, work boots, leather sandals, sunglasses. They were a peaceful crowd, but there was a familiar playfulness that was missing. It was a warm day and some of the men had taken off their shirts, but there were very few flowers or beads or Indian-style pajamas. They were thoughtful, unsmiling, squinting in the sunlight, shading themselves with sheets of newspaper. There was no visible grass in the park, only people and trees, cut through at the center by the silver water of the Serpentine.

You wanted to be there, but once you saw how many people were there you began to feel a little strange about being a part of something so ambiguous. It was hard to know what to feel—a beautiful day in July, very sunny, the trees in full leaf. It made it worse somehow that Brian had died in such a stupid way. You wondered, were you there to celebrate or to mourn or what? And what were you celebrating or mourning?

No one knew what to make of the set of iron barricades that had been set up about fifteen yards from the stage. It enclosed the press seats and the seats for special guests and friends of the band. Patrolling these barriers was a squad of two dozen young men in studded leather jackets and leather gestapo caps, members of the London chapter of the Hells Angels. Their motorcycles were lined up on the sides of the stage, all the front wheels turned to the same angle. They never stopped scanning the seated crowd, never stopped convening with one another in little groups. The crowd never stopped pretending that they weren't there.

From a tower of scaffolding to the left of the stage, Anger was filming it all on his Kodak Cine Special camera, a gaunt man in black pants, hair wafting in the breeze. He thought that at least a few of the fans would get up and dance to the music on the P.A., even climb up for a quick frolic on the empty black stage, but none of them did. There was the hush and awe of hierarchy. It occurred to him that his time with the band would be in jeopardy now, that they would have less and less time for people like him. After today, their circle would just get narrower and narrower. They would be as remote as pharaohs or Hollywood stars. He saw that the Hells Angels were more than just a defensive force, they were also the embodiment of some punitive urge the crowd had, an urge to atone.

> Brian Jones, 27, was found dead in his swimming pool Thursday, apparently the result of drug and alcohol intoxication. A spokesman for the band says

> that they have decided to carry through with their
> plans to host the free concert this afternoon in
> Hyde Park as a tribute to his memory. Jones was
> the band's founding member. Last month, after a
> series of drugs arrests, he announced that he was
> leaving the group over musical differences.

He had tried not to push too hard, staying in the background, not a participant but an onlooker. An invisible nimbus seemed to surround them sometimes, a kind of electrical field that made them hyperrealistic, unapproachable. They were stars—lights that were out of reach—and he had tried to understand this. But it had been six years since he'd made a new film. He could feel it like a pressure in his lungs, the images impacted, jostled together, superimposed. The smallest effort on their parts would make all the difference.

The crowd before him was religiously large, a kind of death cult in the new Aquarian style. It had little chance of being much else in these years of violence, riots, assassinations, Vietnam. A rock star drowned in his swimming pool. A gunman appeared in a crowd to murder a president, a senator, Martin Luther King, and in the process somehow became infused with the romance of the person he'd killed. It was the logic of thanatomania, not a sequence of cause and effect but an underlying current, a unifying style. With each death, the mystery of death took on more and more glamour, the romance making the human world feel less and less bound to the earth.

He remembered a dream Anita had told him about just a few months ago, at Keith's country house. In the dream, she was in the desert in California, walking on the sand beneath a cloudless blue sky, when suddenly she'd lost her sense of hearing. There was no sound. She knew then—though there was no mushroom cloud, none of the obvious signs—that the world had ended. At that same instant, hundreds of dragonflies appeared in the air, all of them flying in the same direction. Their bodies seemed to be made of glass, a glistening blue, as if she could see the sky through their transparent shells.

"It went on for a long time," she said. "It was like if I kept walking, everyone might still be where they were supposed to be and we'd all just go back to the way we were before. Only I knew it wasn't true. I knew everything had changed. There was just this endless little moment where I didn't have to face what had really happened yet."

Anger had looked down at his hands, thinking even then that in some way the dream was about Brian. The three of them were sitting on some Moroccan carpets spread out on the grass, and when he looked back up, the different planes of Anita's and Keith's faces were flashing orange or black in the lantern light like fun-house ghouls.

"A dream of heaven," he'd said, meaning timelessness, uncertainty, unknowing. But Anita had looked down at her hand on her knee, not liking the word.

"It wasn't like that," she said. "It wasn't like anything I've ever thought about before. It was strange. I don't know where something like that comes from."

Keith brought his dangled hand to the collar of her leather coat. She looked up at Anger, her face angular and lean, a face out of Dürer. Then Keith leaned forward slightly, offering him the end of a joint.

"People always think the world is coming to an end," Keith

said. "But it never does. They wish it would end sometimes because they can't control it. But you never control it. All you can do is react."

They were crammed into an armored car, a dark container with bench seats that inched its way up the narrow park road through the crowd. Their journey from the Londonderry Hotel to the stage in Hyde Park was less than a quarter of a mile, but it would take them almost forty-five minutes. Their new guitarist, also named Mick—Little Mick—was staring down at the floor as the van shunted from side to side, jostling his body. He was nineteen years old, a wiry-haired boy in a kind of swashbuckler's shirt with puffy sleeves and a set of crossed laces at the collar. He had been in the band for less than three weeks and had never played with them anywhere but in Keith's basement.

The G up high, then C, down to E^b, C, A^b, double bar for the suspended fourth, watch the third finger. Shuffle on C, suspended on the F, down to C, B^b, G, chorus.

Across from him, Keith sat with his head slumped over on his shoulder, his eyes half-closed. He hadn't been to bed in two days—no rehearsals, just a long binge that still hadn't stopped. He remembered Anita passing him the joint after they'd taken in the news about Brian, then the long drive to London, dropping her at the flat in Chelsea, then two days later—this morning—walking across this same park a little after five o'clock. He wasn't going to stop. He didn't know if he was strong enough to survive the kind of life he was going to try to survive, but it was who he was. Every day he was more certain of that. Anita was eight and a half months pregnant with their child. She was out there somewhere in the crowd now with Marianne, the two of them sitting in the sun, getting high. A part of him was distracted, angry, as if Brian were still alive. The band had not played in front of a live audience in three years, and now Brian had just died, making it even harder.

Mick was sitting with his hands in his lap and looking straight ahead at nothing. He had a summer cold. His throat was so sore that he could hardly speak, much less sing, but he was purposeful in the way of someone who knew he couldn't fail. He was going to walk onstage in front of half a million people, and to do this was like walking onstage naked. It was an act of surrender that had to look and feel like an act of conquest. His sign was Leo, the sign of Strength in the tarot deck. Its glyph looked like an omega, the sign of infinity, or of the apocalypse, depending on whom you asked. The band's support staff had a code name for today's events. They were calling it the Battle of the Field of the Cloth of Gold.

Memories of the riots outside the Democratic convention in Chicago, the riots in Paris, the riots in Berkeley. The crowd was getting high and doing crossword puzzles, and a few of them were playing guitars, and they didn't know what to feel about the sight of the armored van moving up the path through the crowd. Its way was cleared by six motorcyclists in spiked helmets and leather jackets, an imperial guard armed with beer cans and knives. The words "peace" and "love" had been used so many times by now that they meant almost anything, including their opposites. It was what gave the words their charge. It was why some of the men in the crowd were wearing olive drab fatigue jackets, like GIs in Vietnam.

Tom Keylock announced over the P.A.: "Ladies and gentlemen, the world's greatest rock-and-roll band."

A subdued kind of cheering started. They whistled and shouted encouragement and then they stood up to take in the view and then the applause thickened into a diffuse cloud of noise.

Anita stood up with them. Her eyes closed and her smile loosened into something dreamy and approving as Marianne pulled her back gradually into her arms, all four of their hands on her pregnant belly. Anita wore black kohl on her eyes and a purple gypsy dress and a crown of Moroccan coins around her straw-colored hair. Apart from her belly, she hardly looked pregnant at all. As Anger filmed her, he was struck once again by how much she looked like Brian.

They were the world's greatest rock-and-roll band. Even a year ago, no one would have made such a claim, but now it seemed obvious. They had a backlog of more than two hundred songs. Country songs, blues songs, rock-and-roll songs. Mick and Keith didn't know where they came from, only that the flow had been unstoppable in the last year or so. During that time, Keith had taught himself to play the guitar in several different tunings, the notes all in different places on the fretboard, moving from one accident to the next, everything working. They'd written riot songs, war songs, murder songs, drug songs, and these had turned out to be exactly the songs people wanted to hear. It was toilet music, dirt music, the music of 1969.

From his place on the scaffolding, Anger considered stopping the film. Mick had come onstage alone, and he looked all wrong—he looked lost. His long hair fell into his eyes like a sheepdog's and he wore a gauzy white gown and black lipstick. He had a large, solemn-looking book in his hand, possibly the

Bible, and there was something priestly about him as he tried to quiet down the crowd.

"Now listen," he said. "Cool it for a moment."

Behind him, there was a large cardboard cutout of Brian, standing in the sunlight like a figure on the wall of a temple. He wore a fur coat and half a dozen brightly colored scarves, making the Hindu greeting of two palms pressed together before his chest.

Mick read something archaic and strange. He read it in a prim, unconvincing voice that made it sound as if he didn't know or even care what the words meant.

> The One remains, the many change and pass;
> Heaven's light forever shines, Earth's shadows fly;
> Life, like a dome of many-coloured glass,
> Stains the white radiance of Eternity,
> Until Death tramples it to fragments.—Die,
> If thou wouldst be with that which thou dost seek!
> Follow where all is fled!—Rome's azure sky,
> Flowers, ruins, statues, music, words, are weak
> The glory they transfuse with fitting truth to speak.

To the crowd, it maybe sounded like Shakespeare. Anger recognized it as Shelley's *Adonais*. But what did Mick mean when he ordered them all to die? Did he mean that Brian had found some "white radiance of Eternity," or did he mean nothing at all? Mick was the Prince of Darkness or the Angel of Light. It was difficult to say why he was so hard to stop looking at.

Keith sniffed from his canister, once for each nostril, then let the silver straw dangle down from the chain he wore around his neck. He picked up his guitar and slung it over his back as the crew flung open the doors of two large boxes at the front of the stage. They were full of butterflies—moths—and they flickered for a few moments in a daze above the crowd, half-suffocated, then wafted down like white confetti on the massed heads and the black-painted stage.

The Hells Angels leaned back against the iron barricades, legs crossed, passing each other beers. The band tuned its guitars. The cardboard cutout of Brian smiled unchangingly at the crowd, a billboard advertisement for a children's play about a magic prince.

It started with a flat, basic drumbeat, so slow that the song felt as though it was about to collapse before it even started. Mick was trying to move in time, a half jog, half chicken walk, wading through thick sludge. He'd taken off his white gown and was wearing tight cotton pants and a sleeveless mauve T-shirt. Keith didn't look at him. His guitar part was one chord, so useless that he didn't even face the crowd but stared down at his strings, as if waiting for something better to happen. Mick stared at him: it was too slow. He was almost ready to give up and start over. He clapped his hands and waved his head from one side to the other, a rueful smile on his face, but then Keith finally got to the first riff, a major-key country riff slowed down to one-quarter speed. He mangled a few double-stops in the middle, but now it started to make sense. The point of the song was its big gaping holes, the ragged dead spaces between the sounds. It was always about to break down, a half step behind. The drums leveled out at the same slack pace. Keith leaned back, head nodding, then stepped forward on one long leg, a black-haired ghost in bullfighter's pants, a crescent moon dangling from his ear.

It was the band's new sound. Mick put his hands in his hair and pouted and stood on his tiptoes. For a moment, he looked like a street drunk yelling denunciations at strangers. His first words were incomprehensible, but it didn't matter. They were all looking at him now. He scowled and pointed his finger, then mouthed a kiss: a dictator for half a second, then a dancer out of *Swan Lake*.

It was a series of vibrations amplified through electric circuits, a current of sound the crowd could feel on the skin beneath their hair, in the cavities of their chests, in their rectums and their groins. It registered in their bodies, in the pulse of the blood, but also in their minds, the part that was always changing, as senseless and illogical as a dream. The band was making sounds, the sounds were coming from the stage, but they were no longer themselves, the people in the crowd were no longer themselves, no one was even thinking about it anymore. They might be a nobody from Romford with the wrong kind of accent, or a mechanic's son with ruined teeth, or they might think all the time about what people had and what they were missing out on, but nobody was thinking about any of that while they were in its grasp. It was basic, energy and sound, life intensified for a few moments, its chaos made plain, the self slipping outside the body, joined in sound to other bodies. It was a feeling everyone had always craved, had always been warned about, a connection to something like the deeper self that used to be called the soul.

When Anger got home, it was almost two in the morning. His lover Will was asleep beneath an afghan on the broken couch, surrounded by eight-by-ten color prints he was supposed to have arranged for Anger into little booklets to promote the yet-to-be-made Lucifer film. Anger set his things down carefully in the glow of the TV, trying not to wake Will, but it wasn't long before he stirred.

"You missed something good," he said.

He looked to his side, slightly dazed by the pale, clustered lights from the TV. The rest of the room was shadowy, the walls dimpled, water-stained, dirty windows reflecting back the TV light, like glass plates for some abstract etching.

"It's not my thing," Will said, shifting beneath the blanket.

"Yeah, well, there were half a million people there."

"The guitar player was the one I liked. The one who died. He was the only one I responded to."

Anger looked at the stack of mail on the table, but there were no personal letters, no checks. He sat down in a chair and rubbed his eyes, head bowed.

"Are they giving you anything back?" Will said.

"They're doing my film. I don't know what you're talking about."

"I mean the real film. The one you had in mind before. Not the film of you following them around documenting every time they wipe their ass."

Will reached for a cigarette, groggily alert now. He was intense-eyed, with long sideburns and a crooked jaw that looked as though it had been imperfectly repaired after a childhood fall.

"They're my unconscious agents," Anger said. "My hench-men."

Will pushed his hair behind his ears, then lit up. "You're not joking, so why pretend you're joking? Even if you were, it isn't funny."

"They had a half a million people there."

"Which means what? That because it's interesting to you, it must be important?"

"It is important."

Will sniffed, looking down at his hand on the blanket, which had fallen down so that it made a kind of wide skirt beneath his rib cage. Through his thin T-shirt, his shoulders and the cleft between his pectorals stood out in shadowed relief. He had a body like Bobby's, articulated and firm. Anger wondered what was the matter with him, why the sight of Will always brought to mind Bobby.

"I went around to all the shops this afternoon, all the galleries," Will said. "Nothing. I may go back to school."

"You don't have to work."

"Or I may go on the dole."

He squirmed upward and brought his hands into a clasp behind his head, his cigarette still burning. Anger looked at his biceps and the fringes of hair showing where his T-shirt pulled back from his armpits. He felt his age like a physical force between them, his body time-wracked, exposed.

"You didn't get very far with those booklets," he said. "We'll have to do them tomorrow."

On the floor were the eight-by-ten prints. There were pictures of the band, close-ups of electric guitars, wide-angle shots of students rioting in Paris, Black Panthers brandishing machine guns. There was a picture of the Sphinx, looming in the desert with its lion's body and pharaoh's head.

"I got distracted," said Will.

"I'm just saying that we'll have to do them later. It isn't hard to see that you got distracted."

He stood up. He kept his back straight, his chin slightly raised, arms at his sides, hands clasped behind his waist. He made himself look at Will, standing there in his black pants and silk shirt. It was difficult, this role that was his to play now, though he had always known it was there waiting for him: the preoccupied husband home from work, or the father, the closed-in man in need of conciliation.

"I almost kissed him one night," he said. "The one you liked, Brian. I was that close. But he was so lost. When they're that lost, it isn't interesting anymore, is it?"

He reached out and cupped Will's chin in his hand, turning his face, and Will stared up at him.

"You don't have to work," Anger said. "You shouldn't demean yourself. You should live by your wits."

"Like you."

"Not like me. I'm just saying you should take advantage of what's there. It's stupid not to. It's the way the world works."

Will put his hand on Anger's wrist. "It's the way I was born. A parasite on men with no money."

The bedroom was so small that it was filled up almost entirely by the dresser and the double bed. In the dark, the walls seemed to breathe and expand, and the foil stars on the ceiling shone dimly at the edges. Will's body was a silhouette that moved and turned, smoothly curved beneath Anger's hands. Anger felt his chest, his rib cage, his nipples, the tautness of his balls. There was mercy in the dimming of his vision now, desire returning him from his mind to his body. He moved up onto his knees as Will lay beneath him on the sheet, his face turned on the pillow. Will's arms stretched down at his sides, hands tensed into claws, and his calves pressed down against Anger's shoulders, flexing as they brought him closer.

Afterward, they were silent, breathing, and the film began to assemble itself in Anger's mind. In the darkened bedroom — in the space between consciousness and forgetfulness — it didn't matter if any of it made sense or not. What mattered was the images themselves: thin clouds passing over the pyramids in Egypt, a woman dressed as Isis standing against the bright sky, Bobby in a top hat climbing a pile of stones as the sun struck the head of the Sphinx. They came whether he wanted them or not. They were signs of the demon inside him, from the Greek *daimon,* the guardian spirit, not the self but the soul.

"We've just been talking about the tour," said Keith, turning in his seat. "The mad people over in America. The bloody war and the bloody astronauts."

Mick had just come downstairs. They were at Keith's country house. Anger was standing at the window, peering outside. He turned back to face the room, the candles burning on tall, wrought-iron stands, sending up filaments of smoke above the carpets. He watched Mick sit down on the arm of Keith's couch, not even looking at him, looking immediately at the journalist. There was always a mild feeling of vertigo whenever Anger played this role, the room's specter, his presence meant to suggest to the journalist questions he would not feel comfortable asking.

"It will be the biggest tour anyone's ever done," Mick said.

"Football stadiums. Hockey arenas. You can play these enormous places now and actually be heard."

Anger sat down in one of the chairs by the window and looked at the magazines. Across from him, Keith's bodyguard was rolling joints at a corner table in the faint glow of a lamp, another character for the journalist's benefit. On the cover of one of the magazines was a picture of the actress Sharon Tate, who had just been murdered along with four of her friends in Los Angeles. Anger leafed through the photographs, listening fixedly as Mick and Keith talked about the American tour. He still found the pictures grisly, even though he'd seen them now a few times. The killers had used knives, rather than guns. They'd stabbed each of their victims more than a dozen times, then written messages on the walls in their blood, strange incitements to rise up, to destroy. Sharon Tate had been eight months pregnant. It occurred to Anger that she looked a little bit like Anita. They were both blond, both in their twenties. It wasn't hard to imagine the murders, or something like them, happening here at Keith's house.

They talked about politics, music, astronauts, Richard Nixon. It was a litany Anger had heard before, heard from them and read about in magazines. They talked about the war in Vietnam, how it was galvanizing the young people over in America, bringing them together, giving them something to rise up against, and how they wanted to be a part of that. Then eventually they came to the part where they talked about Brian, what it felt like to be going on the tour without him, what it had been like playing in Hyde Park two days after he'd died.

Mick looked down, finding himself a more comfortable seat on the couch, then leaned forward and passed the journalist a joint. Like everyone else now, the journalist was trying to look like Keith. Even the women had the same thin body, the same patched and torn clothes, hair that rose in a slapdash spray that they were always teasing with their fingers.

"You felt bad because he was your friend," Mick said. "But he wasn't equipped for it. It isn't easy—there's no way to explain why, it just isn't. You always hear this about people getting famous. Some of them get on the wrong track or they can't stomach it or something. They get lost. After a while, they're just passing through it, gliding by everything or haunting it or something. Brian was never able to enjoy it."

The journalist looked down at the wire that connected his microphone to his tape player, straightening it with his hand.

"It was almost like the moment he began to get what he wanted, he gave up on it," Keith said. "Because it happened very early on, right toward the beginning, when we were just starting to make a go of it. It didn't help him, the success. It made it worse."

Anger steepled his fingers in front of his chin. They were going to be talking about their interest in the occult soon. It was going to be his chance to get himself into the journalist's article, to talk about the Lucifer film. But he didn't want to talk about it. It wasn't something you could talk about anyway. Right now, the thing that was occult was the way Mick was slouched down on the couch, one knee up, his forearm resting on it, barely moving. It was the smoky room, the way they splayed themselves out on the furniture, the long hair in their faces. It was the way they were more alive now that Brian was dead and the band was entirely theirs.

"I mean, we're curious about these things," Mick was saying.

"There are things in the songs. But most of it is just people's fantasies. Fantasies about the way we live our lives, which people want to think is 'evil' or 'satanic' or whatever they want to call it."

"Which they were saying at the very beginning," Keith said. "Back when we first started—five boys with slightly shaggy hair, some guitars. That was 'evil.'"

Anger nodded faintly a few times. He examined his hand, not looking at anyone. "It won't seem so funny when you get to America," he said. "There's a craziness there. Sometimes it's out in the open, sometimes it's more hidden."

He stood up, smoothing the sleeve over his left arm. It was one of those situations where his fussy poise worked to his advantage. Even his age worked to his advantage. He opened and closed his hand at the edge of his thigh, looking at Mick.

"That's what I would worry about if I were you," Anger said. "The way you're going to instigate people over there. The sincere ones, the hippies. They're serious about things like 'evil' in America. People still go to church there. They're much more black-and-white."

He brushed off his lapel as he walked across the room. They weren't talking. It wasn't that they were troubled by what he'd said, it was just that they were mulling it over, letting it become a part of the room, the smoke, the dim light of the candles.

Outside on the porch, he found Anita. She was leaning back in her chair, her baby in a stroller beside her. There were several people he didn't know, or whose faces he had seen before but whose names he had forgotten.

"You could move to France," someone was saying. "They can't follow you there."

"Or just not pay."

"Or send a bomb."

He sat down in a wordless, unobtrusive way, fading into the conversation.

"You don't have any matches, do you?" Anita asked. She had let her hand rest lightly on the sleeve of his jacket, speaking to him without quite looking at him, not wanting to tune out the others.

"There's a candle right there."

"No, but it's for a trick. You need matchsticks."

"A trick."

"You're useless. What are they talking about in there?"

"Nothing. Ideas."

Her eyes moved across the table to one of the boys sitting there. His chair was pushed back so that his face was out of the light, his posture hidden. Beside him, Marianne was scrolling up a cigarette paper into an empty tube. She stood it in the center of an ashtray and lit the top end on fire. It burned slowly at first, unspectacularly, but then the flame shrank down to a thin rim of embers and it rose up into the air, a weightless glowing ring. It hovered for a moment over everyone's heads. They all looked at it.

Anita turned and looked at the baby. She smiled at him with spontaneous pleasure, mouthing some quiet nonsense at him, the mumbo jumbo of a spell.

After a while, Mick came outside. He stood by the doorway, in the dark, lighting a cigarette. He didn't look at the people on the porch. They were pretending not to notice him. They were trying out the trick with the cigarette papers now, chin on the elbow, thick-fingered, uncommitted. Each time the trick worked, they admired it. Each time it failed, they admired the smallness of the failure.

Mick pushed his scarf over his shoulder, exhaling, and walked off onto the lawn. Anger got up and followed.

"Have you given it any more thought?" he said.

Mick looked out into the darkness. "I don't want to talk about it right now."

"It's usually not like this. It's usually the other way around. It's usually the actors who keep bothering me. I'm not used to bowing and scraping like this."

Mick pushed his hair out of his eyes. His face was not so much ugly or beautiful as forceful, implacable. "I've been getting death threats," he said. "People watching me, people sending letters. There are police cars in front of my house some nights. All I want right now is to get out of here and out on the road. I don't want to think about anything else right now."

There was a moat that cut around Keith's property, separating it from the woods and the farm fields to either side. In the distance behind it was a lake, a charcoal smear gathering width as it spread from left to right. It was lit by a full moon centered above a clearing between two banks of trees, a thin disk with the fine texture of rice paper.

Mick started walking away, off toward the trees.

"Maybe it scares you how much I've been thinking about it," said Anger, following after him. "Maybe you think I won't leave you alone."

"I think you'll leave me alone when I want you to."

"I wouldn't be so sure about that."

Mick turned. "Come on, Kenneth, we'll take a walk. I'll show you something. You haven't seen this place before."

They were just outside the ring of light coming off the porch, a third of the way down the lawn. Mick walked toward the trees, one hand placed lightly on his back, just above his waist. It was the way a woman might walk after a day of housework, the wide cuffs of his pants shimmering at his ankles. He didn't look back to see if Anger was following. There was nothing hurried in the way he walked, nothing but certitude and boredom.

When the lawn ended, they reached the moat. Its brick retaining wall was sunken in thick tufts of grass, and Mick stepped up onto the ledge and balanced himself with his arms, walking the curve above the water. The ledge was only a few inches wide. He seemed to be tottering a little on purpose, accentuating the danger. The drop to the water on the far side was at least ten feet.

"They think that Keith is the wild one," he said. "I'm the cool one, the deliberate one, faking his way through it all. That's what a lot of people think. That's what a lot of people want to believe."

He jumped off the near side of the ledge and landed in the dirt. He pushed his hair out of his eyes, then placed his hands on his hips the way Anger's were, seeming to mock him. His face was almost invisible. Anger was standing at the edge of the woods, half in darkness, breathing a little heavily from the walk.

"I have different lives," Mick said. "You know, some people know about one life and some people know about another and none of these people ever gets to piece together the entire picture. That's what they call 'faking.' I don't worry about it anymore, if it's faking or not. I can say what I like to the journalist and I can say what I like to you right now and I can say what I like to the Queen Mother and you can all go fuck yourselves if you don't like it. That's the way it is for me now."

"Always faking," said Anger.

"It's not hard to see what you've been wondering about all this time, Kenneth. What you've been thinking. Do you want to come over here and find out if it's really true? Isn't that what you want?"

It was dark enough that Anger didn't have to look into his eyes, but he did, his body tense, his mouth set at a strange angle as if preparing to laugh. There was nothing in Mick's voice to suggest that he was joking, but that was the danger of course. He thought he might grab Mick by the back of the neck—ambush him, pull him against his chest—but it was harder than he thought. Once he got close enough, it was hard to move at all. He reached for Mick's body—his hip, anything—but Mick backed away, smiling, watching Anger's face.

"Maybe some other time," Mick said. "What do you think? You can imagine whatever you like, Kenneth. Maybe you'll get to know me better than anyone else ever has. But maybe you won't. Maybe the more likely scenario is that nothing will happen at all."

"I'll see you later," Anger said.

"Right."

"Are you coming back to the house?"

"I told you before, I want to be alone. I'm staying out here."

"You're a shit."

"I know that. I've been one for a long time."

Mick stepped closer, his hands crossed behind his waist. "Don't get moralistic," he said. "You're going to say that there's nothing inside me, that I have no soul or whatever, but it isn't that simple. Nothing is ever that simple."

He put his hand on Anger's face. His eyes were blank, examining Anger's expression not with curiosity but with the confirmed suspicion that everyone was exactly what he knew they were. There were no surprises. It would have been just as easy for him to kiss Anger at that moment as not to kiss him. It would have been the same no matter who Anger was, whether he was a man or a woman or a figment of Mick's imagination.

"Good night, Kenneth," he said. "We'll talk more tomorrow."

"We'll have to see."

"We'll talk about the film. I still want to do it. Don't think that I don't want to do it."

Anger turned away. He looked at the branches above his face, oak branches that were so still they were almost artificial-looking in the moonlight. When the breeze came, the leaves moved like lifeless hands, shaking and stopping, shaking and stopping. He waited to hear Mick walk off, wherever he was going, then headed in the opposite direction. The pale leaves jostled on their branches, a mimicry of living movement that was utterly without mind. All he could see of the porch and the people on it were vague, elongated shadows, almost like mirages, disturbing the glow from the candles.

He was awakened the next morning by the sound of rifle fire. There was no clock in the room, nothing to orient him at all but the dark mahogany bed and the Gothic chairs that reminded him he was at Keith and Anita's house. When he looked out the window, he saw the abandoned lawn, a plush rolling green that led out to the trees and the moat and the lake beyond. It was a sunny day. There was a quilt left out on the grass, a single leather sandal, a whiskey bottle with a black-and-white label, nothing else. He heard the rifle again: a firecracker pop elongated by its report. It was coming from out in the fields or in the trees where he'd been last night. He realized then: it was just Keith, Keith and his friends out playing with their guns.

He looked across the room at the wrinkled shopping bag he had brought with him yesterday. In the bag were two top hats. One was black like the one Bobby had worn in San Francisco. The other was an Uncle Sam hat with red and white stripes and a blue brim. He held them both in his hands, looking down at them quizzically. He had brought them to give to Mick, props for the Lucifer film, but also stage props for the band's American tour. They would be good for large crowds, visible from a long distance. He could see Mick onstage in either of them, moving toward the microphone, raising his fist. The devil in the top hat—they were associated somehow. The god of power—money, politics, war. The sly, sophisticated con man who in the end was just a bewildering reflection of all the people who were looking at him.

Something hit the gutter on the eave above his window. It clanked down onto the stone porch below, then rattled for a few seconds and stopped: an empty tin can. From the distant fields, there was another round of rifle fire. Were they shooting at the house?

THE LOVERS, 1969

FOR MORE THAN A YEAR, Bobby had just been drifting, moving up and down the coast, playing music in bars, not thinking very much about where it would lead. He had managed to keep some of his musical instruments, some of his good clothes, the black top hat he liked to wear onstage. He had pawned almost everything else he had of value, including the 16 mm camera he'd stolen from Anger, which had brought him less than forty dollars. No one had offered money for the Lucifer film, and so he'd just kept it for a while, moving it from place to place, not knowing what to do with it, until eventually he'd lost it, like so many other things, still thinking it might be worth something someday.

In his ruffled sleeves and top hat, he bent over his guitar now, his legs crossed, listening through his hair for the underlying pattern in the endless, coiling melody Charlie was playing. Beside him, Charlie looked feral, his face and hair visibly grimy, black grit beneath his broken fingernails. He was moving through a strange progression of chords, his song at first a blur of lullaby and muted groans, then an improvised poem that, like the music itself, made no literal sense but was full of suggestions: a desert road, darkness over the Santa Susana Pass, a night ride into the city, clouds passing over Devil's Canyon. They had just recently met, so Bobby wasn't used to this phenomenon of Charlie being the uneasy center of the room whether people were looking at him or not. They were in a Mission-style house in Benedict Canyon, not far from Beverly Hills, at a fashionable party full of record industry minions and full-fledged stars. In the living room, the girls Charlie had brought with him all wore five-inch Buck knives fastened to their belts. They were sunburnt, their clothes stained, their hair tied back with bits of string, and this raggedness made everyone in the house aware of them — anonymous girls who looked alike, sweetly vacant, conspiring. Bobby could see his girlfriend, Kitty, in the darkness in the corner of the room, huddled next to another girl named Leslie. Kitty's fingers were entwined in a cheap necklace on the floor between her feet. He didn't know how to read anything about her anymore, whether she was really lost or just manipulating him by acting lost. He leaned in and tried to follow the unpredictable curves of Charlie's music, the most unusual music he had ever played. He used all the technique he had to make the song even stranger, elongated and off-center, avoiding the simple pentatonic scales of blues and rock for the mysterious spirals of the Dorian mode, the Mixolydian mode. The music reflected back a range of tensions in the room, all the social hierarchies that no one wanted to admit existed anymore, drawing them out, magnifying them. It was not aggressive — it had an ethereal, dreamy sound — but it spread a malevolence that came at first as a faint surprise, then blossomed into something so familiar that it seemed obvious. It was the music of dim rooms, of red wine in gallon jugs. It was the music of slow violence unfurling in a secluded house in Benedict Canyon.

It was an amorphous party in the style of the time, a place an intruder could walk into without much chance of detection, much less confrontation. People were gathered in the kitchen, surrounded by ashtrays and bottles, and every bedroom had a shrouded group whispering in the shifting glow of tea lamps inside paper sacks. When he'd first seen Charlie tonight, Bobby had been fighting with Kitty in the backyard, struggling with her wrists in his hands, trying to wrestle her into being quiet. She was spitting insults at him in a muffled shout, scattered and fierce, and he'd turned to see a small figure in the darkness at the edge of the bushes, his hands crossed behind his waist, his long hair and slightly hunched figure somehow suggesting a crone beneath a shawl. When he stepped closer, his angular face was like a daguerreotype from a hundred years ago, a bearded man in deerskin pants and shirt. He gestured at his forehead, pointing with his index finger, and told Bobby to stop acting like a pimp, some low-life pimp slapping his whore around in an alley. There was a small moment of jockeying over how serious he was being. It was hard to see Charlie's face beneath his hair in the darkness. But as he stepped closer it became clear that he wasn't joking, that he didn't like what he was looking at, his eyes appraising Bobby and Kitty with a barely curious scrutiny, as if unsurprised by the lack of anything interesting or distinctive there. Bobby adjusted the top hat on his head, letting Kitty go, and she pushed her hair behind her ear, embarrassed but oddly still as Charlie stood in front of her, one hand on her shoulder, the other one caressing her cheek. He was the comforter now, menacingly strange, his stern face somehow enhancing the biblical overtones of the pose. It was a con, Bobby felt certain of that, but he didn't object, sensing some cynical game just beginning to unfold, knowing that if Charlie had seen through him, then he had at least seen through Charlie too.

It was September 9, three days before the band was to leave for the American tour. They had finished one album, the next one was already in progress, and Keith was sitting outside his house on a plain wooden kitchen chair, playing his guitar. It was early afternoon and the sun was hitting everything at a tilted angle, the wind tossing the boughs of the trees, filling the air high above him with a sound like thousands of rattling plastic bags. Some friends were playing golf on the lawn, using plastic balls that wafted back toward them in wild curves. He looked out at the old carpets on the grass, the shabby furniture, all the things he would be leaving behind for the next three months, and all of it looked perfect. The golf cart sagged in the high grass beside the moat, a purple banner trailing behind it like a giant, colored serpent coiling in the wind.

"You don't even see me sometimes," Anita would say. But it wasn't true, he saw her all the time. She was upstairs now, getting her things into suitcases, the bedroom a heap of clothes and jewelry, magazines and cosmetics. He could see her standing with her hips canted forward, one hand on her thigh, the other on her cheek, looking down with pensive hostility at the mess. She was not coming on the tour. She was going to a drug clinic in St. John's Wood.

She had given him a lot of things to forgive lately. She had slept with half the people he knew—that was what he had signed on for, he knew that. She had even slept with Mick, because she was crazy, or just to hurt Keith, or possibly just because she wanted to. She was threatened by Keith in some way. Maybe she had reason to feel threatened, because after all he had forgiven her even for Mick. She didn't have as much power to faze him as she'd thought. He had forgiven everything except the scene last week, when she had taken too much heroin and blacked out for close to an hour.

Every sound had a slight flange to it, a little sag at the middle, as if he was manipulating time, bending it and stretching it. He chopped out a rhythm of big chiming chords and heard all the textures of the different notes lined up in rows. It was a sad song, but it didn't feel sad to play it. There was nothing that needed to be done right now, nothing he could do anyway, nothing but the sight and sound of his friends beneath the trees and the ability to communicate it through the notes of his guitar. He was high in a way that slowed down the apprehension of sound just enough for him to hear little textures beneath the surface, a graininess of copper wire, steel wire. If music was just an escape—an evasion of "reality"—then how did you account for this moment when the wind and the light on the trees and the sounds of his friends' tapping golf clubs permeated him so entirely that he seemed to embody these sensations, to encompass everything outside him so that there was no "him" and no "outside"?

She came down in her buckskin jacket, bare-legged, her head tilted a little toward one shoulder. "I'll be ready in a few minutes," she said. "Will you tell Tom?"

He nodded, closing his eyes, still strumming the guitar.

"I'm just going to take what I take," she said. "It's too much to think about. I don't know how people pack."

"I think there's a sheet of paper somewhere," he said. "Candace sent it. Addresses, phone, all that. The itinerary."

"I'll just ring her. I can't be bothered with a sheet of paper."

She was standing in front of him, her hand in his hair. Her eyes moved slightly from side to side as she stared at him. "You're not coming with me, are you?"

He looked down at the patio. "I'll tell Tom you're almost ready," he said. "I'll be in in a minute, all right?"

It came back at the strangest times. It had been two months since Brian's death and most of the time it still wasn't real, except at times like this. This was the period when Keith was smashing up cars on the M1, falling asleep with lit cigarettes in his hand, staying up for three nights in a row, shooting rifles from the cockpit of his Hovercraft. It didn't look or feel like mourning. In most ways, it was the happiest he'd ever been.

When he was a boy, maybe eight years old, his aunt had bought him an atlas of the United States, one of those wellmeant gifts that triggers an unexpected enthusiasm in a child. He would linger over the maps before he went to bed—the legends, the statute miles, the shapes of the states, the words "Pacific Ocean." He could see with his eyes how huge the places must be—Texas, Wyoming, California—the shaded areas of their mountain ranges, the pale blue contours of their shorelines and lakes. Stockton, Mariposa, Bakersfield—the names had nothing to do with the rows of brick houses outside his window. They led him through moviescapes of rubbled forts, horses in the sand, riflemen, cattle. He knew it was out there, a physical reality, not a dream. He had the maps, the names, the borders and geography. He was a boy who went to school in a cowboy costume with holstered toy pistols and spurs.

Right up until the time he'd died, Brian would call in the middle of the night, as if he were still a part of the band, as if they were all still friends. He had made so many tapes, why did he keep erasing them? Could he come over and play Keith his new tape? All his best songs went wrong because he waited too long, kept picking at them, second-guessing himself. Or maybe it was time for him to strike out on his own, start something new, a different kind of band.

Keith would hold the phone uncomfortably between his shoulder and his ear, sitting on a kitchen stool in the dark, playing his guitar. In the living room there would be a throng of people—friends and hangers-on, people whose names he knew and people whose names he didn't—listening to music, smoking, laughing, sulking. Brian's voice would lapse into silence, a child trying to tell a story but getting lost in the mire of details, or sometimes it would intensify into weeping, into outraged, paranoid tears. Keith would talk him down with a persistent stream of factual information: records he had listened to, meals he had eaten, places he had driven in his car. It was always he and not Anita who fielded these calls. He was the one who was always awake, always smiling, the center of things even when he wasn't in the room, always feeling situated in his skin by three or four o'clock in the morning.

"You just have to get something down and then we can work with it," he would say. "You have to stop thinking so much. Mick doesn't hate you, he doesn't even think about you, I tell you this over and over. No one thinks about other people half as much as you do."

. . .

Keith put on a Chuck Berry record in the library. He stood in the half-lit room and gripped the counter with his right hand, staring down at the record player, waiting for it to start. He watched the record spin and listened and didn't move, standing there in his sunglasses and his scarf and his cowboy boots, a cigarette burning in his hand. When it came on, it was loud. He could feel the warmth of it beneath his skin, the soothing pulse. He heard the clean, bright twang of the guitar, the thick bash of the snare drum, the rattle of the upright bass: a song about high school, girls, hamburgers, cars. He heard the piano with its splashy laughing trills, felt the stupid joy of it, and knew that this was why he had to go to America again, to make this sound. Even after it was over, he felt the perverse certainty that nothing else mattered, nothing was more important than this three-minute song.

The room upstairs was bright but cool, a country room that smelled of moss. The light came in through a screen of trees and made a mottled, watery pattern on the walls, the wooden beams, the faded tapestries that hung from wrought-iron bars. Anita was on the floor with the baby, leaning toward him on her hands and knees. It was one of those moments when their eyes seemed telepathically joined, both mother and baby smiling, but just faintly—more than just smiling, communicating. She rattled the ball with its tin bells, and he lay there on his back, trying to reach out with his hands, watching her eyes. His tiny feet curved inward on bowed legs, a few inches above the ground, as if resting on an invisible stool.

"I've found him a job," Keith said.

She didn't look up. It was a running joke, already old. "You've found him a job," she said. "What is it, factory work?"

"It's physical work. Heavy lifting."

"Quarrying. Building houses."

"Has he got his documents sorted?"

"I haven't asked him."

"They'll want to see documentation. Credentials."

He sat down on the floor, sprawling, his head next to her knee. The baby had that drunken, slovenly look now, his head leaning to one side. It was as if he were puzzling over how to breathe or what breathing meant, how it felt.

"When he moves his head sometimes," she said, "his eyes change. They look just like yours. They become adult eyes all of a sudden."

"He hardly ever cries. It freaks me out a little."

"He cries when I leave. But I never really leave."

"You must flog him. Hit him with a paddle. Cane him."

"It's crazy what people think of, isn't it? What they do."

"Are you all right?"

"I'm fine. You know how I am."

"I didn't mean to say I wasn't going with you. I'm going with you. You know that."

"I just don't want to be here after you leave. The empty house. All that. I just don't want to have to deal with all that, that's all."

"I wouldn't want to have to deal with it either."

"It's also that I've been good lately. I don't know, two weeks, maybe a little less. I think I could stick it out anyway, but not here. Not with all this stuff around." She shook her head, bored with the topic.

"You'll be all right," he said.

"I know it. I know."

"It's just dope."

"Yeah, and you're one to talk."

"I'm just taking the piss. What else is there to do?"

She leaned her head on his shoulder. He encircled her in his arm, looking out at the baby. He felt her arms go into a loose clasp around his waist, her body next to his, and he could imagine her face, not crying, but looking straight ahead, just thinking. He never thought he would be able to keep her, had only wanted to, hoped to, but now she rubbed his thigh with the side of her hand, then she scratched his jeans a few times with her fingernails. She sat up and kissed him, her lips moist where they came together, her eyes closed. She opened them and stared into his eyes, her face almost touching his, and he saw how unlikely it all was—this room, this house, this woman, their baby. None of it should have happened, it all had. There was no way to explain it, it was only luck. It would never stop.

On August 6, they found Bobby asleep on the side of the road, his car broken down on the shoulder of Highway 5 in the desert north of Los Angeles. He had been awake for more than two days before that. It took him a moment to remember why he was there, whose car he was in. Outside, the sky was a bluish gray. The sun cast a plane of yellow light on the dashboard. He stared at the cop, and the cop told him to put up his hands, not to move.

There were cuts and scratches on his hands, his arms, his face. There were bloodstains on his pants and shirt. They pulled him out of the car and spread his legs apart and had him lean forward with his hands on the roof. He watched them search the glove box until they found the registration with his friend Gary Hinman's name on it. When they asked him who Gary Hinman was, he said he didn't know. He was smiling by then, not realizing it, thinking of the beat-up piano he and Charlie had dropped off at Hinman's house a few months ago, the joke of that transaction. He was remembering his plan of a few days ago: to sell Gary's car, to get the money that way and then go to Canada somehow, but he couldn't remember how he had lost sight of the plan, or how he had ever expected it to work, or why he'd driven here to the middle of the desert. He couldn't believe that the last few days had occurred.

"Don't move so much," one of the cops said. "Look at your leg. Your leg is twitching. Just relax."

They cuffed his hands behind his back. He squinted against the sun, stumbling off-balance in the dust, his dirty hair falling into his eyes. He understood that he was going to jail now, but it was impossible to understand what he had done in the last two days, to match it up with anything he knew about himself. When he thought of Gary Hinman, all he could picture was the outside of his house, the A-frame with the broken door, the beat-up cars on the lawn.

"I'd like this to just be the first part," Anger said.

Mick was still looking at the flickering white blank on the wall. He hadn't moved since the film ended, and it was only now that Anger realized how disturbing it was. He'd made it up of some leftover scraps he had of Bobby in San Francisco; some scraps of the band in Hyde Park, the Hells Angels in front of the stage; some scraps of himself—all of it pieced together like the shards of an explosion. It was not the vision of light he'd started out making three years ago, but the vision of what he'd seen in those three years, all of it that he'd managed to preserve on film.

"It's not what we talked about, I know," he said. "This is just the chaos part, the prologue. It's just the beginning."

"I don't know why you would show me something like that."

"It's just a film. I've been working on it for three years. It's a long time. You get inured to it."

"What is it called?"

"It's called *Invocation of My Demon Brother.*"

Anger switched off the projector. The room was lit now only by a small hammered tin lamp on the desk. Mick was perched on his stool in a white blouse, a scarf around his neck. In his lap, he had the book of pictures Anger had brought over, the promotional packet meant to explain the yet-to-be-made film, the optimistic sequel, *Lucifer Rising*. It was a collage of Egyptian ruins, Northern Renaissance paintings, AP photos of anti-war rallies, troops in Vietnam. Interspersed were pictures of the band—glamour shots, but also advertisements for their old records, rigidly staged. There was a close-up of the archangel Michael from Van Eyck's *The Last Judgment*. There was a flying saucer above a darkened moonscape, tinted orange and green in the night sky.

"Everything is falling apart right now," Anger said. "That's what we know. This revolution or whatever they're calling it, it's really happening. Whether it's only chaos, or if it leads to something better, we don't know yet. That's why I want to make the next film. I don't think it has to be only chaos."

Mick was looking down at the book, a forgotten quality about his unmoving lips. It was opened to a picture of his own face, framed in yellow with the omega-like glyph for Leo. Above his head was a tiny Marine helicopter inscribed with the same sign.

"I've been asking you for a favor," Anger said. "I've been asking you for a long time now. It would take two days. Maybe less."

"It's been a busy time," Mick said. "You know that. You know this whole story, Kenneth. There was Brian, then we were in the studio, now we're leaving for the States. The tour. Rehearsals."

Anger took the book out of his lap. He put it down on the table and turned away from it: the glossy cover, the careful lettering, the fussy four-color printing. On the cover were two Egyptian gods, Isis and Osiris, signaling with their two raised arms the coming of Horus, the child god. It all looked slightly ridiculous now.

"I thought you were going to do this for me," he said.

"I want to do it. I just can't do it now." Mick sat up, not looking at Anger, twisting his neck a little from side to side. "We should go downstairs."

"It's just a film."

"Right, and what we do is just music." He leaned forward on his stool, his forearms resting on his knees. "You want my name, my image, I understand all that. It helps us both. The Lucifer bit—that's what we're into now. But I don't know why you'd show me a film like that when we're about to go out on tour."

Anger reached down for his briefcase, looking at his hands as he picked it up and put it on the desk. He closed his eyes and tried to stop it, but the film was playing itself back in his mind now, sped up to an absurd jumble, a spasm or an assault. An invocation draws forces in. It can lead to an evocation, which spits the forces back out. He didn't know what had happened with Bobby yet, nor did he know what was about to happen with the band on their tour, but it didn't matter. It was already present on some level in the film. He opened the briefcase and put the spools inside. Then he closed it and flipped the locks shut.

GIRL TELLS OF
TWO NIGHTS
OF SLAUGHTER

Links Death Cult to Eight Slayings
Tate Murder Finally Solved

DECEMBER 1, 1969.
Murder suspect Susan Atkins, 21, recounted today how she and a band of hippies broke into the Benedict Canyon residence of Sharon Tate on the night the screen actress and four friends were murdered. She said that on August 9, a man, two women, and herself entered the house dressed all in black to carry out the raid.

Miss Atkins has also admitted to being present the next night, August 10, when the same group broke into the Griffith Park home of Leno LaBianca, owner of a chain of grocery stores, and murdered him and his wife, Rosemary.

The lawyer of the pretty, dark-haired girl, Frederick Cobb, described the August 9 killings: "A man cut the phone lines with a pair of bolt cutters, then entered the house through a side window. He then let the others in through the front door. The victims were tied up, then beaten and stabbed."

Cobb said that his client told him that Charles Manson, 34, ordered them out on another murderous raid the following night, August 10, at the LaBianca home. He insisted that his client "had nothing to do with the murders" and that she admitted only to being present at the scene. He described Miss Atkins as being "under Mr. Manson's sway. [She and the others] revere him as a fatherlike figure. He has a hypnotic power over them."

The houses of the victims were selected at random, Miss Atkins stated. Her story ends months of uncertainty in what had become some of the most publicized and frightening murder cases in recent history.

Miss Atkins appeared yesterday in Santa Monica Superior Court to face charges in yet another murder, the July 31 slaying of Gary Allen Hinman, a Topanga Canyon music teacher. Police now believe that the Hinman murder was the first in a series of at least eight homicides related to the Manson group. Also charged in that crime is Robert Beausoleil, 22, who will stand trial later this month. Beausoleil, a rock musician, has pleaded innocent. He has denied any connection to Manson and his followers.

Miss Atkins stated that the crimes were "an act of war. I was told to go and I went. We had a basic way of living. You didn't think about what you were doing, you did it."

Manson was arrested two weeks ago in a roundup of more than 30 hippies in Death

Valley. He was taken yesterday to Municipal
Court for a preliminary hearing on charges
of receiving stolen property. The bearded
cult leader stared blankly as witnesses gave
testimony about six stolen motorcycles he is
charged with receiving. He did not speak
with Deputy Public Defender Ross Kuzak,
who represented him.

ALTAMONT, 1969

THE CROWD COULD HEAR the band's helicopter before they found it in the sky, the deep burble of its rotors. It got louder and louder, narrowing in focus, building to a whine. They looked up at it, the large black ship with a swinging arm above its body. It was impossible not to admire it for a moment, a Bell UH-1 Iroquois, a "Huey," the same kind of helicopter being used in Vietnam.

It was December 6. The crowd had been gathered there for a day and a half already, staking out their spots, waiting for something they couldn't quite envision. There were people with cameras and people flashing peace signs, people walking with backpacks on their shoulders, people handing out leaflets. They wore football jerseys, jean jackets, floppy leather cowboy hats, mirrored shades. Some of them wore nothing at all. In their nakedness, they looked like mendicants—earnest, emaciated, begrimed. They lay on sleeping bags, blankets, cardboard boxes, stood up with their hands on their hips to look out over the crowd to the distant stage. It was a free concert for half a million fans, the biggest concert on the band's tour, the first time they'd been in San Francisco in three years. All that week the news had been about a series of brutal murders last summer in Los Angeles and the arrest five days ago of several suspects and their leader, Charles Manson, who had already become a new kind of star. Nobody knew what to think about the story, whether it was to be believed. Nobody could explain the strange glamour of it, why the killers were fascinating while their victims were hardly even real. It had already been a day and a half of wine and Quaaludes, seizures by the medicine tent, fistfights, barking dogs, but it was possible not to look at any of that if you didn't want to look at it. Some of them broke out into fits of dancing and singing, buoyed by the bright, sunny day. There was a procession of people in flowers and beads who pushed a colorfully painted cart through the crowd, its spoked wheels as high as their shoulders. Inside the bed was a blue cow made of papier-mâché, like something from India. In spite of everything they knew about the band, in spite of everything the band embodied, the crowd was thinking about Woodstock, the glow of having been there. They all wanted this to be something like that, and they were already a little frantic, wanting a good spot, not wanting to miss out.

Someone with blood on his shirt was walked across the field by two people who led him by the elbows. A sixteen-year-old boy sat in the straw drinking wine, staring right at him, not seeing him, brushing something off his sleeve. The helicopter circled above it all, waiting for its chance to land. Then, as if in escort, a group of motorcycles arrived, coming in a long line between the hills, forty or fifty of them, some of the riders with girls on the seats behind them, some of them drinking from jugs of wine. As they got closer to the crowd, they shifted into low gear so that they were half walking, half riding. They were different from most of the fans, older, dressed in black clothes and boots. At either side of their line, people picked up their things and stood up, not even realizing in that moment how afraid they were. Some of them nodded their heads in solidarity; some of them smiled to their friends as if they were somehow a part of it.

The motorcycles had saddlebags and mirrors and gas tanks painted black or blue. Behind them came a yellow school bus with a banner draped over its side that said HELLS ANGELS and bore the regalia of the different local chapters. More than a dozen people stood on its roof, drinking beer, shoving one another around, held in by a metal rail. One of them wore a black top hat. He was a tall, thin man with a beard, his clothes covered with dust, raising his arms like a scarecrow as he danced.

The crowd went back and back, farther than you could see. Even if you wanted to leave now, it would not be easy. There were so many people lolling around, playing flutes or blowing bubbles, their faces so open it was hard to look at them for very long.

ANDY: They were going to make a record—that was something you were always hearing about back then. But that's what nobody understands. Charlie wasn't interested in making a record. I don't think Bobby ever really understood how far from all that Charlie was, all that rock-and-roll crap.

DAVE: It was a ramshackle hundred acres set up in the hills above L.A. Lots of dogs. A couple dozen horses. At night you would hear the coyotes. You could walk for miles out there and never see another human being.

LISA: The trees, the dry riverbeds, the mountains. The mountains would get this fabulous yellow color, with these gray bushes up the sides. Sudden, powerful rainstorms. Rain that would just pour and pour all night. You'd forget what century you were living in.

DIANE: We raised artichokes. We would sell them in town, and then for a while we had the tourists come in and we'd run it as a dude ranch. We'd put on these long-sleeved flannel shirts, and we'd take these people out on trail rides. Cook them pancake breakfasts. At night, we'd make a fire and sing songs.

DAVE: One day Bobby drove up with one of his girlfriends and this dog he had, a big white dog. This was probably toward the beginning of 1969. By then, there were more and more people starting to hang around, living in the various outbuildings and the old bunkhouses.

LISA: He had that kind of crooked face, like he was up to something. That long black hair, the clothes. I think everybody was kind of in love with him. Even Charlie was sort of in love with Bobby.

KATHY: Riding the horses through the desert. Getting up early so you could be out there when the sky was still purple and then you'd watch it all turn orange. We all got to be good riders. Learned how to saddle them, put the bridles on.

DIANE: I don't know how to explain it. I just knew that everything in my life up to then had been this painful, unnecessary lie.

KATHY: The mountains were just shimmering with light. Birds shimmering out of the rocks. You'd find these dried-up old trees—weird, religious trees. We just took off our clothes and made love in the dirt, just balled all day, like no one had ever done it before.

DIANE: Locked up in your body all the time, like it's separate from you. Jealous of it, guarding it, protecting it. It's such a release to not say no. Such a giving thing to make love with someone you never thought you could make love with. Making love instead of picking and choosing, hoarding yourself like you're made out of money.

KATHY: It was a way of being almost interchangeable. You're growing out of yourself. Getting closer to God.

DIANE: We would play a game where we were a Panzer division, out looking for Allied tanks. North Africa, the desert. We had field radios and maps and Charlie would come out sometimes and give us directions. He had binoculars and these *National Geographics* describing the battles, and he and Bobby would drive around the desert, kind of checking out what happened.

MARK: It was some kind of hide-and-go-seek thing, only there was no one there to find. Riding those jeeps at top speed through the desert, driving over the washes, over rocks. You began to get really involved. The radios wouldn't work. You'd run out of water. You'd get frustrated, lost.

KATHY: Charlie would tell you, "You're just like a prom queen, you're a prima donna, you always need help," and then you'd start acting like that. It became a pattern.

DIANE: You started to try to read his mind. There was the sense that he was always watching you. Not in judgment, but like he was trying to get inside you to understand you.

KATHY: It was like he was awed by how alive we were.

DAVE: Barefoot on the rocks. You learn to walk more carefully. You cut yourself, and you learn to pay attention to where you're going.

MARK: At night, the emptiness that waits for you out there. No sense of time. If you think about it, you start to panic. You panic in the space of a second, but then you learn to relax into it. You see that time is elastic, that time is all in your head.

DIANE: The stars. Tiers and layers of stars. You see more of them as you keep looking. The sky gets bluer, less black. They start to swell and pulsate. All that darkness weighing down on you, that light moving farther and farther off into space.

KATHY: I remember just throwing all the kindling on the ground. Throwing it down and kicking at it and screaming. Minutes and minutes of furious screaming. Just this outlet of rage. And then when it was over I just laid my head on Bobby's shoulder and cried. I just held him for a long time and wept.

DIANE: Because we saw what was coming next. It was always the cops or always the war or always someone trying to hustle us or rip us off. And then people wonder what we're doing out in the middle of the desert. Why we carry knives and need guns.

DAVE: In San Francisco, there was no place left to live. It happened very quickly—the ghetto feeling, the heaviness. By the time they were calling it the Summer of Love, it had been over for a long time.

KATHY: You'd see their bikes lined up in the sunlight, the way they leaned to one side, the front wheels all at an angle.

DIANE: A few of them wore colors, but it wasn't uniforms, it wasn't flashy. Most of them just wore jeans. Not necessarily big, but tough. It was the small ones, the wiry ones, I was always more scared of. They were the ones you could see going off.

LISA: Mostly it was just drinking beer, having a good time. The bikers were friends. When they were around, the mood was light, we were safe, it was just a party. Everyone relaxed. For a while, they made everything better.

DAVE: People were coming from all over by then. They'd

heard about us. Nobody knew who to trust or what they wanted. Charlie was trying to get the bikers to stay around, he wanted to keep them happy. He wanted them to be protection. I think Bobby thought he was going to be one of the boys. He thought he was as hard as the bikers, as hard as Charlie, so he started scoring them dope, sneaking around, getting all wrapped up with the bikers. That was how it all got started.

KATHY: The sound of those engines. The pipes. Do you think we were afraid of that sound? I used to be just like a little girl on the back of Danny's motorcycle. Even my bones were ringing with it.

DAVE: Whatever he saw in the bikes, the bikes as a way of life. I don't know why Bobby got involved with what he got involved with. I can't explain that to you, maybe you should ask him. We had our own thing going there. The outside world was less and less a factor to us. It should have been enough. All I know is that Bobby started to come around more and more once the bikers came.

When the police found Gary Hinman, he looked as though he had been posed deliberately to frighten them. He was slouched in a chair, his torso and the side of his face smeared with blood, his ankles and wrists still tied up with extension cords. There was blood on the linoleum of the kitchen floor, smudged and imprinted with the marks of tennis-shoe soles. Messages had been written on the walls in blood: incitements to rise up, to destroy.

He was a music teacher—Gary Allen Hinman—a graduate

student a few credits short of a master's degree in sociology. In his living room and his bedroom there was a library of textbooks, Marx's *Das Kapital*, several books on Buddhism, transcendental meditation, gardening, jazz. Because his kitchen had been ransacked—all the drawers pulled out, papers scattered on the counters—it looked at first like a drug deal gone bad, just another hippie killing another hippie. There was not much of an investigation until a few days later, when another seven people were murdered in a similar fashion, wealthy people who were not hippies or drug dealers at all. They had been bound by ropes or cords before being stabbed to death, sometimes fitted with a noose or a hood in some elaborate rite of sacrifice. Because the meaning of the killings was impossible to ascertain, it became more ominous. The news brought panic, bewilderment, fascination. When the killers' faces were at last revealed in newspapers and on TV—offhand or contemptuous or even smiling—they looked beatific, or simply empty, young people severed from all ties to the ordinary world.

It had started when someone that Gary Hinman had not seen in a long time showed up in a sweat, his face pale, almost gray, a boy who had lived in Hinman's basement last year for a few months, Bobby Beausoleil, with his white dog. When Hinman let him in, he offered Bobby some tea, but Bobby said no, he'd take a glass of wine, if there was any wine. He hadn't slept last night, he'd had nowhere to go. He told Hinman that he needed a hundred dollars. He didn't ask for it, he just insisted that he needed it, his voice quiet, almost resigned. He stood in the kitchen in his borrowed clothes and Hinman didn't understand what had happened to him, how he had become this vagrant in an army coat, a bruise on his face, circles of sleeplessness under his eyes. He thought of Charlie, the day three months ago that Charlie and Bobby had dropped a used piano off on his porch, something in their manner giving Hinman the first indication he'd ever had that they were anything other than his friends.

He told Bobby he didn't have any money, what was he talking about, but Bobby just looked down at his glass of wine, the stem rising from the web of his fingers on the kitchen counter. He insisted that he was in trouble, he needed the money, he owed it to some bikers, Danny and Ray from the Straight Satans, Charlie's friends. He said that he had sold them some mescaline and now they were saying it was cyanide, it was a burn, they wanted their money back, and what did Gary think they were going to do? Did he think they were just going to let him go? Did he think Charlie was going to just let him go?

Hinman had a mustache and a beard—marbled and crusted with blood when they found him, blood that looked more like dark syrup—and a bald spot at the back of his head. He looked older than he was. He had had a little bit of a crush on Bobby last year, not sexual but an attraction, a desire to help, and Bobby was always at loose ends, always driving up and down the coast with nothing to eat, no money, this beautiful white dog that he managed to feed and that he loved like a little boy loved his dog, a white Alsatian. He didn't have a hundred dollars. He told Bobby that he would try to help with at least some of it, but he lived from paycheck to paycheck—Bobby knew that—and he had maybe twenty in his wallet. He grew plants in his garden, corn and beans and lettuces and tomatoes. He had fed Bobby for a couple of weeks last year, different casseroles and soups he would have made in bulk anyway, it wasn't a problem. A few months ago, he had even bought the used piano from Bobby, the one on the porch. He had always tried to help, and that was why it made no sense now for Bobby to shout at him, angry, but then with tears in his eyes, standing so close, shouting for the money that Hinman didn't have, knowing he didn't have it, hating him for the stupidity of not having it.

And so the pistol came out of nowhere. The blunt force of the pistol grip—the wood and steel against the skull—and then the blood coming down through Hinman's hair. It seemed to happen almost in reverse. Right before, there was something in Bobby's eyes that told Hinman that this wasn't just about money, that it could not be explained by anything as rational as a hundred dollars. Bobby hit him on the side of the head with the pistol frame clenched backward in his hand, not once but three times, cutting open his scalp, hitting him with the gun and then kicking him when he was on the floor. *It's a hundred fucking dollars, Gary. I know you have it somewhere. Don't be a fucking Jew about this, it's just a hundred dollars.* They just sat there on the floor for a while, neither of them moving, Bobby breathing hard, a glaze on his face as if he was going to be sick. For a moment he seemed to become aware of how things had changed in that kitchen, aware of how they had once been friends, but that was when Hinman knew it wasn't going to stop, that Bobby was just steeling himself for another round, that Hinman's own weakness, so naked and exposed, was making it necessary for this to continue. When Charlie showed up a few minutes later with two girls, Susan and Mary, everything began to move forward with a kind of dream logic, each step like some confirmation of what Hinman had always known but was realizing only now.

Charlie had a knife, almost as long as a sword, in a scabbard at his side. He was wearing a shirt with big, loose sleeves
that Hinman recognized as one of Bobby's. He just stood
there with his hands crossed in front of his waist, looking
down at them like a bored father: two boys in a fight, blood on
the floor, Bobby breathing, Hinman breathing. He didn't say
anything, he just turned his head slowly to one side, as if
searching for a better angle from which to judge their inanity.
Then he went into the living room and left them there, Hinman watching as Bobby leaned over his knees on the floor,
staring into space, trying to think his way through this. The
girls stood silently by the kitchen counters, their fingers
hooked in the belt loops of their jeans, not sure what was expected of them yet. It wasn't just a question of money, Hinman knew for sure now. The money was something like an
excuse they had all made to help them arrive at this moment.
He could see that Bobby wasn't thinking clearly, sitting there
with the pistol in his hand, not moving. Then Bobby left the
kitchen and came back with the extension cords and said to
the girls, "I have to talk to Charlie for a minute. You watch
him. Don't let him move."

He saw his chance then. It was just the girls. They looked as
scared as he was. He started twisting himself up onto his feet,
his head throbbing and his vision blurred, but he couldn't do it,
he just kicked himself slowly in a meager arc on the floor, his
sense of balance gone. A black sheet of pressure forced his eyes
shut and pushed out against his eardrums. The girls were
screaming, *Goddamn it, Gary, why don't you sit down? Why
are you doing this? Why don't you just do what he said?* One
of them hit him in the back with a chair. He could hardly feel it

through the pain in his head, his eyes closed, his face pressed down against the linoleum floor. She hit him again—groaning, sighing, making a sound of disgust— and now he felt a bar of pain across his shoulder blade. They came back into the kitchen, and Charlie was standing over him, his foot on Hinman's chest, prodding him a little. He turned to Bobby and told him that this was important, he had to do this right, to call him when it was finished. Then he reached down for the long knife at his side and drew it out of its scabbard, crossing it over his body like a skilled swordsman, the point in the air behind his shoulder, and in the same motion brought it back down on Hinman's head. It was as if the side of Hinman's face had been torn out by a rake. He felt nothing but pain. He screamed, but the screaming came from another room. His fingers did not recognize the sticky slime that had been his ear, and it took several minutes before he had returned fully to his body.

It went on for a long time after that, Charlie gone, Hinman tied up in the chair, the girls crying. It took Bobby eight tries before he finally drove the knife far enough into Hinman's heart to kill him. When it was over, they wrote graffiti on the walls in Hinman's blood. They didn't know why they did this. They had been awake for more than forty-eight hours by then. All of it for a hundred dollars. All of it for no reason at all.

At every show it was the same, but it was never dull or repetitious, it always seemed new. They would keep the fans waiting, sometimes for as long as three hours, as if to establish in advance that there were two sides, star and fan, and that this was what both sides needed if they wanted the experience in its purest form. Mick would walk onstage first, his vaudeville smile made faintly ironic by his sudden emergence from the darkness. He would shield his eyes with the flat of his hand, trying to see out past the spotlights, pretending to survey the crowd but unable to see them.

We'd like to thank you all, New York, or Cleveland, or Chicago, or Miami. We're going to start with a fast one now, a rock-and-roll number, and we'd like you all to get up and groove.

He would lick his lips, smiling, adjusting the microphone stand without having to look at it. Keith would stand by the drum kit with his head bent down, kicking his way free of his cord. He was so thin by then that it was hard to believe he was alive, the bones of his face as delicate as the bones of a monkey's skull. He started with a riff of doubled or tripled notes that twisted off in different directions, dissonant almost to the point of randomness. At the first sound, Mick would raise his arms over his head and thrust his pelvis, his face in profile. He would turn back to look at the crowd. Before long, their faces would be mirroring every movement of his face. Even in the upper decks, they would see the red, white, and blue of his top hat. They would see the lavender scarf that fell past his waist, the thin body dressed all in black, the omega sign on his chest. They would climb up on each other's shoulders, press up against the stage, and sometimes it wouldn't be enough. Sometimes they would have to get up on the stage themselves, lunging at him, grabbing him by the shoulders or the head, trying to bring him down.

———

Their helicopter circled above the fans for several minutes before it landed. Behind them, they could see the traffic backed up for almost two miles, a line of cars cutting between rolling hills that were a grayish tan, like frost-damaged wheat. There was always a surprise at how big a crowd was, but this one looked even bigger and there was no stadium to give it form, just a colorless sprawl, hemmed in on two sides by wire fences. There were the towers of scaffolding for the lights and the P.A., the low black stage with its amplifier stacks, the fans scattered like bits of rag across the fields. From the helicopter, it seemed unrelated to them, a refugee city without plan or logic. They watched and didn't say anything, looking down at the row of trailers to the side of the stage as the pilot banked to the left and began their descent.

On the ground, the pool cues were already coming down in sudden flurries, like hunters gathered around prey. From a few yards away, it looked planned, a tactical use of force. All the bikers had them—pool cues and cans of beer. Everyone had seen their share of news footage from Vietnam—the nighttime raids on village huts, the impromptu executions in the city streets—and this was something like that, the freedom to do whatever you were compelled to do, the unresisted urge.

It was late when Anger came out of the Sloane Square tube station. He started walking up the King's Road with a shopping bag in his hand, passing huddled groups of nighttime stragglers, closed shops. London still made no sense to him, even after all this time. It was a mix of austerity and nostalgia, history fenced in by concrete, glass, prim rows of Victorian brick. In the streets, the black cabs were like a stubborn denial of time, impossible to take seriously.

He turned left on Oakley Street and headed southeast toward the river. It looked a little like Greenwich Village, only in front of the buildings there were rows of iron railings interspersed with thick stone pillars that looked almost like fortifications. He couldn't look at London without thinking about World War II, the devastation. The older the buildings were, the more they brought to mind a ghost city that existed in parallel to the city he was in at the time.

He saw Bobby laughing, spitting on the floor, utterly lost. By now, the image had become a vague tightness behind his ribs, an emptiness in his stomach. It was with him all the time. He supposed that was how much he was still attached to Bobby, imagining that Bobby was thinking of him too, that they were somehow connected.

It was so much worse than anything he'd imagined. He would not have foreseen the blood on the walls, the crazy deliberateness, the mutilated bodies. That was how the Lucifer role had played itself out. That was who Bobby was now, the brute fact of his crime. That was all he would ever be.

He took a right turn onto Cheyne Walk, the only one on the street now. Mick lived in number 48, a white Georgian building three windows wide. On the second story was a wrought-iron veranda that looked almost Spanish, like something out of a Goya painting. There was a streetlamp in front of the gate, which helped him to see the keys in his hand: two ordinary keys, not even on a ring, keys that he might have plucked at random from a junk box. A few lamps had been left on inside the house, but he knew it was empty.

Once inside, he stood for a while looking at the living room: the tapestried chairs, the low tables, the hammered brass lamps. Everything was almost in silhouette, the light was so dim. He remembered the time a half year ago he had looked at the pictures of the murdered actress, Sharon Tate, and how it had reminded him of the band. He remembered thinking that the murders seemed like the kind of thing that might easily have happened to them. He remembered looking at the picture of the actress on the front page — blond, in her twenties — and thinking how much she looked like Anita.

They were always so stoned. That was how he'd managed to steal the keys and make copies, returning the originals before anyone even noticed.

He went upstairs to the library, the place where he'd showed Mick the film three months ago. He took a glass of water upstairs with him. The house was dark and silent, and there was something about the ordinariness of the glass he took that made it more difficult to be there. He put the shopping bag down on the desk beside the reels of film and stood there for a moment before he turned and opened the cabinet. The projector was on a sliding shelf. There was a screen that pulled down over two stacks of bookcases, like something from a spy movie. He spooled the film into the projector and switched off the desk lamp and took a sip of the water. Then he sat there in the dark with the film playing and tried to imagine it: the phone lines cut, Bobby and his friends appearing in the library, breathless, on the verge of laughter.

We're here and there's nothing you can do about it, their faces say. *We're here and we're not going to leave.*

When they came out onstage, it was dark. The fans had been waiting for almost three hours since the last opening band's performance. There were Hells Angels everywhere, on the amplifiers and in the middle of the stage, in the front row of the crowd, pushing them back with pool cues and with their motorcycles. Keith bent over his guitar, crouched by the drum kit. They'd heard what it was like from the opening bands, but even now that they could see it for themselves they were still going to try to play their way though it, inured by this point to riots, crowds, warnings, threats. Keith stood upright to hit his first chord, nodding his head. Mick gripped the microphone with both hands, collapsing and rising, collapsing and rising, but by the middle of the first song the stage was so crowded they couldn't go on. Everyone was looking at a brawl on the ground. Mick stood there in his devil's suit and top hat, unable to understand what was happening. In his motionless bewilderment, he looked for a moment even younger than he was, a stranded boy in a plastic costume.

"Everybody just cool out," he said. "Just cool out. Just stop it."

It was hard to see what was going on from the stage, through the lights. Dogs crossed in front of the microphones. When they started again, they saw girls sitting on their boyfriends' shoulders, dancing, glitter on their cheeks, smiling or closing their eyes. They saw the raised fists, the shaking heads, and sometimes it almost looked like an ordinary crowd with the usual few scuffles at the edges. They didn't see the boy pushing his way forward, one of the few black fans in the crowd, dressed in a fedora and a green suit, his girlfriend behind him. They didn't see it when he brushed against a biker near the stage, not turning around when the biker grabbed his shoulder but readying himself, gathering all the anger of being in this crowd, being black in this white crowd, all of it about to usher in this moment of confrontation. They played an old song about a girl, a pared-down version, bluesy but fast, treble guitars against the batter and crash of high-hat cymbals. The boy in the green suit took one last look at the band, knowing that the bikers had him, and then he drew his gun in a sudden flash, jostled by the crowd so that his raised arm pointed for a brief moment right at Mick.

An empty space suddenly opened up in front of the stage. It got bigger and bigger. For a while no one would go near it. It got so big that Mick could see the grass between the motorcycles, lit up by the footlights, and for a few seconds there was something close to silence. Keith grabbed the microphone, pointing at some bikers who were still swinging their pool cues, demanding that they stop, but it was impossible to see what was happening beyond the reach of the lights. When they started the song again, there was a moment when Mick caught the eye of some boy who implored him to stop, who mouthed the words in a way that was unmistakable, and Mick stood there looking at him, taking in what he was saying, thinking it over. He had not seen the body on the ground, stabbed in the neck, pummeled to death by pool cues, a seventeen-year-old body in a green suit. He started dancing in a frenzy, shaking his whole body, looking right into the other boy's eyes, defying him. Even then, there were still people cheering, still people with hungry, solemn stares, still people dancing. There were still people trying to get closer to the stage.

Style has an aura that words only diminish. The words follow, trying to explain, but the glamour fades in the glare of opinions and ideas. There is no more Lucifer now, no more Prince of Darkness, no more Angel of Light. There is a return to what was always there before, the silence.

The front door seemed to recede back into the distance as Anger looked at it, making up his mind. He had framed it with newspaper, putting up sheets around the lintel and the jambs, tucking them around the edges and fastening them down with tape. He had covered the doorknob with more tape, and he'd taped the hinges and the sides of the door itself. It looked violated and alive now, a demented shrine. A newspaper picture of Charles Manson stared numbly out at the room, his body slumped to one side, flanked by policemen. There were pictures of Bobby, Susan, Leslie, Tex, Patricia—the girls with their shy, ecstatic smiles, the boys with their thoughtful, intense stares.

He spread some more newspaper on the floor, making an improvised carpet from the doorway to the coffee table. Then he took the first can of paint out of the shopping bag. When he opened it, it looked like oil on top, gold oil that was streaked with lines of dark or gilt specks. He turned it slowly with the wooden stirrer, cross-legged on Mick's floor, bringing up the pigment until it was burnished into a consistent brownish gold, honey-thick, gleaming in the lamplight.

It would not be something that Mick or any of the others would understand. When they came back, it would just be there: the door painted gold, a kept secret, resonant with silence. Maybe it would seem threatening. Maybe it would seem benign. He didn't know. He didn't know if they would think of him right away, or at all.

The paint went on unevenly, sometimes too dark, dense with glitter, sometimes a sticky, almost translucent smear. He went over a thin patch while it was still wet, but the result was streaky and he moved on to another area. It was important to do it precisely. It would take several coats to get the finish right. It had to look like the door had not been painted but had simply materialized, cast in gold. When it was done, he would peel away the tape and the newspapers and pack them up in the shopping bag to take home with him. He would look at what he'd done: the ordinary door transformed, the violation of the break-in softened into something that was not quite a violation at all. The fact that he had done it and not just thought about it would make the moment when he walked through the door last longer than an ordinary moment. It would stay in his mind for a long time, this disappearance, this ambiguous farewell.

It is raining in the theater now. There is the rumble of an explosion, so loud that Bobby can feel it rattling inside his body, pressing at his bones. In front of the screen, Anger's silhouette strides across the stage in its robe, an image flickering above him, a zodiac glyph, then an image of Mick's face, singing. There is a flag at one side of the stage, a Nazi flag with a swastika at its center, and Anger lifts it in the air, displaying it, shouting words that Bobby can't understand. The dream calls for blood. That's why it has always mattered, why it recurs. There is no end or purpose to it, only greater speed, the pull toward the glistening in the darkness. He lights the flag on fire, holding it away from his body. The music behind him is an adrenaline thud, a racing heartbeat, a dream of violence unfolding in a pink neon haze. On-screen, Mick and Keith play a song to half a million faceless blips. A biker whispers directives into another biker's ear. An image of Lucifer begins to coalesce. He is a red curtain over still water, a blue gas flame reflected on chrome, a black sky pocked with green specks of light. He is a dead boy spread-eagled on the ground, his arms tattooed with anchors and skulls, blood in his hair. A plastic skull rotates on a pedestal whose base is the intricately spoked wheel of a motorcycle. It bleeds into a massive image of Anger's sweating, frenzied face, and as Bobby watches, he knows that this will never end, that neither he nor Anger will ever leave this room.

Projected now is a picture of Bobby himself, sitting cross-legged on a wooden crate, raising his arms in the darkness without knowing why. Patterns of light crawl across his face, generated by a slow strobe held behind a black card punched through with holes. The light bleaches out his features, makes him look even younger than he is. He raises his eyebrows and opens his eyes wide in what might be self-mockery or just an effort to speak. He can't remember anymore what he would have been trying to say. He can't remember what it was that he and Anger were trying to accomplish. His image on-screen lifts his arms in the air as if to absolve him of responsibility, or as if to ask what happens next, what he should do.

It is June 6, 1968. Mick is standing by himself in a vocal booth, one hand pressed to his ear to hear himself better above the backing track, as the tape begins to roll. The news around the world that night is that Robert Kennedy, five years after his brother, has just died of the gunshot wounds he sustained the night before. It is as if the decade itself knows that it can never return, that it has only these few years to live out its own extremes. The light on the sound buffers is a dim beige, a pre-dawn staleness of smoke. Mick hears the music: a flat patter of bongos, a resonant thud of conga drums, a locust-like hiss of maracas. They've spent three days in the studio, fumbling, grasping, finally to arrive at this moment when it works. He backs up and lets out a yelp, a monkey screech, saturated in echo. He makes grunting noises from deep inside his chest, rising on his toes so that his body shakes, his hand moving down his hip to his thigh. On the monitors, the piano strikes a wide, sustained D chord and the song suddenly spreads and hovers, Mick's lips tensed into a sneer as he begins his delivery, a song about the Devil, about violence, death magic, its glamour and mystique. His head is silhouetted by a floodlight affixed to the ceiling, so that the split ends of his hair glow a bright white, like the filaments in a lit bulb. He is Lucifer — in that moment there is no better word for how he has changed. He is an escape from everything drab, the music behind him shot through with exotic colors that have as little to do with darkness as a stained-glass window. An electric bass thuds out a pattern of syncopated triplets and eighth notes, matching the repetitive pounding of the drums, and with each note comes a twitch in Mick's legs, a jangle of his spine, a defiant lifting of his chin, a hundred little signs to let you know that it's not fake this time, that for the three minutes of this song the god will be real. He raises his arms, all sinew and muscle. The decade will pass, forty years will pass, and maybe you'll hear a snatch of it through a car window, the sound of it still a surprise over a stranger's radio, the old song sent around the planet in waves that never end.

PART FOUR

Q: Do you believe in God?

JOHN LENNON: Yes, I believe that God is like a powerhouse, like where you keep electricity, like a power station. And that he's the supreme power, and that he's neither good nor bad, left, right, black or white. He just is. And we tap that source of power and make of it what we will. Just as electricity can kill people in a chair, or you can light a room with it.

—from a press conference given in Montreal, December 1969

RISE, 2002

OVER THE YEARS, Anita kept in touch with Anger sporadically. She had put some money into his last film, in the seventies, but he wasn't easy to be with and so for periods of time she would let the friendship lapse. The last time she saw him was five years ago, when she was in Los Angeles. His apartment was over a dry cleaner in a two-story stucco building in the run-down neighborhood of Echo Park. Some boy let her in. He didn't introduce himself, and after answering the door he disappeared into another room. It was very dim inside, the curtains drawn, the walls painted a harsh red, the ceiling a glossy black. All of it was lit by old lamps that cast a pale bronze light that would have been the same shade day or night.

Anger was sitting in a chair in the living room, his legs crossed. He wore a black suit and black police shoes. He must have been at least seventy, she thought. There was a thin trace of eyeliner around his eyes.

"Hello, Kenneth," she said.

She bent over and gave him an awkward sort of half hug, more a patting of the shoulders, and he felt resistant and dry. He looked down at his hands. Beside his chair was a Japanese folding screen and a nightstand cluttered with plastic cups.

"I was expecting you a little later," he said. He turned away. "But you're here now."

"Yes, I'm here now."

"It's been a long time."

She sat down and put her bag on the floor. The room was decorated with old Hollywood memorabilia: pictures of stars from the silent era, Day-Glo posters from the thirties and forties, a pair of brocade curtains with gold tassels. There was a still from Anger's own film, *Inauguration of the Pleasure Dome*, which showed a close-up of a woman's face, lit by a pink light, her red hair cut short like a man's. Jezebel, Anita remembered. The Whore of Babylon. It was such a long time since she'd last seen the image, more than thirty years.

"Would you like some tea or something?" Anger asked.

"No, thanks."

"The host is supposed to offer the guest something to drink. It's a gesture of hospitality."

"I'll have some tea, then. Whatever you want."

The room had a museum stillness when he went into the kitchen. Everything was immaculately silent, watchful. He came back with the tea on a tray: a blue and white ceramic pot, two bright green cups without handles. The cups were ornamented with tiny white and black cranes. In the dimness of the living room, they almost glowed.

She told him she had moved back to London, back to Chelsea. She hadn't seen Keith in a long time. They had split up many years ago. She was glad to be back in London, though. New York had never felt like home.

"And what about you?" she asked.

"I've been here."

"For how long?"

"Long enough. I've been trying to work again. There's not much to show for it yet."

He told her he'd moved back to L.A. at the end of the nineties. When he'd lived in New York, he'd been badly mugged several times. It was the crack years, and he'd lived through all that in East Harlem, 110th Street, in two rooms with sealed windows. It was a different city then. He'd been glad to get out. They talked about New York for a while: the way it had changed, both of them saying disparaging things that they didn't really believe. Overhanging it all was the awareness that in the years they'd both lived there, probably ten years, they had never seen each other at all.

She looked around at the room, at the images of Valentino, the gaudy illustrations of science-fiction characters. There was nothing you could say about the past that didn't ring false, she thought. She didn't feel regret or nostalgia about it. Mostly she was happy that things were less urgent now, less intense.

"You're one of those people I was always curious about," she said. "Why you disappeared. Why you stopped doing films."

"There's nothing to know."

"You called me a self-absorbed bitch in one of your interviews. I read those things."

"I say a lot of things."

"We weren't thinking, most of the time you knew us. You never really understood that, how little thinking we were doing."

"I thought you were beyond thinking. I thought you were interesting to watch. I just got tired of it. Struggling, I mean. The money. Thinking it was important to make films."

He closed his eyes for a moment, then he raised them, looking at her with a slightly hostile appraisal. "We're all still alive," he said. "That's the surprise. That was the one thing the world was always counting on, that we would all just die."

Her eyes fell again on the picture of the woman with the short red hair. The image had been made decades ago, and yet even now the way the woman looked was daring. If she were alive at all, she would be in her seventies or eighties. Probably she was dead. Time — it had become a big subject for Keith and Mick, a vein of pathos in their last work that was any good. For a long period of her life, she'd had no sense of it — it had had no power to scare her. Later it had seemed that time went back so far that nothing could ever last long enough to matter very much. She would think of geologic time, or the time reckoned by astronomers. But it was better not to think about time at all.

"You've been feeling bored," he said. "That's why you came here."

"No, not really. Things have been going well."

"Wondering what the point of it all is. Wanting to stir up the old ghosts."

"They're still there. It's just that there's no point in talking about them anymore."

He bent down to sip his tea, showing the crown of his head. She saw the tattoos on his wrist, the dark ink mottled and slightly faded. It occurred to her, as it had often occurred to her in the past, that the way he looked and acted was a pose, a kind of private joke that kept him at a distance from the world. But it was a long time to hold such a pose. Surrounded by his movie props, he seemed more than ever like someone she would never understand. The room was thick with his past, an agglomeration of dust and souvenirs. It was hard to imagine him leaving it.

In the Lucifer film, the sequel to *Invocation of My Demon Brother*, there is a scene in which a woman who looks just like Anita climbs a mountain in the closing dusk, a full moon overhead, clouds passing in front of it. Ahead of her in the darkness are four torches that lead the way over a narrow suspension bridge that connects two stone cliffs. She crushes a sprig of lilac blossoms in her hand, throws them aside, staggering a little. The path is made of large stone blocks that slant and buckle, leading to the high span of the bridge and the ancient monolith that lies beyond it. Her role is Lilith, goddess of the unacceptable, the dying, the discarded. She looks like Anita, but in fact she is Marianne, dressed in rock-and-roll clothes: a black fur coat, platform shoes. It is 1972 and, like Anita, Marianne has a heroin addiction that there is no reason to believe she will ever overcome, though she will overcome it, both of them will be all right. She forces herself up the hill, the gray light on her face, her hand at her throat, head down.

When she reaches the summit, it is just before dawn of the winter solstice, the year's lowest ebb. The sun begins to shine dimly on the rocks, casting a purple glow over the horizon, the hills below. There is a raised stone at the edge of the cliff that she stands on, a perfect circle cut out of its center. Every year on this day, at this moment, the circle's circumference is entirely filled by the rising sun, the beginning of the new pagan year.

She can hardly look at it. It's been a long climb and she feels faint, nauseated, in need of dope. She raises her hands as directed, trying to embrace the sunlight coming in through the hole in the rock, but she looks almost repelled by it, her eyes narrow with censure. She used to be fascinated by things like the monolith—by magic, mysticism, fantasies of all kinds. Now there is physical pain, craving, no more idle wishing for life to seem more mysterious or important than it is.

She sits down, half collapsing, bracing herself with a hand stretched out beside her hip. Her head hangs down from her shoulders, her black fur coat twisted around her back. She closes her eyes and waits for it to stop and doesn't move.

It went on for a long time. It was like if I kept walking, everyone might still be where they were supposed to be and we'd all just go back to the way we were before. Only I knew it wasn't true. I knew everything had changed. There was just this endless little moment where I didn't have to face what had really happened yet.

When she wakes up, she's sitting in the sand before the pyramids of Giza. She is wrapped in a pale linen shroud, her skin and clothes covered in dust. She is a shade, no longer alive. Motionless, speechless, perhaps faintly smiling, she holds a lotus blossom in her hand and she stares at it, chin raised, as if staring continuously into a mirror. Her face looks like Anita's, so it also looks like Brian's, a sixties face, a kind you no longer see.

Isis awakens on a white cliff. Osiris rises from his cave, his face painted blue. They salute each other across a desert valley, each raising a single arm in the early morning light. They are so beautiful that it's tempting to forget they are actors: her naked breasts, the gold bands around his arms. They go through a series of benedictions — he raises his staff, she raises hers — and then they disappear, as does Marianne, nothing left now but rocks and sand and the ruins of the ancient temples. There is a dreamlike calm, the calm of barren landscapes under sunlight, clouds passing over, as if all of the turmoil we call history has taken place on some infinitely distant, even imaginary plane.

The sun is beginning to set. Time is moving more quickly now, the film almost over. There is a psychedelic image, flying saucers coming over the desert, vintage crafts of nuclear orange, neon green. Their beams shine down on the empty expanse of sand, on the ruined temples, on the rubbled face of the Sphinx. They hover and rise like some last wish, not darkness but a final surge of color.

ACKNOWLEDGMENTS

Among the sources I consulted while doing research for this book are: *The True Adventures of the Rolling Stones* by Stanley Booth, *Up and Down with the Rolling Stones* by Tony Sanchez, *Keith Richards* by Victor Bockris, *Faithfull: An Autobiography* by Marianne Faithfull, *Blown Away: The Rolling Stones and the Death of the Sixties* by A. E. Hotchner, *Helter Skelter: The True Story of the Manson Murders* by Vincent Bugliosi, *Hollywood Babylon* by Kenneth Anger, *Anger: The Unauthorized Biography of Kenneth Anger* by Bill Landis, *Kenneth Anger* by Alice L. Hutchinson, and the films *One Plus One* by Jean-Luc Godard and *Gimme Shelter* by David and Albert Maysles.

In the interest of concision, I have invented various documents that appear throughout the text, including letters, newspaper articles, oral testimonies, and interviews. The book *Dream Plays: A History of Underground Film* and the occult treatise referred to as *The Sephiroth* are also both fictitious.

I would like to thank Bill Clegg, Pat Strachan, Jayne Yaffe Kemp, and Dan Franklin for their help with this book. I am grateful to Edmund White, John Dalton, Marshall Klimasewiski, Eugene Constan, Christopher Quirk, Amy Madden, Carroll Moulton, Ernie Hulsey, and David Winner for their friendship and support through many years of writing. I would also like to thank my family, and especially Sarah.

Reading Group Guide

A NOVEL BY

ZACHARY LAZAR

A conversation with the author of *Sway*

Zachary Lazar talks with Christopher Sorrentino for *Bomb*

In your imagining, all of your characters are doing something secret, something taboo, which each wants to put on display.

I was thinking about the imagination as something that intrudes into what we call "reality." That dichotomy has always interested me, perhaps because as writers we don't usually get to see the products of our imagination take on such enormous dimensions as the people I've gathered together for *Sway* did.

Do you posit a link, if only in Manson's mind, between such creative acts and his own weird vision—that he may have thought, or, God knows, still thinks, that his murders are inchoate works of art awaiting interpretation?

I've looked for reasons why the Manson murders have fascinated me, all these years later. For one, they have this perverse aesthetic quality to them. They were orchestrated in a way that is calculatedly terrifying. Writing in blood on the walls, some of the stuff they would say to the people while they were killing them—you couldn't script a more terrifying scene. And there's Manson's past as a would-be rock star, which may have been what instigated this whole set of murders: a lashing out by someone who didn't succeed as a legitimate artist.

It's difficult to try to separate Manson from that Laurel Canyon milieu in which he tried to ingratiate himself. I think we both want to steer clear of the facile insinuation that ritual murder is some sort of extension of the popular culture — but there is that tenuous link.

Yes — the murder I describe in the book is one done by Bobby Beausoleil, and it's much more mundane. It's basically a drug deal gone bad, but that's what started the whole series of murders. When Manson sent those girls to Sharon Tate's house later, he told them to "do something witchy." I mean, what a strange thing to say, and it essentially translates into "be creative." There is a very perverse creativity being spoken about there, something that's uncomfortable now to talk about.

What about the "helpful commonplace distinctions" made pointless by the Rolling Stones, both in their music and in their essence. You're referring in particular to racial and gender boundaries that they simply ignored. You also refer to "a language of pure connotation, of suggestion and innuendo" to describe the attitude, the look, the style in general that began to emerge at that time among young people. How does that collage of intimation and reference differ from the knowingness of today's culture, which is perhaps more cynically referential?

There was a freedom back then that explored its own vagueness. Everything hadn't been done before, and certainly not a thousand times over as it has been now. Currently, you can't do much of anything without nodding at something that came before. Music, especially, is largely referencing older styles, putting them together in different combinations. Which is what the Rolling Stones did, actually. The difference is that they seem to have taken it on faith that what they were doing had meaning and potential, a kind of potential we would never dream of music having now.

The extent to which the changes in the culture as a whole took root and spread throughout the '60s through the music followed, in effect, the unvetted creative decision-making of young people. It's hard for me to imagine a song by Band A or Band B lasting 40 years, not in the way that "Sympathy for the Devil" has, as you point out at the end of Sway. A song that still sustains that power—that sense of a different world opening for us—is certainly different from what we would expect from pop music.

Yeah—it's remarkable that it still works, that it doesn't come across as completely stupid. I was thinking about *Spinal Tap* when writing the book. That movie is so funny and it does such a good job of undermining all the bombastic qualities of rock and roll. But I wanted to *get* at this thing. I'm amazed that "Sympathy for the Devil" still has a power beyond irony.

From the blurring of those distinctions came a kind of anything goes sensibility—sometimes quite liberating. But Sway gives the sense that at some point the cup ran over. Suddenly it isn't as simple as dancing naked in Golden Gate Park—it's Charles Manson exhorting his followers to "do something witchy."

Yeah . . . there's that famous Whitman line, "Unscrew the locks from the doors! Unscrew the doors themselves from their jambs!" And the William Blake quote about the road to excess leading to the palace of wisdom.

Cleanse the doors of perception, that kind of thing. You use several such quotations as epigraphs to your book's sections.

William Blake was full of those exhortations to do anything and everything to expand the realm of consciousness or possibility. Of course, he was William Blake. Walt Whitman was Walt Whitman. You take a bunch of 17-year-olds and give them that kind of advice, it's not surprising that some things happen that are not only far from sublime but in some cases sociopathic. A lot of different forces came together in the '60s that allowed young people to get into more trouble than they ever could get into before, all of which was sanctioned by a philosophical outlook. You had it in the 50s, to a certain extent, but not on that scale.

Your book's title suggests multiple meanings: there's the Stones song of that name, there's swaying to the music or to the flow of events, and, of course, "sway" in terms of someone's exerting influence over someone else. How much did the idea of control interest you when you started writing the book?

The title was one of the first things for the book that I had. The multiple meanings of "sway" referred to control in the dynamics of the band, which is a little political machine; Manson's control over his followers; and also the control that your time period has over you, whether you're aware or unaware of it, or whether you want it to or not.

What's the difference between a Richards and a Beausoleil? Talent? Charisma? Sheer determination?

Beausoleil had charisma, and probably talent, though not as much as Richards. An artist seems to succeed best when he or she has one foot in the world of the mundane, not just the ethereal. Richards had that in terms of both his work ethic, which was considerable, and his ability to toy with his own myth and have a sense of humor about it too. If he had failed as a rock star, he would have become a bartender or something. He would never have fallen under the spell of a Charles Manson.

Christopher Sorrentino's interview with Zachary Lazar was first published in *Bomb* (Spring 2008, number 103). Reprinted with permission.

Questions and topics for discussion

1. From the Rolling Stones and Bobby Beausoleil to the eerie soundtracks of Kenneth Anger's films, music is central to *Sway*. What does music from the 60s signify to you? What does it signify to the novel's principal characters? Discuss the different implications music has for the Stones, Anger, and Beausoleil.

2. *Sway* follows three individual stories that eventually converge. Discuss the points of convergence and the events leading up to them. In what ways are the novel's characters and their experiences in the three separate stories similar? Do you think one storyline is the most representative of the 1960s?

3. How do you define masculinity and femininity? Discuss the manifestations of each in the novel, especially with regard to the Rolling Stones, Bobby Beausoleil, and Kenneth Anger. Discuss the role that gender plays in the characters' private lives and in their performances.

4. Both the group and the individual figure prominently in *Sway*, most notably with the Manson family commune and loner Kenneth Anger. Compare the motivations and ideals of each. How does the author use them to critique both individuality and collectivity?

5. Anita Pallenberg can be considered a muse to the Rolling Stones in 1968 and 1969. In *Sway*, how did her forceful

personality both inspire and mature them, despite her romantic inconsistency? How is her character further revealed during her late encounter with Kenneth Anger?

6. The *Sephiroth* appears at various points in the novel. Discuss its main tenants. Why is it important to the characters and how does it relate to the novel as a whole?

7. In many ways, the Rolling Stones' vacation in Marrakech is comparable to the extremes of Kenneth Anger's films. How does this trip alter the lives of the band members, particularly Brian Jones? What role does hallucination play in both their lives and their art?

8. Lucifer is normally thought of as a symbol of evil and darkness. How is he transformed in *Sway* into a bearer of light? What are some of the many, perhaps conflicting permutations of Lucifer in the novel? Discuss the role Lucifer plays in "Sympathy for the Devil" and *An Invocation of My Demon Brother*.

9. The 1960s have been mythologized and idealized as stories have been passed from one generation to another. Identify some of these generalizations. Discuss your own preconceptions of the era. How were they reinforced or transformed by *Sway*?

10. All of the characters in the novel succumb to the sway of someone or something. Why are they swept up? In what ways are they influenced and what are some of the consequences of their actions "under the influence"? Do you think their impressionability is a comment on the decade as a whole?